THIRTY PIECES OF SILVER
Destiny Sealed With A Kiss

I0662420

Dorothy Davies

THIRTY PIECES OF SILVER
Destiny Sealed With A Kiss

Fiction4All

From Immortality
Olton Pools, Sidgwick and Jackson Ltd.,1917

There in the midst of all these words shall be
Our names, our ghosts, our immortality.

Dedicated to the memory of Judas Iskariot, surely one of the most maligned and hated people of the last two thousand years. All that he did was ordained for him to do; he carried the burden of his 'betrayal' with strength and dignity.

Judas' dedication:

This, my life story, is dedicated with the greatest and most overwhelming love any man can give another, to Jesus himself. I followed him with love when we walked the earth plane; I give him my love and service now.

And to my channel, who welcomed me and accepted me and gave me her time and her love. Thank you. It is impossible to say more.

Comment from Judas:

It is hard for me to believe I am doing this, that I am giving the world my story. For the best part of the last two thousand years of your time, in the eyes of the Christian church and its adherents I have been one of the most hated and reviled people who ever lived. I have heard my name used as an insult so many times it has lost the power to hurt. I know that had I approached anyone during that time to put my side of the story to the world, I would have been scorned and persecuted. So I waited and watched and then finally approached this channel, confident that I would be accepted. And glory be to God, I was. I am.

This loving soul calls me Jude, not the hated name. She smiles when I come into her presence. She says that wonderful word 'welcome' which I cannot hear often enough, each time I come to her. Having been so long in the wilderness, it is difficult to accept that this is happening and yet it is. How impatient I was for my story to be committed to her machine! She told me she would write it as soon as she could, alongside the other books, rather than make me wait. I would have cried tears of happiness if I had not forgotten how to cry. I am locked up inside, a hard ball of unhappiness. I almost wrote bitterness but that would not be the truth and this had to be the truth. Nothing else would do. My channel will know when the unhappiness is gone, for then I will be able to cry.

I was asked to decide how to tell my story. As a book, as a narration, as an outpouring of emotion, where to start and what to choose? It was important; I knew that from seeing how the other authors worked. I had so much to say and wanted to say it all in one go, knowing that could not happen. There is just so much time that can be devoted to writing.

I have to say this: remember that what you read in the Gospels is translation from translation and in that much has been changed, altered and amended. Nothing is as the original writers intended it to be. Why else are we here, asking this channel for the chance to write it properly? And much was suppressed, too. The early church seems to have had its own ideas about all of us. Come to this book with an open mind. I have had two thousand years in which to recall every step of that journey, the one I took with Jesus. Mine is as close to the truth as you will get. But for the rest of the story, what happened before I arrived and what happened after my death, you will have to wait for the others who are coming to write their books. I can only give you what I experienced myself.

I commend this book to you, my readers, in the hope you will gain a new insight into my life and my times. It was difficult, heart wrenchingly difficult, if I can say such a thing, to do what I had to do. Know this, I loved the man then, I love him now.

Judas Iskariot

Chapter 1
Early Life

Kerioth: sun baked village, small white houses, parched land, livestock tended by hand else it would not survive, sat alongside the road to Hebron, the centre of our world. Kerioth: place of companionship, of boys to run and tumble with, of my four brothers to share a home with, of strict rules, both secular and religious and loving parents who cared for us before themselves. Proud they were, proud people with ancestry that went back into the darkest recesses of time. Grandparents would quote the family history by rote and were listened to with awe when they did.

Kerioth: the one place seemingly not invaded by the Romans. Only there could we live, walk, worship and be ourselves without a Roman guard watching our every move.

Hebron was the centre of our world. Small flat roofed buildings, tiny winding streets, many without names for we knew where they went and only used those which went to places we needed to go. Hebron was fascinating; bazaars, people of all races and many languages, people with all manner of clothes, bright, colourful, decorated with beads and embroidery and fine threads. In Hebron you could hear everything and understand nothing but the music which layered over all conversations and street noises as if it were a comforting blanket. There never seemed to be an end to those who wished to make music, to lift the spirits with delicate melodies and to make the feet move in time with lilting dancing sounds. Hebron was history, business, commerce, trade, learning, socialising, registers kept of this and that and everything else.

Hebron meant Romans, too. Guards at the gates, guards on the municipal buildings, soldiers tramp-tramping through the streets, demanding all get out of their way and let them pass.

Romans. We hated them. We were polite, we greeted them when we had to, we ignored them when we could. We behaved in public so as not to be harried away to some court or other and never seen again. We had heard of Roman atrocities although few of us had seen them at first hand. The rumours of them were enough to terrify the hardest heart. Rome held Hebron and Judea in its mailed hand and the hand tightened all the time. We heard enough of trying to make the tax payments, of trying to pay off this official or that to ensure life carried on, to know the Romans were bleeding the area dry. What they would do when there were no people left to work, when there was no money left to pay, was anyone's guess. Everyone fought to put that moment off as long as possible. No one wanted to find out what the Romans would do to the inhabitants of Judea when that happened.

My childhood was idyllic, apart from the Roman presence. I loved my brothers, my parents, my extended family of cousins and uncles and aunts and all manner of relatives, grandparents and all. There were those related by marriage and those who were associated with the family not by marriage but close enough to be given family titles. They were from nearby villages as well as Kerioth, some even lived in Hebron itself. It seemed as if there was ever people around, gossiping, sharing the work, bringing food and gifts, being part of the daily round of my life.

And then there were the patients. Father was a doctor, a good one. His fame had spread beyond our small area and people came from Hebron to be treated. His knowledge of herbs was extensive and his potions effective, or so it was said. He had the ability to heal. I know now not all of it came from his herbs and potions but from the man himself. As a child I did not know about healing, but having watched the Man working, I realised what had been happening all through my childhood. Some things you tend to take for granted when it concerns your parents. As far as I was concerned, people came with illnesses, left with potions and sent back messages saying they were better. He did not do the miracles of Jesus, no people made to walk who could not walk but the healing was there and the sick and injured came to Kerioth to find him and purchase his potions and pills.

One room in our house was set aside for this: it was redolent with herbs and tinctures, with shelves full of tiny containers stoppered tightly with wax and bearing seals to say what was inside. As a child I would gaze on them and think they held the secrets of the Universe. I said this once to my father and he laughed.

"Perhaps they do, Judas, perhaps they do, for who knows what wisdom God had when he created those plants for us to use for healing?"

It meant nothing to me at the time. Now I understand. Now I see healers and herbalists at work, I see those who massage with different oils and understand that plants can - and do - heal. I have to ask you, why do you take chemicals when plants can do the same thing without harm? And you answer, this we call progress, to dismiss that which is natural and use that which is unnatural. So be it.

My mother was the centre of the home. The centre of life. Everything revolved around her, our day to day living, our schooling, our growing up, our coming and our going. Father might be head of the house but somehow, I know from looking back, it was Mother's gentle guidance which directed us all. I am telling you this for one reason: you need to know how much I was impelled to leave when I first heard the Man speak, that I walked away from this tight, loving, close family and went to serve an itinerant preacher. Such was His power.

We had tutors to push us to learn the arts of writing and adding, of calculating and of understanding the world as it was known at that time. It meant learning of the vast area occupied, there is no other word for it, by the Roman Empire. No one outwardly openly said it, but the teaching was there for all to read it, if you could read the subtext. We had a land, the Romans invaded. We had a life; the Romans took it over. We had cities, the Romans claimed them. We had ancient names, the Romans made them their own. One tutor, bolder than the others, talked of a hope that one day a leader would come to rouse the people and throw off the oppressors. We hoped for that day to come.

Before then, we simply had to get on with life as it was. Romans and all.

I grew up not knowing which direction I really wanted to go. My brothers had already made up their minds by the time they entered puberty. One followed Father and decided to be a doctor, another went further and said he wanted to be a surgeon, as the inner workings of the body fascinated him. My third brother decided to go into Law and the youngest one felt himself called to the synagogue and eventually become a Rabbi. I was undecided for some time until Father suggested I look into work as an actuary, which covered many fields. For me it presented a challenge I could not ignore or resist, the chance to work in a field where there were many different conditions to be assessed before advising a client to make a decision on investment or any other matter. It seemed far ranging enough to be of real interest and that is what I sought. As soon as schooling was done, I was enrolled in an office in Hebron and began the long task of learning this new way of life.

At first I travelled back and forth each day but after a while I thought to have my own home in Hebron, if it could be arranged on the money I was then earning. We looked around and, with family help, I secured a place in which I could be content. It was no real effort to cook a meal or sweep a floor or make up a bed for myself. I grew plants in containers which I watered daily; I had herbs and flowers in pots in a little courtyard and delighted in the growing of them. The blooms enchanted me; the herbs were useful in my simple meals. All else I bought from the shops and street vendors when they visited the road where I lived. I was content in my home, more content than I expected to be. There I spent my time with the Scriptures, studying the laws and the sayings, reading widely of the philosophers of old who seemed to have much to say to me.

For all of this quiet contentment, a part of me remained restless, unsatisfied and even lonely. I have never before spoken of this, not even in the most confidential of conversations with the man I came to love. No one knew of this secret loneliness, I could not bring myself to talk of it even to Him though we walked together some moonlit nights and talked of many things when he could not sleep and needed someone to walk and talk with. Then we discussed the philosophers I had studied and I found that his thoughts matched mine. Once he said, with great pleasure, it seemed to me, "Judas, of everyone who is with me, I feel you know my mind best of all, for your thinking and mine accord on these topics." I remember my heart swelling with happiness at his words, for they went deep into that lonely core I held and eased it a little. But not entirely, the ache went too deep for that.

That was much later in my life. Before then there is much to talk of.

When our studies were done and our place in our future professions assured, my brothers and I began to look for brides. There were many to choose from, every family we associated with had beautiful or attractive marriageable daughters. Within a short time, no more than a year, my four brothers had found their life partners and were married. They set up homes and were successful. I stayed unmarried for I could not find the one person who satisfied me in every way. Each time I courted someone, I found something lacking in their personality or their general being. I could not say what it was and my mother despaired of my finding a wife. I knew at times I was a disappointment to her in that regard but equally I did not want to marry someone just because they were on offer to me. That would have been unfair to the girl who could, if she searched a little more, find someone who truly loved her and could give her a lifetime of devotion. That was the one thing I could not come to terms with: binding myself for a lifetime to another person. It simply felt wrong to me. Maybe I sought too much, I told myself. Maybe I should lower my sights, accept the defects in the personality and learn to overlook them. Somehow that argument never worked and I was alone where my brothers were content to be married and began producing children. That too was a tie I did not seek. I wondered at times if there was something wrong with me. I adored their children, played with them, handed them back when the visit was over without a pang in my heart. Not one touched me to the point when I thought 'this is something I have to do, have my own child.' I loved the little fingers tugging at my beard and hands, but it was easy for me to walk away. That told me much about myself and my need for a wife and partner. It is hard for a mother, one who wants a tribe of grandchildren, to see her eldest son remain unmarried but that was the way it had to be. I saw myself then as a lone person, I do now. It's not that I didn't like people, I did, I do, but I preferred my own company and my own thoughts. I did not like to indulge in idle chatter, socialising small talk, as it were. I felt if people had nothing meaningful to say they should not say it. I liked this very much about the man himself. He only spoke when he had something to say that was worth saying. This made visiting my parents somewhat difficult at times; Mother did so like to chatter and I found it boring so I tended to let it drift over my head. I believe she knew well I was not listening but talked to me anyway and somehow, by some osmosis I did not fully understand I somehow learned enough about my brothers, their wives and, later on, their children so that when I visited them, or we came together for the feast days and festivals at our parents' home, I could speak intelligently about them, use the right names and comment on their abilities for their age and so on. The family seemed impressed with me, but I thought I was nothing more than a sponge, absorbing useless information and then releasing it when pressed or crushed or both. I was pitied, not having my own wife and children, without anyone realising it pleased my heart and mind not be bound to another, to have the freedom to come and go as I wished, eat when I chose, eat what I chose, sleep when needed, stay up all night if the mood took me, walk for hours if I felt restless, with no one to answer to about my movements. I wondered how many would envy me if they were to think on my lifestyle and compare it with their own.

And so my life continued for some time. Quiet, calm, fulfilled, content and even happy at times, this is the way it was. Work, home, family, religious duties which I attended with gratitude in my heart for all that I had, all that God had seen fit to give me, and back to home again, where I could read and study and think. I was complete – I believed.

I had no idea how wrong I was.

Chapter 2
John the Baptist

From time to time strangers appeared in our area, hermits with wild hair and long beards, ragged clothes and outrageous claims to contact with the Divinity. Many people would go to see them, some to mock, some to take pity and give them food and drink, others to believe and go home wondering about their own souls. If they touched one person, their task was done. I didn't bother with them, I felt they were – what can I say? This is being written with hindsight when everything is so clear to the person relating the story. From my perspective now I would say I felt they were incidental, that I was waiting for something – or someone - without knowing precisely what it was I waited for, apart from the certain knowledge I would know when it - or they - arrived. I did not expect someone to knock on my door and announce they were the one I was waiting for but it was close to that feeling. And so I dismissed the other hermit prophets as no more than scaremongers in their own way, but they did perform a useful task, they prepared the way for the one who came with his talk of redemption, of absolution, of the one who was to come.

We all knew when John the Baptist arrived for there was no way the region as a whole could not have known. The news spread like fire through a parched woodland, leaping from village to village, from person to person, 'here is come a true man of God.' Some called him a wild man; others called him a true prophet, yet more called him the Messiah himself, the one for whom we all waited. The promised one of God. The leader come to set us free from our servitude to the Roman Empire. To set us free from the servitude of our own sinful lives.

Perhaps.

I held out some hope but not too much, for fear of being bitterly disappointed if he failed to live up to my expectations. Not only mine, I hasten to add, but the many of us who lived under the thrall of the Romans. For there had been false prophets, the hermits who had come from the wilderness before had come with promises and wild accusations and none had the ring of truth, no matter how much we wished that they would bring it to us. I was one of many who looked beyond the teachers we had in our synagogues and meeting places, for they had learning but no fire. It would take a charismatic man to combine the two and set the spark which would bring down the hated ones and put us back where we should be, in charge of our own destiny. Charismatic men were few and far between, it would seem. Each of the hermit prophets were like straws in the wind when we sought strength and fortitude.

The reports of this man, John the Baptist, were different. People spoke of the fire in his words, of his flashing eyes, some said blazing eyes, yet more spoke of the intense feeling they received from just being near him. It seemed this prophet, this hermit and wild man, was different from the others. I decided to go and see him and arranged my mealtime so I could go without starving myself. I did like to eat, I admit this freely. I also liked to eat at regular times. Again I tell you something of myself so you know how much I gave up to follow him when he came, for there was little chance of eating regularly and at times little chance of eating at all if we could not find people kind enough to donate food and drink.

Whilst I am on that topic, I must also say I liked comfort. My own bed, my own chair and table, my books, my garden, my whole way of living was comfort. I had good clothes and footwear. All this had to go. You cannot carry comfort with you on the road. I gave it all up without a second's hesitation. I assure you, whoever you are, reading these words, if you had come into contact with him in the flesh, the living breathing walking talking healing preaching Jesus, you would have done the same. Many did, women as well as men. I was honoured to be one of the twelve.

Again I get ahead of myself. This is my impatience to get to the story of him and how I ended up in His life.

The day seemed hotter than usual as I travelled to the River Jordan. The great watercourse provided sustenance and life for thousands ranged along its entire length, used for bathing, drinking and watering their crops. There was no question of not finding the Baptist, for the crowds were making their way along the dusty paths even as I was. I became one of the many who was on a pilgrimage to what seemed to be one of the great prophets of our time.

I wish I could find the words to convey the sense of anticipation, of wonder, of excitement, this man caused in our region. It was palpable, it was magnetic, it was mesmerising. To think that I, a cultured intellectually inclined man, should be trekking along a dusty pathway with hundreds of others to see one man said much about the quality of the reports coming from the Jordan and flowing across the area, just as the river flowed on its course to the Dead Sea.

The noise as we drew closer to him was incredible. It was a roar, almost, as if of a great wind howling across a desert and finding little resistance in its way. The impact was physical, it hurt my eardrums. It added to the heightened sense of excitement that was rippling through the crowd making its way to the banks of the river.

And the smell of dust, of living people with sun soiled clothes, of children who were playing in the mud at the river's edge and adding that to the mayhem that was the crowd awaiting the prophet's words. On the breeze came a myriad of perfumes, trees, grasses, animals, plants, fruit and more people raising yet more dust to choke and blind the eyes. Why did it not matter?

And then we were there. No, correct that, I was there. Many more were following and had not yet reached the river when I saw him.

It was as if he was a man twice the height of a normal person, such was the power of his personality, his voice and his message. His voice boomed across the water, his hands gestured to match every word, his face glowed with an unearthly pallor that enhanced the way he looked. He wore the traditional skins of the wild men who come from the desert but on him they looked like fine robes. He wore them with such nonchalant ease and seeming grace that you did not realise at first they were hacked about, ragged skins. His hair was long, flowing, catching the sunlight. It had red-gold glints in it, which matched his flowing beard. No one had offered this man the facilities of a barber for a very long time. Again, it did not seem to matter. It was of a one with the man himself.

He gestured and in that moment the huge crowd fell silent. It is impossible, I would have said this to anyone, totally impossible for a large disparate group of people without a leader to stop speaking all at once but they did. I swear this is true. Silence descended on the world. No bird dared raise its voice. The Baptist had spoken. But no, again I am wrong. He did not speak. He gestured and it was as if he held magic in his browned workman's hands.

How, I wondered, did anyone not shuffle their feet, how was it no child snivelled or cried, how did no person cough or sneeze or make any sound that would disrupt this total eerie silence? What kind of power did this man have to control us all in that way?

And then he spoke.

Redemption, confession, tithing, changing our ways, looking up for God and not down for Man. Obey the laws of God.   Honour the law of the land but look beyond it to the Kingdom of God.

In his words were the hint of rebellion.   Now that seems a strange thing to say for there was nothing, nothing there to say he was advocating an uprising and yet I sensed it. I ask myself now; did I look for what was not there? Did I seek to put on to the Baptist that which was not within his chosen/given task?

He stood in the Jordan river and held out his arms for those who wished to be baptised, those who wished to drown their sins in the fast flowing waters, those who wished to be closer to the man of power and fire and they went, one after the other, stumbling, helping one another down the side of the river bank, mothers guarding the children whilst the fathers went into the water, fathers guarding the children whilst mothers went into the water and I wondered why no children went until I realised a child is without sin until they are old enough to know the difference.

And I stood and I did not go into the water.

I watched and I listened and I felt –

Alone.

The Baptist turned and looked directly at me and our gaze locked. It was as if half the region were not there, that he stood in the water, his skin robe flowing with the current, and I stood on the bank, dry, over-hot and wind-blown and there was no one else there for either of us.

In that moment it was as if he read my soul and it was not a good feeling.   Then he dismissed it – and me – with the tiniest shake of his head. The time was not right and we knew it, both of us.

I left him there, in the coolness, with the fire of his speech and the fury of his emotions and the compassion of his heart, baptising those who sought the consolation of the act.   I left him there and returned home, accompanied by a few who had been in the water and whose clothes steamed as they trekked home in the heat.

I was also accompanied by my thoughts but they made no sense. What was he? A leader, a rabble-rouser, a man sent by God to lift the people of Judea against their Roman oppressors? Or a man of God sent to cleanse sins by baptism in the great river and preach of redemption and resolution? What did he sense in me? What did I sense him? There was a question I could not answer. I detected strength, conviction, deep faith but there was something else. Something I could not identify. I puzzled over it the whole way home.

I went back the next day.

And the day after that.

I could not stay away. I had no desire to immerse myself in the river and I knew he would not accept me anyway, but I had to go back.

It was on the fourth day that it happened. No, it was on the fourth day that it began. Someone shouted: "Are you the one we have waited for?" a clear reference to the Messiah we had been promised and who had so far signally failed to come.

"No!" he shouted back. Again there was the deathly unnatural stillness over the crowd, which was larger than before, by many hundreds. "I come to clear the pathway for he who is to come! My task is to prepare for his coming. I am not he! I am not fit to fasten His sandals on his feet!"

"Then where is he?" demanded the same voice. "Too long we have suffered under this regime, too long we are taxed out of existence and pinned down by laws and rules and suffer guards and Romans on our streets and in our buildings!"

"Patience, friend." Now the Baptist's voice had changed from blazing fire to glowing embers. "Patience. God knows when he wishes to make a move and lift the people. God alone knows the right moment. I do not. I cannot demand that he who is to come step forward and take on the role assigned to him by God himself, for he may not be ready."

"We are!" shouted someone else.

The roar which went up must have been heard in Rome. It was dangerous, there were doubtless many spies in the crowd, the authorities would not allow such a gathering without being aware, very aware, of what was being said. It was dangerous but it was right. For too long we had been the oppressed and no one, no one single person, had come to lead us out of the mess we were in. I felt my heart beating twice as fast, I felt a nervous anticipation sweep through me, I felt as if I myself were on fire and wanted to yell with the crowd. I remained silent through tremendous will power, for again I saw the Baptist's eyes turn my way, again I felt the power of his persona and knew he understood more than I ever would.

He held up his arms and silence fell instantly. It never failed to amaze me how he could do that.

"Until the day dawns … be patient, friends. Be patient. He will come and he will have words for you which will lift your hearts and souls up to Heaven. Seek not the way of violence for in that lies total repression and in that lies the total destruction of your being."

"It's the only way!" Another voice joined in and another roar went up.

The Baptist let his arms fall back to his side. "If that is your wish, find your leader and follow him. But do not ask me to be that one, do not ask He who is to come to be that one unless it is His chosen destiny. Remember, we are all of God and God alone knows what is right for us."

"God has forsaken us!" a woman's wail went up, pitiful, heart-breaking in its sorrow.

I saw the Baptist dash a hand across his eyes. Had she touched his heart with her cry?

"I know." It was said with such emotion that the silence grew even more intense. "I know the feeling. Have I not suffered long hard lonely days and nights in the wilderness as I fought for God's words in my heart? Did I not, days and nights and endless times, decide he had forsaken me? Did I not ask for his angels to come and succour me and they did not? And did I not, in that solitude and emptiness and loneliness come to understand that only God knows the way forward? Only God knows what we have to do to live our lives the way we want."

How careful were his words, even in the intensity of his emotions, he was cautious. I admired this man more and more.

He took a deep sorrowing breath. "Only God knows and he is not saying. Not yet anyway. Wait on his sign. Wait on his command, if you like. I bid you all, follow his words, obey the law, do nothing that will bring down the wrath of the authorities upon you. We have a life to live, all of us, and we must live it to fulfil that which he has arranged for us."

It was as if the life had gone out of everyone. No one entered the water, no one spoke. They stood, statues around the banks of the great Jordan River and were silent. They had hoped for more. He could not deliver more for it was not given to him to do it. This I knew and this I longed to say to him. But he walked across the river and climbed out of the bank opposite to the place I stood.

I knew too he would be back on the day following and I knew too I would be there, for there was a message in his words which I could not yet read.

But I would.

Chapter 3
The Man Cometh

Somehow the following day was hotter and more crowded than the other days I had been to see the Baptist. Were the two things connected, I asked myself? Did the amount of people there generate the extra heat, or was the sun hotter than usual? Whatever the reason I was sweating heavily, despite the fact I was wearing my lightest robe, when I arrived at the Jordan River to find the Baptist in his usual place, standing thigh deep in the water. I envied him the coolness.

Person after person stepped down into the water, to be baptised by him in the coolness, to experience – what? They went in with blank or anticipatory faces; they came out looking as if they had experienced some divine happening. So I asked myself what it was that had transformed them, what had gone on in those few moments of total immersion, what had changed them?

Even more than that, I asked myself why I was not stepping down into the water, too. I had no answer. No, I lied to myself, over and over I lied to myself, the worst kind of lying there is, for the soul knows when the conscious mind lies to it and is hurt by it. So I stood on the banks of the River Jordan and lied to Judas Iskariot's soul. I did not step down into the water – because I was afraid of what it would do to me. I was afraid of being changed; transformed, turned into something I was not. I wanted to remain the way I was, I wanted to understand without experiencing it. I held back, let others push past me in their haste to be baptised, stood back when they emerged, dripping and smiling and looking as if they had descended from Heaven or something equally wonderful. I stood back and my heart ached because I could not bring myself to do it. And I wanted to. Oh dear blessed Lord how I wanted to! The

25

two parts of me fought over the decision and the materialistic side won. I watched and mourned instead. I returned to my home and continued to mourn.

Hebron was full of talk over the next few days, talk of the man who had walked through the crowd, which had parted for him as if before a great ruler. He walked with that kind of authority, they said.

I heard many versions of what happened. Mostly they said, those who had seen, those who had heard it from someone who had been right there, I swear they were … that when the man arrived, the Baptist stopped speaking and looked at him.

Then he said; "I am not fit to baptise you."

The man said, "I wish you to do it. I know it is God's wish." And stepped down into the river as he said it. His white robe darkened with the water soaking into it as he stood facing the Baptist. "Do it," He said quietly and yet such was the silence of the crowd, everyone heard the words.

"As you wish." John the Baptist put his hands on the man and lowered him into the water and brought him back up again.

Now this is where the reports vary, from the dove which came and landed on the man's shoulder to the voice from heaven which said "This is my beloved son, in whom I am well pleased." Some said there was no dove, no bird but the brightest ray of sunshine anyone had ever seen which seemed to touch the man as he stood, dripping, in the river. Another said the voice was from the man himself, radiated to all who were there. Others said he would not say that of himself but that the voice was that of the Baptist who reached out with his mind to them all.

Whatever you wish to believe, it seemed it was a momentous occasion and I bitterly resented the fact I had not been there to see it for myself. Then none of the conflicting reports would have bothered me, would not have sent me scurrying from this group to that to overhear another report, another 'eye witness' account which varied from the one I had heard earlier. Why did I do this? Why did it bother me? He was just another visitor to the Baptist, wasn't he? So why did everyone seem to be talking about him and stories seemed to be flying across Judea?

I sat at home, for once unwilling to cook for myself, to water my plants, to tend to anything. I sat with wine and a small lamp and stared into the flame of the lamp and drank the wine and wondered what I was doing in this life.

I had a position and earned money. I had family and friends, religious devotions to follow, discussion groups to attend if I wished. I had the luxury of my home, which was furnished just the way I liked and held many pleasant memories for me of the evenings I had spent there, with books or quiet contemplation.

It was not that like on that evening. The thoughts were wild, were caught in their own web of entanglement. What was I doing in this life? Was I wasting it? I had no wife, no partner, no child to succeed me. Did I want such things? No, I did not. So why did the thought cross my mind that I had no wife, no partner, no child? What demons possessed me that evening? I could see nothing beyond the authoritative figure of the Baptist standing in the cooling waters of the Jordan River, baptising those who came for divine cleansing. I could see no other way to describe it. My mind rebelled at the thought of my own body being lowered into the water, so I asked myself again, what was I afraid of? Would I be asked to give up something of myself if I went into the water? Would the Lord God find me wanting in some way and refuse to cleanse me? But John the Baptist said no one was beyond redemption, no one would be turned away. Why then could I not bring myself to do it? And because of that refusal, I missed a chance to see someone who seemed to have stirred the crowds in a way I did not understand.

It came back to the core of Judas Iskariot. I did not want to change. I wanted to observe and believe and hold fast to that belief but I did not want to change. The fear that consumed me, and I confess there was a fear which consumed me, was that change would come whether I liked it or not. It was a foreboding, a darkness hanging over me. Within that darkness I drank my wine and stared into the flame and neither consoled me.

I went to my bed cold stone sober and sorrowing.

I know, because he told me, that after his encounter with the Baptist, he spent some time in the wilderness. I spent time in the wilderness of my own heart and mind. We were probably struggling with our thoughts at precisely the same time. He admitted as much during one of our talks. I am not sure to this day which of us had the more difficult fight. I cannot comment on his, I was not there. I can comment on mine, if I can walk through this time, for I lived every single moment of it and it was not easy or comfortable.

My problem was simple. Some-thing had entered my mind and would not let me rest.

I went to my work each day, I returned to my home each evening. I followed a pattern of cooking, eating, sleeping, visiting family, following the religious duties imposed upon us by the Lord God himself and I did it all as if I had but half a mind. People commented on my abstracted air, my sense of not quite following what they were saying. My mother asked if I needed any of Father's herbal concoctions for whatever it was that was troubling me. I did need something for that which was troubling me but it was not a herbal concoction for nothing physical could reach that which I was enduring.

What purpose was there to life?

The question tormented me. I watched people struggling to make a living from barren soil, I watched as they tended the small plants, the half-starved animals, the stunted trees. I watched as the well fed well dressed and obviously rich Romans travelled here and there and cast their laws upon us as if they were manna from heaven. They took our tax money as if they were the supreme rulers. Fool that I was, I had to believe they were or I would have gone crazy during that time. Why suffer, why work, why pay others your hard-earned money and go without to ensure they lived in luxury? What point was there in doing all this? What was the insane desire to procreate – surely we, as sentient beings did not have to constantly strive to ensure the continuation of the species? We were not animals. The prayers, the observance of the Sabbath, the structure of the services, the laws of the Torah, nothing made sense to me any more. It was as if a black cloud had come over me and coloured everything within me with its blackness. I had no fire, no passion, no enthusiasm, no exuberance. I was. No more than that. I was.

I realise, looking back, that I was profoundly depressed, but at the time I did not see it that way. I thought I had a sickness of the soul and spent time in prayer, even as I thought it was useless to do that. When I walked with the man in the darkness and we spoke of deep things that had troubled us, he spoke of such times, when prayer is a sort of refuge but the belief in the prayer is not entirely there. He said he endured some of that in his time in the wilderness but he came through it stronger and more clear minded than before. He was fortunate; I went on suffering for a long time.

My black mood became worse when news fled around the city – and I do mean fled, it was as if it had wings and would escape the confines of the country if it could – that the Baptist's preaching against what he called the incestuous marriage of Herod Antipas had finally cost him his life.

They said, the ubiquitous 'they' who seem to be everywhere and know everything, that he had been held in a dark prison where he spent his time in prayer and exhortations against those who held him, those who said they did not hear his words and scorned his efforts to get them to repent and give up their service to the ruler. They said some chit of a girl danced before Herod Antipas and so pleased him he asked what she would like as a gift and she, no doubt primed by those who would see the Baptist gone from life, asked for his head on a silver platter. And got it.

I found myself at my desk staring into the distance, imagining that wild fiery man cooped up in a dark prison cell, wondering what his fate would be, wondering if he would suffer, knowing he had to die, knowing he would die, knowing the authorities had contrived a way to remove him from the scene, for he gathered people to him and the people looked to him to be a leader. It mattered not that he denied he was the one come to lead them, those in power saw anyone like him as a threat. And threats had to be removed, once and for all.

I found myself wondering what it would be like to know life was counted in days, hours, minutes, rather than days, months, years – were the senses heightened or was there nothing but overwhelming despair that it was ending too soon or – as the Baptist had done so much in his time – the feeling that all had been achieved that could be achieved?

Oddly, it was within those philosophical thoughts I found relief from my black mood and strange musings. I began to see life again for what it was, something worth living.

Chapter 4
A Change Of Life

Something had changed in me. I could not pin down what it was, analyse it and criticise it and fight it so that it was defeated. You can only fight a known enemy and this one evaded me. I knew I was not the same but how and where was another matter entirely. I could not ask anyone for fear of seeming and sounding foolish. Imagine my going to my family and asking 'do you find me different? If so, can you tell me where and how I am so changed?' No, it could not be done.

For some time I wondered if the words of the Baptist had touched me in some way, but then I discarded that thought. Had his words truly touched me, I would have willingly walked into the water and been baptised. So I though the opposite, was I changed because I did not do what half of me wanted to do? Again, I discarded the thought for it seemed illogical to think that something I did not do had any bearing on my being changed in some way.

I was restless, that was one thing I became aware of very soon. No longer could I sit with book or scroll or wine and music after my evening meal, no longer could I quietly listen to a discussion on points of law in the synagogue, none of these things held my attention for longer than a few moments. I needed to be moving about, going somewhere, even if that 'somewhere' was no real destination. I had to be active in some way. I began walking the streets of Hebron at all hours, avoiding the Roman guards who would interrogate anyone they thought was not being lawful. Not that it needed much for them to believe that of anyone, I had found. Hebron is a maze of tiny streets and alleys; it was easy to avoid a guard if you were alert enough to see them before they see you. I became adept at it.

But the walking did not satisfy whatever the restless demon was which had taken possession of me, for such was the way I viewed it. I knew it was not true possession, I had none of the outward signs of demonic activity within me, just a – searching was the only word I could find to describe it. Searching for something but I knew not what it was.

I mourned the Baptist for I felt if he had lived, he and I might have been able to talk and he might have given me the answers I sought. But it was not to be, or he would not be lying in some pauper's grave, with or without his head. His followers were scattered, afraid of the Roman guard, afraid of persecution. Where was the man who would stand up to them, to demand that they keep to their rightful place (out of Judea), that their taxes be moderate, not excessive and that their laws be reasonable, not pernicious as they were. I sometimes dreamed I was the one. I knew what I wanted to demand but I also knew in truth that I did not have the charisma or the authority to persuade people to follow me. I knew it and it was a mournful thing to me that I could not do it. I was not lacking in courage but I did not have the leadership qualities such an undertaking needed. I had a good knowledge of the law but not to the extent of some preachers and teachers.

I felt inadequate.

That did not help the restless demon, he lived on and projected me into the streets night after night and on the days following the Sabbath, too. I walked many miles and learned nothing but that walking is tiring and at times utterly boring, for there is too much time in which to think and in thinking to feel sorry for myself. It was not a good way to spend my time.

Instead I began to visit those who were learned in the writings and the Law, to listen to their lectures and ask questions and discuss points of contention with them. In this way I learned and they were pleased to display their

32

knowledge by responding to every question with a full and detailed answer. If this led to yet more questions, they were more pleased, these sage men who nodded wisely over grey/white beards and whose eyes were lost in the crinkles and wrinkles of age and experience and who looked at me as if I were a youngster fresh from the cradle who knew nothing. In truth I knew a good deal from my private studies but not as much as they, for I had to work for a living and they studied the law and the prophets for a living. That is a very big difference.

For a while this satisfied the restless feelings I had, I resumed 'normal' life, work, home, visiting family, attending religious ceremonies and conducting a comparatively quiet life. For a while I told myself this was right, this was the way forward, that I could be content with that.

In the darkness of night, alone in my bed with nothing but thoughts for companions, I knew this to be only partly true. There remained an aching void which wanted to be filled but I knew not what would fill it.

Time and again my mind would replay the images of the Baptist standing in the River Jordan, a wild man with a message of redemption, of the pathway to God not being through material possessions. It was an old message told in a new way. Time and again I would wonder at his ability to defy the authorities without recompense, for he insulted them and sent them away and they dared not, at that time, touch him for whatever reason. Fear of the crowds? Since when had Romans been afraid of crowds? Had there been an uprising, the Roman army would have put it down with its usual indifferent cruelty and surprising efficiency. It seemingly took the 'demand' of a young girl who danced with erotic attraction to cause the Baptist to lose his head and his life. I wondered long what happened to him during that time, how he suffered, what he prayed. Why, I did not know for there was no advantage to me in knowing even if I could find out. Who would I ask, anyway? The guards would not know and would not speak to me even if I tried.

I asked myself why I had this obsession, for I realised that is what it was and had no answer for myself. I could not ask anyone else and get an answer, for I did not wish anyone else to know my secret thoughts and obsessions. Some things are best kept to oneself.

It was a small step from the Baptist to the person he baptised, the one about whom so many rumours went flying around, the one I tried to track down, without success.

I thought about this man, wondering if he was preaching anywhere and if he was, would I be able to hear him and learn from him?

But before I could seek him out, I was sure I could if I searched long enough, my mother died, very suddenly.

We had no advance warning, no illness preceded the death. One moment she was living, the next she was not. It was as if the heart went out of the family, for she had been the centre of it all and we could not replace that centre. My father went into deep mourning, my brothers were shocked out of their complacent lives for the first time and I grieved long for the one person I respected more than any other.

And I asked myself, in the dark hours when thoughts tumble rather than proceed in an orderly direction, why I felt as if a significant tie had been broken to allow me my freedom. It made no sense and I dismissed it. I had no intention of giving up my life for anyone, even if my mother was no longer the centre of it. Father would still need support. Would he not?

And yet, the restless demon which had possessed me spoke of open spaces, of strangers waiting to be greeted, of new teachings to be heard and perhaps, perhaps – a new leader to be found to lead us out of servitude and submission and into the freedom that we, the people of Judea, sought.

Where he was, who he was, how I would meet him, was in the hands of whatever is known as fate, whether that be the great God himself or those who work for him in various ways, his angels, his workers. I had no way of directing any meeting, it had to be left to 'chance' and the direction of those who wanted it to happen – if indeed they wanted it to happen.

There was a tiny, almost minuscule, thought which emerged and then retreated into whatever dark corner of my mind it lived. The thought said there would be a meeting and that it would be momentous and that I had a major part to play in this person's life. Because none of it made sense, for who could know of such a thing, I dismissed the thought completely, just as I had the other strange one that said a tie had been broken and I had my freedom. I had no such thing. I was bound by familial ties and the responsibilities of paid employment, I had a home which needed to be paid for and tended and commitments at the synagogue which had to be fulfilled. There was no such thing as 'freedom' in a conventional life; we all have ties beyond that which we immediately appreciate. They are otherwise known by the word 'responsibilities' and they cannot be cast aside at a mere whim.

Or so I thought.

Night after night I sat with my scrolls and papers, my readings and my wine. Night after night I fought the demon which spoke of other places and other people and told it to leave me and allow me some peace.

It ignored me. It bothered me. It pestered me to give it at least thought.

After some three months of this, I gave in and put aside all the scrolls and readings and sat in silent prayer instead, asking for guidance.

Nothing happened the first night, or the second or third, but on the fourth night I had a vision which deeply disturbed me, for it meant I would be completely changing my life and I was not sure I was ready for it.

I saw, as clearly as I saw my own family when I was with them, a man standing by the side of a lake. He looked at me with piercing eyes and said; 'where are you, Judas? I wait on you. The work is begun.'

I felt drawn to him, whoever he was. I felt as if I knew him already, as if he and I shared some destiny that was concealed from us both. I felt stupid and annoyed at the same time, for all of this was illogical and fanciful and surely the result of my disordered thinking over so many weeks. How could anyone know of me when I did not know them? How could someone be waiting for me and what work was the man referring to?

More than that, why was I giving the vision time and thought?

Over-riding all these random thoughts was one which was driving out all the others – the one which said, where is he and how can I find him?

It was only when I voiced this thought aloud that I realised I had not asked the question 'who is he?' as somehow I knew. It was the man everyone had spoken of, the one I had missed when He went to the River Jordan to see John the Baptist, the one who had received the accolade of the Lord God himself, if the people were to be believed.

When I accepted that, a great calmness came over me as if the restless demon had finally departed. That night I slept without dreams that I recalled and without thought of the morning.

The next day I arranged to take an indefinite time away from my employment, stating I needed to investigate some religious truths which were bothering me to the extent I did not feel I could do my work conscientiously. Fortunately for me, this is a widely accepted reason to take a pilgrimage and deal with inner demons, so no questions were asked. Provided I did not want money during my time away, they were content to let me follow my conscience, as they thought.

In truth, I was about to follow my convictions. Whether I would ever return was another matter entirely. I had no idea where that thought came from, but I accepted it for what it was, a truth.

Then I found myself closing down my house, putting my affairs in order, visiting my family and telling them I was going on a pilgrimage. My father put this down to my grief, holding me tight in a manly embrace and saying he understood. He did not but it was not for me to argue with him at such a time and in truth, I could hardly rationalise my motives myself, let alone to someone else.

When all this was done, following nothing more than an inner compulsion, I set out for Galilee.

Chapter 5
Meeting The Man

In the heat, the Sea of Galilee from the edge of Capernaum was a welcome sight. It cooled the body just to look at that vast expanse of water, with fishing boats either on its surface or along its beaches and coastline, catches being hauled ashore in gleaming silver heaps, men with sweating faces doing a hundred tasks, none of which made sense to me, being a land person with business skills rather than practical ones. I walked among them with bewilderment at their strength and their ability to do so many different things, repairs to their sailing vessels, mending nets, collecting up the hauls, trading and storing and there was a sense of inadequacy in being there. I felt as if at any moment someone would shout 'who do you think you are?' or 'come and give us a hand here!' and I would have to admit I knew nothing of what they were doing. I could not recall seeing such much activity before, so concentrated on one thing, fishing, and could have wandered all day, just looking, but I had something to do.

I had a man to find. He of the eyes and the knowledge of who I was and the fact I was needed, apparently. Or was it all in my mind and there was no person calling me? I would not find out by standing stupefied at the industry I saw around the shores of this great sea.

The question was, should I ask someone, or should I just follow my instinct and see where it led me?

The day had slid away toward eve through my meanderings. I found an inn by walking the streets of the well-laid out town and finding one that appealed to me. There I made provision for my shelter that night, realising I was both hungry and thirsty, not to mention tired. But for all that, I was drawn back to the water even as I knew I had to attend to bodily needs, or I would be in no fit state to meet with the man when I found him.

It was growing dark; the waters were changing colour from their deep vivid blue to one of a purple hue when I finally broke the enchantment which held me on the shore. I went back to the inn, there to drink and to eat and to listen to the chatter of those who clustered there, seeking relief from their day of toil and trade. Talk it was too, of ships and boats, of nets and fish, of dubious dealers and traders who were honest enough to pay good coin for fresh fish and complaints, endless as we were all used to, of the taxes imposed by the Romans on every part of life. Talk that was of good honest toil, a vast distance from the papers I covered in fine script day after day, papers which served what purpose? From this distance I could see no reason for my employment, yet whilst I was there, it seemed to serve a proper purpose. Would that we could all stand back from our work and see whether it has value in the world in which we live!

Tired and overwhelmed with impressions, I went to my bed but could not find the strings to pull sleep to my overactive mind. I could see and smell the fish, the boats, sense the roughness of the clothes of the fishermen, the brightness of the robes of the women who bargained for the fish they needed, the high pitched excited voices of the children who swarmed around and over and through and sometimes beneath the barrels, boats and nets which adorned the area. I found myself visualising everything I had seen that day, wondering at the difference between Hebron and Capernaum, not in size but in character. Where Hebron was a place of learning and business, here it seemed to be a place of trade and toil. There was more colour here, more vitality, for businessmen do not wear colourful clothes, nor do they indulge in avid talk. Their speech is measured and quiet, the discussions discreet and often unstated between those who know each other well enough to take a word as a bond. I was reacting, I believed, to the sheer vitality and energy of this small place which, despite its size, seemed to contain a mass of people and much activity.

Where, in that great kaleidoscope of activity, colour and humanity, was the One I sought? Or was He, even as I thought it, seeking me?

When sleep finally came, my dreams were fevered, strange, but with a central theme, the piercing eyes of the man who had called me, the one I had come to find.

In the end it was simple. I broke fast in the morning, collected together my few possessions and walked out into the countryside. I saw a great crowd of people heading in one direction, just as they had been when I followed them to the riverbank to see the Baptist. A sense of excitement pervaded the people, it was almost tangible, in their talk, their gestures, their swift anxious footsteps.

"Hurry!" they called to one another, "Hurry!"

And we did. In the heat of the morning, for it grew hot very quickly, despite the cooling influence of the Galilean sea, we walked swiftly to –

A gathering. I was drawn there, knowing what I would find, no, correct that, WHO I would find. He was standing, gesturing to those around him, saying something which sent them scurrying off in all directions. Then he turned back to the crowd gathering in front of him, looked across at me - and smiled.

I was lost.

In that moment I knew I was lost, that life as I knew it was over, that here was my destiny. Whoever and whatever he was, I was his, for life.

"Forgive me a moment, my friends." His voice was deep, resonant and surprisingly strong for he carried no weight on his slender frame. "Someone has arrived I have been waiting to speak with. I will not keep you long." I needed no further bidding. Everyone else had managed to find a place to sit, a small area to claim for themselves. I realised I was the only one left standing. Self-consciously I began to make my away around the outside of the group, but saw it was quicker to walk through the seated people, which is what I did. I walked with all the speed I could muster, as if drawn by a force I could not understand, toward him.

Some of those he had sent on tasks had stopped in their leaving and were staring at me, not with hatred but with curiosity. I was not like them. He stood, patiently waiting, with the gentle smile that captivated me and transformed his face from solemnity to glowing happiness.

When we met physically, when he enfolded me in his arms, it was the coming together of two great forces. He whispered "at last!" and then let go, stepping back and waving a hand toward the few who had remained to stare. "This is Judas," he told them. "Judas of Kerioth. He has answered my call." He turned back to me. "Judas, I am so pleased to see you. I will introduce you to everyone later. Right now these people have come to hear me so I must speak. Please, sit here and listen and wait for me." The other men walked off, smiling, I was pleased to note. Maybe they did not mind an outsider joining their group. Maybe it was his words which drew us together as one. All I knew was, for the first time in my life, I belonged. I belonged in every sense of the word, for his greeting said I had arrived where I needed to be, for whatever reason which no doubt God would reveal to me in time, coupled with the smiles of those who had remained to see who I was and why I was attracting so much attention.

I sat, grateful to be part of the group. I sat and I heard him preach. To this day I could not tell you what he said, for I was too overwhelmed by the fact I was there, that I had not mistaken the vision, that he had called me but I knew not why. I studied those around him, realising for the first time there were women in the group. Those who had been sent on errands had returned; they came with smiles, greetings and comfort, offering me water, bread, hard cheese and some fish. All this I accepted with gratitude, as much for the need of food as for the companionship it signified.

I studied him. The frame might have been slender, but there was a strength, an inner power which radiated from him, following his gestures, his turn of the head, His voice. He stood in rough sandals on earth which was baked by the sun and it was as if that earth was the finest carpet ever woven. He wore a plain robe tied with a simple girdle and it gleamed as if made of the finest silk. His close trimmed beard shone in the sunlight, as if coated with the finest of oils. His hair, dark brown and thick, also shone.

Something he said in his speech, for it seemed to be that, must have included those of us around him, for he turned and gestured to us all, once again with the smile which transformed the solemn face into one of lightness and – something I could not analyse. His eyes were dark brown and held an inner glow, indefinable but all knowing. I placed him as much about my own age, thirty years or so but unlike myself, He looked work-worn and experienced in the ways of the world. I felt myself a mere callow youth beside him.

Like a love-struck fool I sat and watched and didn't listen to the words but the sound of his voice instead and knew I would not return to Hebron again, that my home, my career, my family, were lost to me and that it did not matter.

Most of all, it did not matter. I had found my destiny - for better or for worse.

And I wondered where that thought came from.

When the crowd had gone and the sun began to set over the Galilean Sea, the man turned to me and held out a hand which I took, feeling a shiver of energy run through me. He smiled and looked into my eyes, just as he had in my vision.

"Now we can speak, Judas of Kerioth. I am Jesus, late of Nazareth, now an itinerant preacher come to convert the people of this land and speak God's words."

"How do you…"

"Later." He held up a hand. "First, let me speak of you to my friends and of them to you." He sat down on the ground, taking the flask of water from one of the women who brought it over to him. He smiled at me. "This is Joanna, Judas of Kerioth, lately the wife of Chuza the steward. If you do not know of him, it matters not. Suffice to say Joanna is no longer the wife of Chuza the steward-" He turned and smiled at her, a different smile, one of infinite tenderness and care, "-but a devoted follower. One day I will tell you – or perhaps she will tell you – of her great service to John the Baptist."

Joanna was beautiful. Her face was a picture of serenity underlain with strength, her eyes were shadows of blue and her smile enough to blot out the sun. I berated myself for the nonsensical poetic words which sprang to my mind but I could not stop myself from feeling that way.

"There's Miriam, she who is tending the fire. She's a widow who has been outcast by her husband's family and come to walk with me for a time. She will find her true vocation – maybe another husband - before long. Until then, she has a place with us."

Miriam must have heard him for she smiled, waved and continued to feed the small fire with twigs and dry grasses. She was a solidly built woman with a sweet face who seemed to have a placid nature. I thought it would not be hard for her to find another man ere long.

Jesus pointed to a sturdy looking man with a weather-beaten face and thick blond beard who was working to assemble a small shelter. He had long blond hair tied back with a leather thong. "That's my stalwart friend and companion, Andrew. He and his brother John, who is busy getting bread for our meal at this moment, were the first ones I called, the first to give up everything and walk with me. John will be back soon. He's quieter than Andrew, which says a lot, as Andrew himself is as quiet as a tomb even when he's being noisy!" I smiled. It was obviously a group joke, one I would discover as time went on.

"The ones who were leaving when you arrived, Judas, were Simon Peter, someone I think of as my rock and Philip and Nathanael. They are getting provisions for our evening meal. We are a small group but we will grow. I have others to call." It was said so calmly and with such assurance and authority, I had no doubt that whoever he called would drop everything and come, as I had.

"How did-" I began again but again he stopped me.

"These are things we will speak of in time, Judas. Not now. There is much you need to know, much I need to tell you but the time is not right. For now, please accept you are part of our group and that I need you to be here. You and I have much talking to do but we have time in which to do it."

And so I found myself part of the group. I was welcomed by all, when Simon Peter and the others returned, I had greetings and welcome and a few questions, not many, about what I did and why I was there. I fended off the 'why I was there' question by simply saying I had been 'called' and saw Jesus nod when I said it. At that they stopped asking; no doubt they knew well what I meant for had they not all been called, each in their own way? Had they not given up their livelihood to be with him? I discovered they were fisher folk who had simply walked away from their boats, their nets and their lives to follow him. If anyone had told me this before I met him, I would have said they were mad. Now I understood. His power was compellingly strong, his aura of authority and leadership was overwhelming and irresistible. No matter where he led, they – and I – would follow.

That night, in the coolness of the wind blowing across the water, we ate and drank, we talked and laughed, we listened and we shared.

Whatever lay ahead, I told myself, I was ready for it.

Chapter 6
My New Life Begins

There was no time for further talk that night, as Jesus was obviously tired. He rolled himself in a thick cloak and found another for a pillow, then, closing his eyes, he appeared to go straight to sleep. The rest of us found a place to rest, whispering our goodnights to one another and exchanging smiles. I had never known such companionship; it melted that which was hurting me deep in my heart, that which I had not realised was hurting.

But again, sleep would not come, no matter how I tugged on its strings. Too much had happened, too much needed to be absorbed. I watched the constellations march across the blue-black sky, saw the moon do its stately dance, distributing its silver light to all without recognition or acceptance of any differences in race, wealth or gender. It shone on Romans and Judaeans alike. I realised, with a sharp pain, that I had been watching those who approached Jesus after his preaching, asking for healing, dividing them in my mind into those who had and those who had not and knew that this was wrong. He had made no distinction between any of them; to him they were just people who had been hurting, physically or mentally. He had cast out demons from some, held the hand of others and sent his energy into them so they walked away strong and tall where they had arrived limp and lethargic. I knew I had to change my thinking if I was to stay part of this group.

My first lesson, I thought, with no doubt many more to come.

I thought on the healing, wondering how it worked, how, with nothing obvious happening, no giving of potions or pills, the people went away seemingly cured of their afflictions. Was this God's power, was this the way it was done, with the touch of a hand and the bestowing of a blessing? Was that all that was needed to cast out demons and devils and make the cripples walk straight and the deformed stand upright? I had to find out. I needed to know. To me, watching them walk away or stop close by and examine themselves and stand upright and praise God was nothing short of a miracle. But it was one that went on and on and on...

The night wind brought the scent of fish, salt, grasses, ash from the fire and olive trees, touched with animal and human scents. It was a surprise to me how alive I found all my senses to be. I was aware of the hardness of the ground, of the tufts of grass I was lying on, of the gritty sand I would feel if I stretched out my fingers. I could hear the sea making its presence felt against the shoreline, hear night calling birds and small animals fighting for survival. I could hear the steady breathing of those I found myself with, those who huddled around a small slowly dying fire as much for the comfort of being with others as for the warmth left in the embers.

I could only see the constellations, the moon and the red glow of the fire. I knew the others were there by the sound of their breath. I could not see them despite the silver rays of the all-seeing but blind-to-all moon.

I asked myself: So, Judas of Kerioth, what do you make of your meeting with these people, with the man who called you and who has obviously captivated you?

I answered myself: these are honest, hardworking people with skills I will never have. They are fishermen and workers with their hands. They are women with cooking and nursing skills. By comparison my skills with food are minimal and as for nursing – I wondered how I knew they would be good at tending the sick. No one had said. The group was one of friendship, co-operation, loving and giving but – it was in existence because of the man at its centre, Jesus of Nazareth. He of the all-knowing eyes and words that soothed and comforted. Even when he spoke harshly, when he denounced and dismissed the demons which possessed the unfortunates, his voice was soothing and comforting yet the demons departed at his bidding. He was wise, his every sentence seemed to contain a thought we could accept and use in our lives. He spoke of the sick who came, how they needed a touch that was nothing but love and that would heal them. No one seemed surprised when he said we would all, every one of us, be able to heal in the same way, provided we had faith enough to do it. At the time I wasn't surprised and I should have been. But he spoke in such a way that it was a matter of fact, not to be argued with. We would do it. He had spoken. 'How' was in God's hands, obviously.

The talk was light, easy, comfortable and absorbed the attention of everyone. No one appeared restless or impatient, no one attempted to cross-question or contradict anyone else. Somehow he personified calm and it reflected on us all.

And I lay awake during the long, endless night, watching the march of the stars and the dance of the moon, wondering if he slept, or whether he too was busy with his thoughts and perhaps prayers.

Prayers. I had not thought of praying, perhaps I should do so. But no, my mind refused the standard formulaic prayers that were part of my life. Somehow that had gone, somewhere between following the crowd and then walking through the crowd to be accepted by someone I had only seen in a vision, all that I once held dear had gone. It left an empty chasm which was to be filled, I sensed, by the words of this strange man, someone who had power in his voice and a depth of knowledge in his mind that few people possessed.

Power. It came back to that. Why else would such a disparate group of people leave all they had to walk with him? It was no life, camping outside, eating when they could, sheltering when they could, washing in streams and at the water's edge instead of from a bowl with a fine thick towel to dry yourself and a fresh set of clothes hanging waiting to be worn. Now clothes would need to be washed and dried outside, washing would be something done when anyone could do it, for it seemed the emphasis was always to be on the preaching and the healing and that was everything.

Priorities. My second lesson. Priorities. People first. Healing their minds with the words, their bodies with the touch, bringing them to God through the simplest of means. Speak to them of that which they would understand, not the high flying talk beloved of the biblical scholars, but simple words. This I remembered from his preaching earlier, even if I could not recall the individual words he spoke. I remembered the simplicity of them, the way the crowd, unusually, remained silent.

As they did for John the Baptist, I recalled, and then wondered what Joanna had done for the Baptist and how she came to be with Jesus and why her husband no longer wanted her. I wondered if I dare ask or whether she would tell me herself. She interested me, she had such radiant beauty and elegance in her movements, she would grace any household, especially one as high ranking as a steward for the Roman ruler of our land.

My third lesson. I could not ask and would not ask, but await each person's story if they chose to share it. I became aware the night was one long lesson, taken in small steps, leading me on to a fresh understanding of myself and the way I would live in future. For I had no doubt I would remain with this group. Everything told me I would and everything told me I would find great happiness in doing just that.

Happiness. It had been a long, long time since I knew the meaning of that particular word, if I ever did. Maybe now I would find it.

And I wondered, just in passing, if this man was the leader we had been waiting for.

When dawn broke I finally tugged hard enough on the strings for sleep to find me. I heard, just, Jesus saying 'leave Judas to sleep for a while, he has had much to think on this night.' And again I wondered, before I drifted into a dreamless state, whether he had been awake and aware of me.

When I woke, the sun was high in the sky and someone had rigged a canopy to protect me from its burning rays. I felt – complete, as if I had been living this way all my life and that a simple blanket canopy was my usual form of shelter. When I sat up, I found Jesus sitting just outside, staring into the distance.

I walked quietly away to attend to my ablutions, then returned to my small area and sat down again. Then he turned and smiled at me.

"I have bid the others give us time to talk, Judas. Soon enough the crowds will be here again and I will be needed. Before then, I know they will hold the people back as long as they can. Now tell me, did you think long last night?"

"I did."

"And you learned things about yourself, that I know. Were they displeasing to you in any way?"

"No. I learned I had to put aside preconceptions and accept people for who they are, not what they are."

He smiled and his eyes seemed again to bore into me. "A good start. Few reach that conclusion so quickly. I'm sorry, I have not thought to let you break your fast."

"It doesn't matter, there will be time for that when you are needed."

"I thank you for your consideration, Judas. Those who come will not accord me the same courtesy. I have to say, for they come with their needs with no thought of mine. So be it, it is part of the ministry to which I am called. What else did you learn?"

"Priorities. That people have to come before everything."

"Yes. That was learned, or you would not have said what you did. And the third thing?"

I started, wondering how he knew there were three things. "To accord each person their privacy, not to ask questions much as I am curious about each of them."

"And that, my dear friend, is probably the wisest thing you learned last night. Each person is complete of themselves, they guard their privacy even when their profession is writ clear in their clothes and their manners. But – not all fishermen are dullards, not all clerics are devout, not all women are natural mothers. We, each of us, are individuals and we preserve a small part of ourselves as our individuality. We share only part of it and that when we want to, not when we are asked. You decided and learned well, Judas of Kerioth. I am well pleased. And to answer your final question, the one you would not ask, in light of that which you learned, yes, I was awake all night and I followed your thoughts by the way you tossed and turned and found no rest on the hard ground. For it is alien to you, you had a life of comfort and security. All this is alien to you and in that lies another lesson which you will discover in time. Where you are is not what you are. You can be yourself in the poorest of homes, the most dire poverty, the most jewelled and golden temple. Whatever is about you is incidental to what you – the real person – are. If you remember that, you will do well. I did well in choosing you, too."

"How did you know of me?" I had to ask, that question above all others burned in my mind.

"I know everyone I want to call to my ministry. I know them because I am linked with every one of them in some way. How, I do not know, for it has not been revealed to me. I am like a man in the dark with a glimmering ever-dimming lantern, seeking the pathway of righteousness to bring others to the Kingdom of Heaven. Where I go, who I call, what I say, comes from God and not from me. I follow his words and his directions blindly, knowing they are right. If I had not that faith, I could not do the work he has given me."

"Master, we can hold them back no longer." The tall shadow that was Nathanael looked apologetic and sad, but Jesus smiled at him and gave him his hand so he could be helped to his feet.

"My beloved friend, our talk is about done. Friend Judas here has much to think on still, but he will be good for us. Be kind and help him break his fast, he has had nothing so far this day. I will go and see to the people that are come."

He walked away with a firm step and as much vitality as he would have had if he had slept the entire night and was rested and well. I watched him go and wondered how he could do that. Then I looked at Nathanael and he smiled.

"There is food, Joanna saved some for you. I will bring you something to drink."

"I thank you. I am sorry I held everything up this morning."

"Jesus does this with each new arrival, lets them 'sleep' when he knows we, each of us, have our thoughts to sort out and he knows we do this best in the night hours. Then he counsels us and walks off as if he had done nothing." Nathanael looked toward Jesus, who was already healing and speaking to the gathering crowd, which was growing larger every moment. "I love the man."

"I do too."

"Yes. You would not be here otherwise. Now, let me get you that drink."

I sat and watched, mesmerised, as the healing went on and talk went on and the people sat with radiant faces to listen to his words. I could not hear them, I was just too far away to catch more than the occasional phrase, but I had his words to me to consider, to store and to treasure.

Life changing words. Mesmerising words. This was one extraordinary man, no wonder the crowds came and kept on coming.

The cold thought wormed its way into my mind.

The authorities would not be content to see these gatherings. There were likely to be storm clouds ahead.

I wanted to help fight them if they came. That for me was a major decision, for I had avoided confrontation with everyone up to that time. It was not only awe of the Romans but fear of the Romans which had instilled in me a need to avoid trouble. Now I was actively saying I would help fight if they came. What was happening to me?

Chapter 7
The Group Grows Larger

There seemed to be no end to the people who came to see Jesus. I, who had seen the crowds gathering to hear John the Baptist, thought I had known what a crowd was. Hebron had been crowded at times but nothing like this densely packed collection of starved human beings, starved that is of teaching that would satisfy their hearts and minds, not of food, for few were haggard through hunger. Most were well fed and some were even richly garbed and over-fed, I would have said. But then, it was not for me to judge.

I stopped myself then, thinking how much I had already learned. In my 'past' I judged instantly, always on appearance, never on personality.

"What of the religious laws?" someone shouted as Jesus paused for a moment in his preaching. "Would you have us ignore the laws?"

"Have I said anything that contradicts the laws?" he asked in return. "My mission is not to tear down the laws, but to show you the way to the kingdom of Heaven. Listen, my friend and hear the words I give you.

"Man is not able to live without laws, whether they be of a religious nature or made by those who rule us. Without guidance, without rules, man would not of his own accord respect his neighbour, give to the poor, observe the Sabbath or do any other thing which is right. You will say in answer to this, of course he would, for the great God demands it of him. Yes, he does, but how does each person know of what the great God demands of him? Only through the laws. Within each man is the desire to feed well, to live in comfort, to provide for his family, to walk safely in the streets and be in his home at night without fear of robbers breaking in. If each person

54

could do that without contributing his money to the taxes which are levied to pay for the safety of the individual, if he could not have to pay for the food to feed is family or work to provide it, if he could have mattresses stuffed with down rather than straw without working for it, would he not do so? Of course he would. It is a natural thing for each person to want without giving in return.

"Giving is not part of man's nature."

He turned and gestured to his small group. "Each person here has given up something, their home, their livelihood, their family, to walk with me. My friend, would you do that?"

The questioner shook his head, looking a little subdued. He had no doubt thought his question to be a clever one but Jesus had outsmarted him.

"And so I say to you, man needs laws to remind him that the poor are to be taken into consideration, that taxes need to be paid to buy that which he seeks of life, that food and comforts need to be worked for to be appreciated. And overall, in our lives, we need laws to keep us on the straight and narrow pathway of righteousness. Not many give freely; not many are of the right mind that they could walk through life and be forever aware of their fellow man's plight. Those who do are venerated and recognised in Heaven before they arrive there. Does this answer your question, friend?"

The man sat down, obviously having much to think on. I stored the words, believing one day I would write them down, for Jesus' words should be recorded, I told myself. I thought I would be the one who would do it. How little we know of our future, when we walk this life path!

"What of those who devote themselves to the religious life?" someone else asked. "Are they not the people of whom you speak?"

"Not all who take the religious vows do it from purity of mind," Jesus said and there was a distinct note of sadness in his voice. "Some need to hide from the world for the world seems harsh to them and they are unable to live in it. Some have a defect of character which is best kept from the world and so their families advise them to shut themselves away. Some think to contribute their wealth to the place wherein they live and so buy their way into Heaven. Some, a few, do truly commit themselves to the religious life. They, and they alone, will be venerated and recognised in Heaven before they arrive there."

A strange silence had fallen over the gathering, for the vibrancy with which he had begun his preaching had faded with the questions. It was as if by bringing his words into question, they were deflated in some way.

Then I realised I was wrong. His words had not been deflated but the people had, for he had delved into some of their innermost strongly held convictions and shown them as not being as worthy as the person thought.

As if realising this, someone on the edge of the crowd began chanting a psalm and everyone joined in. Soon the whole mood of the people had changed again into one of upliftment and joy.

Jesus stood and listened, an enigmatic smile crossing his lips, his eyes shining. When they were done, he spoke again.

"You see how your mood has changed when you invoke the great God through prayer and singing? I say again as I have said many times, put God at the centre of your heart, your soul and your life and all will follow from that. Put aside that which you treasure most, money and possessions. Retain them but do not take pride in them. Use them without venerating them. Fear not their loss but fear more that your soul will not be cleansed enough to meet the great God when you are called to heaven's door. Seek first the Kingdom of Heaven and all else will be given to you."

Then he held out his hands and the sick, the crippled, the diseased, the possessed, came flocking to him. John and Andrew tried to get them to form some kind of line but such was their impatience to reach Jesus that they were jostling one another. One woman fell heavily and could not rise of her own accord. I ran to her and lifted her up, realising she was no more than bones held together by skin. My whole heart ached to help her and I put my hand on her back to assist her as she walked toward Jesus. Because of her fall, everyone moved aside to let her pass.

I saw a strange look in Jesus' eyes as we approached, surprise, pleasure and compassion. I wondered if all the emotions were for her. As we stood there, I began to sense that the back against which I pressed my hand was more substantial than when I had helped her up. I also realised that this was happening before Jesus took her hands in his.

"You are cured," he told her. "Your condition has been broken into pieces and those pieces will be voided by you and be gone. Trust and give thanks to the Lord God."

"Master, thank you!" She fell on her knees and kissed his feet, before getting up by herself and walking away, looking younger and stronger than before.

"We will speak later, Judas," he said, reaching out his hands for the next person.

I went back to shepherding the crowd, confused, uplifted, frightened, so many emotions struggling for eminence in my mind. What had happened? How did a fragile woman become a substantial one in the course of three steps, for we had taken no more than that, I do swear. Was it something I had done, and if so, what? How? What supreme power came through me at that moment? I was beginning to wonder if I had gone mad in some way and yet, watching Jesus, it all seemed so natural and – believable. They went to him hurt and walked away free. I could describe it no other way.

The healing went on all afternoon, with scarcely a break for him to take much needed water and a little sustenance. When at last the evening began to draw its dark cloak over the land, the people started to leave. James' brother John had returned from an errand - 'attending to business' James told me when we spoke of the members of the group - and the two men walked across the field where the crowd had been, picking up items that had been left behind, a cloak, a rug, a bag, things which the people might claim if they came back again – 'or we can use if they don't,' James said later, when the items were piled up by our shelters.

It was then I realised someone had not left. A beautiful woman with a pale delicate face was sitting with Jesus, her eyes clouded with tears.

When we were gathered round the fire, Jesus introduced her.

"This is Mary of Magdala, my friends. I have cast out her demons but she is unable to return home. She will be travelling with us for as long as it is her desire to do so."

That caused the tears to flow silently. I had never seen anyone cry with such dignity and grace. She was truly beautiful and I had thought Joanna the most beautiful woman I had ever seen.

"Mary, you will be tired out from living with the demons." Miriam touched her shoulder gently. "Come, I will find a place for you to rest and restore yourself. I have not been possessed but know others who have and know how tired they were for a while."

"It is also the knowledge they are gone." Mary had a gentle melodic voice that matched her beauty. "It is hard to accept they are no longer there."

"Of course. The worst illness is missed when it is gone, for it becomes part of us." Jesus touched her cheek with infinite tenderness. "Go with Miriam, she speaks good sense. I am glad to have you with us, Mary of Magdala."

The two women moved away, one supporting the other. We watched them go, knowing how much this meant to each of us, the lesson of the fit supporting the infirm, the consideration and sympathy extended to someone who, although now dis-possessed, still needed care.

Jesus saw me looking and smiled. "I have to tell you something, friends. We have a healer among us, someone who did not know he could do it. Judas, my dear friend, what did you feel when you ran to that woman's aid?"

I stumbled over my words, unsure of myself, not having spoken to the whole group, only to individuals, up to that moment. But a calmness came over me and I was able to remember each step that I took.

"That she was in need, that no one around her sought to help her up. Maybe they were ashamed that their jostling had caused her to fall in the first place. When I got to her, I wanted … with all my heart … to help her for she was no more than skin and bone but I felt she … had a purpose to go on living. I am so glad you were able to heal her."

"I did nothing for her, Judas. Nothing at all but hold her hands. She was already healed when she reached me. Your compassion, your overwhelming compassion, broke up that which was eating her body and she began to recover immediately."

It was my turn to have tears; they streamed down my face and soaked into my tunic.

"I had … no idea … I thought … I thought only to help her to reach you."

"And you did. In doing so, you healed her. I said to you before, did I not, Judas, I am glad I chose you."

He turned to the group. "What Judas did you can do. All of you. Mary and Miriam will be able to do healing, casting out demons, healing the lepers and the sick. But remember this, not everyone can be healed completely, for some are at the end of their life's journey and it is not for us to stop their return to Heaven, even for a day. The Lord God knows when each person is to die but what we can do is ease their passing, relieve their pain, their suffering, their fear. If we do that, we do them a great service. You will be able to do this, just by the strength of your love and compassion. Do not ask yourself how it works, just accept that it does. It is a gift of the Almighty God, it comes directly from Him through you. Accept."

Andrew served each of us with food and drink; we sat around the fire and spoke of trivial things, the glory of the day, the amount of people who had come to listen and to absorb the teachings. One by one we fell silent, as we realised Jesus was more asleep than awake. I recalled, with a shock of horror mixed with regret, that he had lost a night's sleep in watching over me.

He must have picked up the thought, for he got up and stretched. "I was awake last night, for reasons you all know," he told them. "Now I must rest."

He lifted a cloak and put it around his shoulders to protect against the night chill, then he turned to me. "Judas, it was not your fault. It was my decision to watch over you. Do not berate yourself, my friend. You repaid me today with your great compassion."

He walked a short distance away and, arranging his pillow, then lying down. Almost immediately he was still, as if he had instantly dropped into the arms of sleep.

One by one we quietly put away our dishes and went to find a place to rest.

For me sleep was a long time coming – again – for the day had revealed much and I had a great deal to think on.

A healer. Me. Judas of Kerioth. I could, for the first time in my life, be of real use to people. It was hard to comprehend and wonderful to believe. I thought I had a fulfilling life, I thought the world was mine to claim, me in my humble home in Hebron, my scrolls, my food, my wine and my thoughts. Now I realised it was of nothing. That all I had done was be servant to others, arranging their finances, what real help was that when the illness consumed you, when you could not stand straight, when you carried demons inside you that ate at your sanity?

I fell asleep thinking of Mary of Magdala, free of her demons. In a way I was free of mine, too.

Chapter 8
Coming Together

I woke early, just as the sun's rays touched the ground. The rest of the group were still sleeping, small mounds of grey in the morning light. The earth smelled fresh, rich with new life, the dust not having yet risen to clog the mouths and noses of those who walked and thus stifle the scents that surrounded us. I remained still and thought on those I had chosen to walk with. I knew little about Jesus, other than he came from Nazareth, which he told me, that he had some kind of mission, which was obvious, that he had others to call, which he told me, that he had leadership qualities which were obvious. But the others, Andrew, Peter, Philip, James, John, Mary, Joanna, Miriam, Nathanael, what did they do 'before Jesus'? What life did they leave behind? Were there families mourning the fact they had left? Who was tending the boats the fishermen had walked away from? Who was taking care of the home Joanna had walked away from?

Miriam stirred, sat up and looked around her. She saw I was awake and sent me a radiant smile, before getting up and going off into the bushes. I hadn't seen her take a flagon with her but she came back with water, which she poured into a bowl and set to one side.

One by one everyone woke, stretched, smiled or greeted everyone else, then set about rebuilding the small fire and coaxing a few flames into larger ones so food could be cooked.

Jesus slept on. We were quiet, even as we busied ourselves with tidying, preparing, washing and all the other tasks everyone has to do every morning. We were all casting anxious looks in his direction, wondering – at least I was – if everything was all right. I saw Mary creep over to Jesus and kneel down by his side. Then she quietly got to her feet and came back to the fire.

"He sleeps sound," she told us. "There is nothing to worry about."

In that moment all tension went out of us and I realised we had been concerned that he could be lying there dead for all we knew. Only Mary had the courage to go and find out. I looked at her with fresh admiration. This serene quiet woman had fought demons, had obviously not been able to return to her family, had chosen to walk with a travelling preacher and still found it in her to check whether that person had died in his sleep when none of us had the strength of mind to do it. Truly these were exceptional people I had met and I wondered afresh at my ability to be part of the group, an accepted part of the group.

Tentatively we began to talk much as we had done the night before, of the people who had come, of the healing which had gone on, how I felt about healing someone. Slowly, perhaps unconsciously, our voices were low at first and then became animated as jokes were made and laughter rang out.

"I'm missing the jokes." Jesus, sleep tousled and still looking tired, came and sat down by the fire. Miriam moved over to give him more room.

"We thought you sleeping, Master."

"How many times do I have to tell you my name is not Master, James? Do I call you servant or follower? Come, we are as one and we use our given names. Yes, I was sleeping but my friends were laughing and joking and I heard you in my dreams. Then I heard an angel saying 'wake up, you fool, for you miss the fun!' and here I am."

The laughter was free flowing and invigorating. I asked myself, when was the last time I laughed? When was the last time I smiled at a woman and knew she would not see an ulterior motive in it? When was the last time...

"Judas?" Joanna was looking at me with a hint of anxiety in her eyes. "Is there something wrong? You stopped in the middle of a laugh, if that be possible, and are wearing a frown."

"Nothing is wrong." I put down the cup I was holding and looked at everyone in turn. "I was wondering when was the last time I laughed, when was the last time I truly smiled and then stopped myself for I did not like where my thoughts were going."

"Why? Philip leaned forward to ask the question. "Judas, it is good to explore all thoughts. It helps us understand ourselves. We need to do that to understand others."

Jesus held up his hand. "One of the wise things which came out of Judas' sleepless night recently was the knowledge that you do not ask questions, you allow that person to tell you themselves, when they feel it is right. That is more or less your thinking, isn't it, Judas?"

"It is."

"Maybe this is not the right moment for Judas to share with us the life he has left behind. Maybe there is a great sadness there which he has walked away from. Should we ask?"

"My apologies..." Philip began but again Jesus held up his hand. "In this group I see no reason for apologies either, unless there is a serious upset or hurt of some kind. Everything we speak of, informally and formally, helps us understand ourselves more and we should discuss it, just as we have now, but when we are ready. Joanna was right to ask, though, for fear of Judas having some physical pain which we should know about. If it is a thought, then that can hurt too but it is a private thing."

"I'm not – I – I have been a solitary man too long." It was hard to say it and yet I wanted to say it. "I lived alone before I came here, my own home, my own

64

company. I worked in an office where laughter was unheard of. I studied with those who are students of the religious laws; there was no laughter there. Now I find I am with people who laugh and talk and share. It is – enlightening, to say the least. No, it's more than that, it's liberating. It was a sudden revelation that caused me to stop, nothing more. Joanna, I thank you for your concern. Philip, I trust we can talk and get to know one another. Jesus, I thank you for your friendship and that goes for you all."

Jesus nodded and then looked up at the bright sky.

"Before we begin our day, I wish to do two things. I wish you all to pray with me, please, and then I want to do something else."

In silence we all sat with bowed heads, making our own private prayers to the great God. I prayed for understanding of the situation in which I found myself, one so unlike anything I had ever experienced before, that it was going to be difficult at times to adapt. I prayed for strength for all of us, knowing without knowing that others were going through the same torment as I was, coming to terms with a new life.

I was surprised Jesus didn't pray aloud, but then he said:

"I don't want to know the details of your prayers, just tell me in one word what you prayed for."

Each of us in turn responded with the same word – strength.

Then I knew why he didn't pray aloud. It was for us individually to accept what we needed most, and we had.

He got up and stood with his arms wide. "I want each of you in turn to come to me."

We did, starting with Joanna and then Mary, Miriam, Peter, one by one we approached him and were embraced. He said something private to each one. None of us knew what was said; it was personal and each person seemed to glow afterwards. I was the last one. I thought it right, I still did not feel I had earned my place in the group. He said, "We share a destiny, Judas. Right now I know not what it is but I will, when my abilities grow. Whether it be good or bad, I know you need to be with me. I thank you for that."

His arms were strong; there was a feeling of security and comfort in his embrace. It was a feeling I was to know many times in the days ahead. I never forgot it.

"Now," he said, full of energy and enthusiasm. "Today we move on. Today we recruit the next member of our group. He awaits us. Let us be gone!"

It was easier said than done, there was much to pack up, a fire to extinguish, food to be put away, a broken amphora to be buried, so as not to leave the place looking as if wastrels had been camping there. All this was done with the maximum co-operation and the minimum of fuss. We each shared a bundle of the communal possessions as well as our own small bag. When we were all done, Jesus took one last look round, smiled and said; "we go."

We walked through Capernaum in a group, Andrew, Peter, James and John walking as guards, protecting Jesus from the many who tried to beseech him to stop and speak, to heal, to just be there for a moment.

"I have to move on," he told them, from the safety of his ring created by his friends, for there were those who tried to touch him even as he stood there, politely explaining he had to visit other places but that he would return. It made progress rather slow for a while.

Philip walked at my right side. "It's always the same," he told me. "The people cannot bear to let him go but he has other places to go to, other people who need to hear his message."

"It also helps with the authorities." Joanna had come to walk on my left. "They do not like crowds gathering in one place too often. I'm sure that had much to do with the death of John."

A sadness crossed her eyes when she spoke of the Baptist and again I found myself wanting to question her but remembered my thoughts and held back from that which I wanted to say. She would tell me in her own time, if she wanted to.

We had been walking for a good part of the morning before we reached the edge of Capernaum, because of the many stops forced on us by the people. Just as we were beginning to make a faster pace, Jesus stopped and pointed to a tax collecting office.

"I need to go there."

"You do not pay taxes," protested Peter, laughing.

"I know, but there's someone in there I need. Wait for me."

He walked away from us, almost regal in a simple robe and sandals. I wondered how he could look so authoritative in such basic clothes. It was something I would wonder for many days to come.

He disappeared inside and we waited in the heat of the morning. Some of us put our bundles down in the dust to wait; there would be time enough to carry them when we resumed our journey.

"Judas, why do I feel-" Joanna broke off whatever it was she was going to say, for Jesus had come back out of the tax collecting office, followed by a man who had a most bemused look on his face and a sort of smile.

Jesus stopped in front of us and gestured to the man. "This is Matthew. He is going to work with us."

We all greeted the newcomer, who seemed dazed.

"Each of these people has given up homes, jobs and families to walk with me, Matthew. I know your inner heart, I know your unhappiness. Will you join me? You have got this far, you have left your desk and your fellows in the office."

Matthew blinked a few times as if he had awakened from a dream, looked at us all and seemed to grow several inches in stature.

"I don't know how you know, Jesus of Nazareth, but yes, I am unhappy and yes, I will walk with you. May I take a short time to pack some belongings and say goodbye to my family?"

Jesus smiled. "Of course. We will be making a meal just outside the town. Come and find us there when you're ready. We will wait for you."

Matthew grabbed Jesus' hand for a moment, then hurried away, smiling. Jesus began to walk and again the four men gathered around him to protect him from those who were coming from their homes to try and speak with him.

"The Master will be coming to Capernaum again," they told everyone. "For the moment he has other places to go. Be patient, pray to the Lord God and he will return."

Jesus said nothing as this went on, just kept on walking, seemingly lost in his own thoughts. I turned back to Joanna, waiting for her to finish whatever it was she was going to say to me, but she seemed lost in her own thoughts, too.

We stopped to eat our midday meal under a tree by the side of the road, which gave us a little shade and protection from the sun. We were gathered around Jesus, something which happened so naturally I realised it was usual for us to do that. We ate in silence, drank water and rested.

"Will he come back?" Andrew asked eventually, the question we had all wanted to ask and no one had dared voice it.

"Matthew?" Jesus looked at his friend with great tenderness. "Why should he not come back?"

"He's a tax collector. He has a position, he has wealth, he has-"

"He has nothing of value. He is a seeker and he will be here very soon."

"How did you know he was there?" Miriam asked.

Jesus leaned forward to talk to us. "It's like a waking dream. Sometimes I see something which is not there at that moment. I saw Matthew in his office, sensed his great need and went to give him the choice: Come with me and find a new life or stay where you are and continue with that life. He chose to come with me." He looked up as he said those words and smiled. "And here he comes now, with a small bag and a big heart."

He was indeed coming, as fast as he could walk, smiling so broadly it was as if he could not contain his happiness. Jesus got up. "Another for the work to come. I am right glad of it, too." He moved forward to greet Matthew and brought him back to the group. He introduced us all.

Matthew stood, still bemused but still radiantly happy. "Whatever it is you have on offer, I will go with you all," he said, almost choking on his emotions. "I know this is right. I knew the other way was wrong."

"You are sure now?" Jesus asked him. "For we are about to move on and I would wish very much that you would go with us."

"I am sure. No matter what, I am with you."

"Then welcome. Let us move on. There are many awaiting our message and our healing."

As one the group once again moved onto the dusty road and set off – for whatever destination Jesus had in mind. No one asked where we were going, or what we would do when we got there. It was enough for us that he knew.

We had taken but a few steps when Jesus turned round. "Someone is calling." We looked at one another in surprise. I for one had heard nothing and was sure, by the expressions on everyone else's face, they had heard nothing either.

Then a small boy came rushing toward us. "Master! Master! Wait!"

"I am waiting," Jesus said. "What is it?"

"This is one of my neighbour's sons." Matthew looked surprised. "Jacob, what is it? Is there a problem at home?"

"No, Master. I am bid to come and ask you to return just this night for a dinner and so that your family can meet the people who are taking you away."

Jesus laughed. "Of course we will come! It will be good to meet the family, Matthew. If you are content to return, of course. Say the word and we will move on if you so desire."

There was longing in Matthew's expression. "I had but little chance to explain, I would be glad of the opportunity. If everyone is happy to come to my home…"

There was no need for words. As one we turned and began to walk back into Capernaum. Joanna walked with me, head down, as if studying her feet as they trod into the dust, small puffs of white rising up each time she set down one delicate foot.

"Judas…"

"Joanna."

We let the others walk ahead of us just a little so we could talk quietly and yet still be part of the group.

"Judas, what do you know of John the Baptist?"

"Very little. I saw him, several times I went to the Jordan and watched him baptise and preach, but of the man himself, I know nothing."

"No, not outward things, not his family, friends, where he was trained, who called him, none of that." She stopped and looked at me, earnestly and intently. "You were there, you saw him. What did you *feel?*"

I thought about this as we walked. The others were chatting to one another with bright cheerful smiles. There was a sense of enjoyment in the occasion and the day. I recalled the brightness of the days when I went to the Jordan River. Before I could answer, Matthew spoke.

"Here we are," he said with pride. We stood before a substantial home, solidly built, with flowers adorning the front. I was struck by its solidity and again marvelled at the strength of Jesus' personality that he could call someone who would walk away from all this.

"We can talk later," I told Joanna. She nodded and smiled as we entered the house.

It was a crush, so many of us arriving at once. Tables and benches were hastily set up outside in the enclosed garden to make room for us all. Matthew's wife, Sarah, red eyed and yet happy, scurried from one to the other, greeting us, smiling nervously, supervising the cooking of the meal and ensuring we were served wine and small cakes.

Jesus called her over when most of the preparations were under way, persuading her to sit with him for a while.

"Are you content to let your husband walk with me for a time, Sarah?"

She looked into his eyes and, as we all did, gave way under the strength of his power.

"When he came to say goodbye I cried, Master. Now I see why he has made the decision. I know it will not be forever. I know too he has to walk with you for a time. I will wait on his return."

"That is not entirely the answer I sought," he said persuasively. "I asked if you were content."

"I was not, now I am."

"That's all I needed to know. Thank you. Matthew has a task to do for me later in his life. I cannot say what it is for it is not yet revealed to me, but when it is, he and I will know it."

"Master, I must see to the dinner. Forgive me."

"Of course." She bustled away; there was no other word to describe it, there was a sense of busyness in her step and a new buoyancy in the way she moved and the way she spoke. She was not losing a husband; she was contributing, in her own way, to Jesus' ministry. Her husband had a task, an essential role in his future. It was enough and would be enough to sustain her through the lonely days ahead. I wondered anew how I knew these things without being told.

More people arrived, friends of the family and people Matthew knew from his tax collecting times. Jesus spoke with them all but said nothing that could be classed as teaching. It was a purely social occasion and he seemed to relax for the first time that day.

There were Pharisees there, too, and scribes. Who had told them he was there I don't know, I never did find out. They were there to try and catch him out, as always. Was he perceived as such a threat to the established order that they were perpetually trying to find fault with his way of doing things?

So I heard, as did some of the others, the mumbling between them. "Tax collectors, tradesmen, those without employment, why does someone who professes to speak the word of God associate with such – the very dregs of society?"

"It shows the true level of his intelligence, does it not, that he would do so?"

What they didn't know was they had been overheard, not only by some of us who walked with him but Jesus himself. Without raising his voice, but with that edge of authority that came when he preached, he spoke to them across the crowded courtyard.

"What would you have me do, oh righteous ones? Would you have me talk to you of the law and what it means? You who already profess to know everything there is to know about God's word? Does the well man seek a doctor or professional? No, they do not. Only the sick need attention and now, only those who are blind to the word of God, those who are lost, those who have strayed, need to hear my words and come back to the true pathway. I am with those who need me, not with those who say they do not."

Grumbling even more, they backed off, for they had no answer for him. But they didn't leave, they stood on the edge of the crowd, for the gathering had turned into a very large crowd indeed. Word had gone out that Jesus had not left and they were there, asking, seeking, waiting, one more chance before he moved on.

When he realised this, he apologised to Matthew and went outside to begin work yet again. We went with him, to protect, to guard and to help where we could. A great roar went up when he emerged from the doorway and he smiled and held up his hands.

"I came for a quiet meal with a friend..." This brought a gale of laughter and then everyone quietened down. "I know you need healing, I know you seek teachings, but I cannot attend to all of you this day. It is impossible for me to say, bring forward those who are most seriously ill, for each of you carries an illness or a condition which to you is serious. I promise you this, I will return and when I return, I will have empowered others to help in the healing so we can reach more of you, treat more of you and help more of you. Is this all right? Will you accept this from me?"

"Yes!" was heard from a lot of people and from others, a sigh of resignation and recognition that they could not be treated at that time. One look at the amount of people who had gathered told them that.

"I will return," he told them again and we went back inside. Jesus sat down in a chair by the cold hearth and looked at Matthew, who was sitting opposite him on a stool.

"You see how much work there is to do, Matthew? I need all the help I can get but I need to choose carefully. Not just anyone, but the right ones."

"How did you know-"

73

There was a tremendous noise from overhead, banging and crashing. Then dust fell in a cloud from the ceiling and daylight shone in. As we stared in astonishment a bed was lowered on four ropes in front of Jesus. Lying on it was a man who seemed to be paralysed. Four faces looked down through the hole in the roof.

"Apologies, friend!" one of them called out. "We could not get through the crowd! Does our friend qualify as 'serious'?"

Jesus roared with laughter and then turned to see one of the Pharisees standing in the doorway.

"What is this?" he blustered. "I saw the men on the roof…"

"A very good way of getting a patient to me. What initiative these friends have shown!" Jesus held out his hand to the man. "Rise up, friend, your sins are forgiven."

The Pharisee's face was a picture of indignation and outrage combined. "What…" The bluster began but stopped as Jesus held up his hand.

"You don't want me to say that? Then I say this: friend, take up your bed and walk."

In that moment life flooded back into the man's limbs. Where they had been unnaturally still, they had movement. He flexed his arms and legs, moved his head, tried to utter thanks but failed. On the roof his friends cheered and began repairing the damage.

And I stood in awe and watched as the once paralysed man got to his feet, bent down to roll up the bed on which he had been carried, walk to the door and push past the totally speechless Pharisee to go out into his new life as a whole well man.

"Apologies, Matthew, again."

"There is no need for apologies. My roof is sound, the man is healed and-" he glanced at the doorway where the Pharisee stood, undecided whether to explode,

74

implode or just walk away with as much dignity as he could muster after such a demonstration of heavenly power, "some people have had a lesson they would do well to remember."

When I looked again, the doorway was vacant. The crowd had melted away, the man and his friends had gone. The afternoon had become calm again.

We moved into the courtyard and had our meal, which was wonderful, considering how short a time Sarah had in which to prepare it. We ate and drank and were at ease with one another. I was still considering the miraculous healing I had just seen and the lesson given to the Pharisee at the same time. And this, despite all the healing I had already seen. Why was it different? What was there to differentiate someone crippled or ill or possessed with someone totally paralysed?

Then it came to me. This seemed more like someone being raised from the dead.

Jesus stood up and beckoned to those of us in the room with him. "Come, gather up the others, it is time we moved on. Matthew, my grateful thanks for your decision to come with us." He went out into the courtyard where I saw him speaking quietly with Sarah for a few moments. She smiled, wiped away a few tears and came in to say her goodbyes to her husband. They held each other for a few minutes and then Matthew picked up the bag he had packed earlier, looked round at his home and smiled.

"It is time, yes."

We all moved out into the street, preparing for our walk out of Capernaum and into new territory - in every respect. We were strung out in a long line, each person walking with one other. Matthew began to walk alongside Nathanael, which seemed to please Jesus, he nodded and smiled when he saw it.

Peter and John were out in front. Peter turned his head and shouted, "Anyone know where we're going?"

Jesus called back, "wherever the road leads us. Find a good place to rest for the night, Peter. I entrust that task to you." Then he turned and beckoned to me.

"Judas, walk with me. It is time we talked."

Somehow we were at the end of the line. I wondered for a moment if he had arranged for it to be that way but I was quickly getting to the point when nothing he did or said surprised me any more.

"What do you know of me, Judas?" he asked.

"Very little. You come from Nazareth, which is a small place, I understand. You have a calling, that is glaringly obvious. You have leadership qualities. You suspect you have humility, that you are not afraid of admitting you don't know something if you don't. I have yet to find that you have been wrong about anything but I am sure you would apologise if you were. You have a great love for people..."

Jesus raised his eyebrows. "You know more of me than I anticipated, dear friend. Let me fill in the rest."

As we walked, he told me of his birth, how the family trekked to Bethlehem for some census arranged by the ever-legalistic and officious Romans, how he had been just another child in just another family until late boyhood when he came to the acceptance that he had a calling. "It happened that I fulfilled the prophesies of the past, Judas. God's doing? I think so, but do I know for sure? Not yet. I am still learning. What I do know is this: the coming of John the Baptist lit the fire within me which is burning now and growing stronger by the day. Being baptised by him was – like being reborn. Before that moment I was half blind, from the moment I emerged from the water, I could see."

"A vision?"

"Yes, very much a vision. One that has built slowly. I saw it like this: imagine a huge wall painting, a crowd of faceless people standing before one man: me. I knew the people but they had no faces because they were not

76

yet in my life. One by one I have found them, one by one the faces in the wall painting are coming alive. There are more to come, women as well as men. We will meet one either today or tomorrow, a woman, that is, who will walk with us. Judas, as this group grows it will require some organisation. Would you take on the responsibility of the money, please? Would you pay for the supplies we need out of the communal purse and keep the records, such as you can?"

"Of course, it would be a good thing for me to do."

"I trust you."

"Matthew would have been a good choice."

"No. Matthew has another task. I know what each of you has to do."

"I accept."

"Thank you. From tomorrow, then, all the finances are in your hands. One less worry for me."

We walked on in companionable silence, the kind you can only achieve with someone you care about, when there is no need to make idle small talk, but you can lose yourself in your thoughts without upsetting or disturbing the other person.

I had a mental picture of the wall painting and marvelled at how he was fitting each person into their place, yet denying he had knowledge of who and where and how. It was all through instinct it would seem, that and an ability to read people. I wondered at his very deep connection with the Divine Being, the Lord God, for it was truly there. He was truly a holy man with a divine mission.

That night, as we camped, a woman named Susanna approached and asked if she could walk with us.

Jesus accepted her with open arms and then looked at me. The thought arrived in my mind – another face had been filled in the wall painting.

Chapter 9
Questions

Why was the Pharisee so determined to intrude on the dinner and the socialising at Matthew's house? The question bothered me. We cleared up our small camping area and walked on, heading to somewhere only Jesus knew, or was he just following an instinct? With him it was difficult to know. Sometimes he seemed to know what he was doing, other times he seemed to be groping in a darkness only he could see, but somehow it worked out right every time.

Jesus was walking with Susanna and they were deep in conversation. We were told she was another family 'outcast', an unwanted widow who had heard Jesus preach and had been affected as well as intrigued by his message. She came with some silver which was gratefully added to the money I carried in a leather pouch. She came with skills as she had some nursing abilities, she said, and was good with children. We were able to utilise both of these as we moved on through the area.

One thing I had noticed was each time we set off to walk somewhere, the pairings were different. No one person cleaved solely to another, no one tried to monopolise Jesus. So it was we walked and talked with different people each time, which meant we got to know them better.

I walked that morning with Nathanael, someone I liked very much. That is not to say I didn't like the others, I did, but as with every group, there are ones you like just that little bit more. Nathanael was quiet, thoughtful and had a delightful sense of humour which burst out at odd moments. He knew the area and the people well, which helped.

"What was that fool Pharisee doing, trying to get in on our evening?" I asked him as we moved on.

As usual he took his time in formulating an answer. I walked on in the sunshine, my bag and the money seeming lighter than they had done the day before. Maybe I was growing fitter and stronger with all this activity and fresh air.

"I think," he said eventually, "he was being paid to find out what we were doing. They – the authorities – were content when we were leaving Capernaum, the 'problem' of what to do with a charismatic preacher was being removed to another place. Then we turned back. They were not happy, believe me."

I did, even though I had no way of knowing how he knew this.

"He had his answer, didn't he?" Nathanael continued. "Jesus outsmarts them every time."

"That he does," I agree with real feeling. There was something deceptive about Jesus, he looked like a mild man, he had a gentle smile and movements which were not threatening, a voice which was calm and peaceful but when he spoke to people like the Pharisees and others who came to question him, there was an edge of true authority which I sensed they did not like. It was obvious to me that some of the questions from the crowds at times were from paid informers. The people who came to listen to Jesus rarely asked penetrating questions, they listened, they absorbed and no doubt went away to talk about what he said and how it had affected them. Their question was usually 'won't you stay?' or 'why must you move on?' They made no effort to try and catch him out in any of his preaching. I asked him about this during one break in our trek and had the expected answer.

"Of course I know what is going on, but be assured, dear friend, God will give me the right answers for them every single time." He had, too.

"If you look round, carefully," Nathanael said after a while, "you will find they are walking with us now, waiting to see what we do."

But when I finally turned to look, they were no longer trailing along after us. Foolish people, what did they think they would see?

Each time we stopped to eat and rest, people would come to us. I never knew how the word spread so fast that Jesus was in the area, but it did and it never failed to amaze me. They came in small groups, they came with their many and varied conditions of illness and possession, they came with their hunger for words of the Kingdom of Heaven and none went away disappointed.

As we sat one evening, watching the flames devour the small twigs Susanna and Miriam were feeding them, a man approached, hands out to show he meant no harm.

"Master-"

Jesus stood up. "Welcome, Thaddeus."

The man stopped just outside the circle. "How... how did you know my name?"

"I have been waiting for you. I need you. I trust you have come to join us, I am not to be disappointed, am I?"

"No, no ... you just took me by surprise. I expected to have to come, tell you who I was and why I was there."

Jesus walked around those sitting around the fire and took Thaddeus into his arms. "Welcome, my friend. I have sat here this eve wondering if you would come back. You were in the crowd earlier, I saw you and I tried to reach you with my words."

"Oh you did, you did! I don't know what good I can be but here I am. Use me."

"I ask no more of that from any man. Come now, let me introduce you to my friends."

And so Thaddeus joined us. He was a middle-aged man, quiet, studious, with a good knowledge of the law and of the scriptures, which complemented my

80

knowledge. He had no family close to him and had for some time been seeking the way to make use of the life he had left to him. Jesus' words had touched him, as they did so many but few took up the challenge. He was friendly and fitted into the group as if he had always been there.

Jesus came over to me and sat down. He stared into the fire and was silent for a moment. I was content to be quiet, listening to the night sounds, the scuffle of wild life, the rustle of leaves, the crackling of the fire and the muted comforting sound of my friends speaking with one another with an undercurrent of love. A quarter moon looked down at us, unseeing, unknowing, uncaring.

"One more to go, Judas, and my chosen ones are complete. One blank face left to fill. He will be here ere long." He stirred slightly and moved his legs as if they pained him.

"How far ahead can you see?"

"Ah, you speak as if I were one of those who can look into the future, dear friend."

"Surely you are, for you know so much of what is to come, who is to come, where your feet should take you."

"So it would seem, on the outside. Inside it is a flickering flame in the lantern I mentioned to you before. The flame sometimes shows me something; other times it obscures what is to come. I believe there is much I have no need to know right now for it would affect the work I have to do if it were revealed to me. So the lantern glimmers and shows me those who are to come, where I need to walk next, which village needs my words and the healing, but no further. That is shrouded in darkness. I just know there is a 'destiny', if I can put it like that, and you are involved in it in some way."

"May God make it a good involvement!" I said impulsively, putting out a hand to grasp his arm. I felt the strength in it, felt the muscles under my fingers.

"Judas, I said before, it matters not whether it is for good or ill, for that is in the hands of God himself, not for us humans to concern ourselves with. What matters is this: God has a plan and each of us has a part in it, for whatever reason. We must be in the right place at the right time to fulfil that plan. Worry not about why and where and what, just walk with me and be that which you are, a friend who can share my thoughts and my work."

He moved again and I had to ask. "Are you sore troubled with the walking today?"

"Do you seek to evade my words, or just showing concern? Or both?" he laughed. "I am tired this day, my legs ache for some reason. The road was rougher than usual, maybe I am not as fit as I thought I was. I wonder how friend Thaddeus will cope with the travelling. He is older than us, we may have to match our pace to his."

I smiled at him in the semi-darkness. The moon's soft light caught his face and made his eyes look like silver orbs.

"I did not seek to evade your words; I understand them well and will keep them in my heart and remember them. My concern over rode my manners for a moment, forgive me for that."

"Judas, there is nothing to forgive. I thought only to tease, nothing more. Now, let us sleep. We have to move on tomorrow, Sabbath it night be but the work will not wait."

I saw Thaddeus roll himself in his cloak and lie down by the fire, close to James who seemed to have befriended him. He was smiling at least as he laid his head on the warm earth. I was glad he was with us. He had much to offer, I was sure of that.

And I, Judas Iskariot, had a part to play in Jesus' destiny. I part wished I did not know this and part glad I did, for it was a good reason for me to be with the group. Oh, I had charge of the money and on one occasion healed someone, but other than that I felt myself to be dead wood. I knew Jesus would not agree. He called each of us for reasons best known to him and to God. I sometimes felt he was keeping things back so as not to worry us. I was sure he knew more than he was saying.

Somewhere in the dark hours Jesus rose and left the group. I was tempted to follow but knew he was not in danger, there were no wild animals around to attack him and any robbers who might be about this night would see he was a simple man with nothing they could take. For all that, I raised myself up on one elbow and watched him walk away, watched his white robe catch the moonlight and then blend into the shadows of the rocks and trees nearby. I knew then he had gone to pray alone and thought, how many nights he had done that, when I had not wakened to see him go? No wonder at times he was tired, it was not the walking as much as the lack of sleep which caught up with him. But then, during the day when could he find time for solitary private prayer and thought? From the moment the sun touched the earth and woke us to the time when the moon's rays covered us in silver and bid us sleep, we were there, his group, his friends, seeking his words, his presence, as leader of the group. There were the concerns of where to stop, what to eat, whether the village would welcome us, how much healing would be needed, how much preaching he could do, whether the 'authorities', whatever form they came in, would bother us. No time for him to be quiet, to look within, to check on that 'lantern' and what it needed to show him for the days ahead. I wanted to try and work out a way that he could have that time, so that he did not lose precious sleep, but it was impossible. There were many of us now and we all had our needs which he cared about.

Somewhere not so far from our small camp a man was deep in prayer to his God.

It occurred to me then that I had not seen the others stop to pray. Did they pray as they walked, as they sat in the evenings round the fire, socialising? Were they feeling themselves free of the restrictions of the laws which said we needed to do this and that, as we had no household, no books, nothing to govern our days?

It also occurred to me that I would benefit from some prayers, too. I got up, quietly and walked away in the opposite direction to Jesus. I found a rock, sat on it and gazed up at the all-seeing blind moon.

"God in heaven," I said quietly. "I know not the connection this man, Jesus, has with you but it is a close one and a very real one and I know he does your will. I ask two things of you this night: one is that you give him the strength to do that which you require him to do to fulfil whatever destiny it is you have for him and the other is that I have the strength, the clarity of vision and the determination to follow through whatever part I have to play in that destiny, whatever it is."

There was more, but after that, it seemed inconsequential and the prayers tapered off. I returned to the camp fire, covered myself up again and wondered afresh at the connection Jesus had with God that he could give up his sleep to pray for so long, for it had been some time since he left the warmth of the fire.

I did not sleep until he returned, quietly, gently, disturbing nothing but the dust. He had already disturbed my thoughts.

Chapter 10
Yet More Arrivals

Next morning I walked with Mary of Magdala, the serene, beautiful, infinitely strong person I had desired to speak to for some time. I did not, these days, interrupt anyone who was walking with or speaking with another member of the group. This day she fell in step with me. We said nothing for a while, just watched the others walking ahead, steadily trekking toward the next village. We seemed to have fallen into a pattern, Jesus leading the group toward whichever village or town he had decided on, with whoever walked with him that day, the rest following on, two by two. Somehow I perpetually found myself last but it suited me well, I could watch for 'observers' and maybe head them off, if it were possible to do that. Jesus was walking with Thaddeus. He made a point of giving a lot of time and attention to every new member of the group, it seemed.

"Judas," Mary spoke in such a soft voice I had to listen carefully to hear every word. "How are you come to walk with Jesus?"

"He called me." It was the truth but to many it would seem surreal, nothing more than my over-active imagination. "I was meditating and praying one night in my home in Hebron when I saw a man looking at me, telling me he was waiting for me, that the work had begun. I packed everything up and went looking for him immediately after that."

She nodded as if it was the most commonplace thing imaginable. "He has that power. I went to him because nothing I did, no prayers, no penance, nothing, would drive out the devils which possessed me. In the space of a few moments he named them and dismissed them. But..." she shrugged eloquently and looked down at her feet. "My family do not wish to know. They do not

85

believe the devils have gone and even if they have, they believe I will invite them back again. So I have no home."

"And family?"

"Husband. Daughter. Mother and father, the usual. No one wanted me. I am dead to them. Now they are dead to me. It is a burden of grief I carry but day by day the grief melts away, for I see the work Jesus does and I want to share it. If I had not been possessed, I would not have met him. Everything is for a reason."

"Jesus says there is one more person to join the group."

"One more man, yes. There are more women to come." I looked at her in surprise for she said it with a certainty that brooked no disagreement.

"Jesus is not the only one who sees into the future, but I do not see as clearly as he does." She smiled and it lit up her face, turned it from calm acceptance and serenity into lively humour and affection. "You are good for him, Judas. I see he is calm when he speaks with you."

"Thank you. At times I feel myself to be dead wood in the group but I know he would not have called me if I had no role to play in his life."

"You do, but I don't know what it is."

I smiled. "He said the same thing."

"Then God is concealing it from all of us at this time. We have to wait and see. Before then, be glad that you are here, for he needs you and you are good for all of us. You are a calm person, where the others can be fiery at times. Peter is especially difficult sometimes, when he does not get his own way. Andrew is a bit better. James is-"

"A working man of high principles and moral standing."

She looked at me sharply. "You're right. You see a lot, don't you?"

86

"I see a group of people, all of whom have left family, wives, mothers, fathers, brothers and sisters, their trades, their employment, to follow a man who calls himself an itinerant preacher. He is more than that, he is charismatic and passionate and devoted to his beliefs and his God. Do you know he gives up some of his sleep each night to pray in the silence?"

"Yes." Her simple quiet answer was enough for me to know that Mary loved Jesus completely, but more than that, unconditionally. There was acceptance of his role in life, to preach, to heal, to lead, and of her part in that life, to walk with him and help care for him. "I see him leave, I see him come back. When he goes he is tired, drawn, older than his years. When he returns he has lost the tiredness, his face is full again, his age is restored to him. Whatever he does, whatever he receives, it is better for him than sleep."

"Does anyone else know that he does this?"

"Not as far as I know. No one has mentioned it. If they've seen him, they've not tried to stop him, which is all that matters."

She stopped in the middle of the road, grasping my arm tightly with fingers so strong they might have been on the hand of a man of great strength. "Judas, I see a darkness at the back of you. Whatever you are to Jesus, it is both good and bad."

"I went on my own to pray last night, too."

"I know. I watched you. When you returned, you were illuminated as if full of shining light."

"I prayed that he had strength to carry through his chosen task and I had strength to fulfil mine, whatever it was."

"It was enough. You can do no more. Don't brood on it, Judas, for it will damage your well-being. Accept that we are all here for different reasons." She looked round, suddenly realising they were no longer walking. "Why have we stopped?"

"We will wait here a while." Jesus' tone made it clear it was not an invitation. We were stopping and that was that.

"We are waiting for-?" James asked.

"The last member of the group to join us."

"The last man." Mary corrected. There was laughter as Jesus turned to her with one of his knowing tender smiles.

"There speaks my oracle, Mary of Magdala. There are more women to come, I take it, O wise woman?"

"There are indeed. Within a week you will be able to say the group is complete. Right now we await the last male, but not the last member."

"I stand corrected, Mary of Magdala. Whilst we wait, why don't we all sit?"

The grass was soft, the sun warm and the air heavy with scents and a hint of salt. The murmuring of voices matched and complemented the buzzing of the bees around the many wild flowers speckling the grass. And we waited. There were passers-by, a donkey or two ridden by workmen and artisans, a fine horse ridden by someone Very Important, in their eyes anyway, for they glanced at us with such contempt and disgust it was almost physical. A Roman contingent marched past, ignoring us as if we were no more than the dust under their feet but no one came who made Jesus react. I wondered for a moment if this time he was wrong.

Just as I thought it, a man was seen in the distance. Jesus got to his feet and gestured to us to stay sitting. He stood on the edge of the road, waiting, a small smile touching his lips, a certain amount of tension in his body. Somehow I knew that although he had seen this person coming, he was not entirely sure they would join us.

It seemed an age before the distance decreased sufficiently for us to see the man, younger than Thaddeus, but I believed older than me, someone who walked with a slight limp and hunched over shoulders, as if he was in pain, looking at the road rather than the surroundings. As he drew close to us he finally looked up and saw Jesus standing patiently waiting.

"Ah, my friend," he said. "I come to ask-"

"And I want to ask you, Thomas, to walk with me."

There was shock written all over the man's face. "How did-"

"Come." Jesus held out his hand to him. "Come. I know why you have walked so far to find me, now I need to tell you why I need you."

They clasped hands and a look I was beginning to know well crossed Jesus' face. It was the emotion generated by the healing because even as we watched, Thomas visibly straightened his shoulders. He stamped his feet on the ground, one then the other, a look of delight appearing in place of the shocked, worried frown.

"That is why I wanted to see you," he said in a low voice. "I cannot-"

"Thomas. I know you have no family now, they are gone to our Father's mansion, am I right?" Thomas nodded. "I know you have been restless and unhappy for a long time. I know that in part you came for healing but also for answers. I am giving you the opportunity to walk with me, to help me in my ministry, together with my friends."

Thomas looked at each of us in turn and I knew what he was seeing, a motley crowd indeed, fisherman, workmen, those who toiled with their minds and not their hands, women who were there to take care of us. I knew what he was seeing but could not decide what he was thinking. Jesus didn't rush him. It was a big decision, to give up everything and join a travelling group that may well run into problems with the Romans at some time. After what seemed an age he nodded, slowly. "If I might return to close everything, my home, my affairs, I will walk with you, Master."

"We will wait for you." Jesus put an arm around his shoulders. "We will walk on to the next village and there we will wait for you. There is preaching and healing work to be done, so I will be occupied for several days. Take your time, but come back to me."

"I hate to leave."

"I know."

"But I have to."

"Yes. Unfortunately, affairs of this world need to be organised before we can work toward the spreading the word of the next. I understand. Some of my friends here did the same thing. Go, Thomas, know we will wait for you."

Thomas turned to us, held out his hands and smiled a quiet, beautiful smile.

"I greet you all. I wish you all peace of heart and mind. I hope for your friendship when I can return and become one of you. Give me two days, three at the very most, and I will return."

There was a chorus of greetings in reply, our good wishes for his speedy return to us. I swear I saw tears in his eyes as he turned to walk back to his home, walking without a limp and without the hunched shoulders.

Jesus waited until Thomas had gone some distance before he sat down. "Thomas will be a walking testimony for us as he reaches his home, as he clears his affairs, as he walks back, for he is known locally as the crippled man and he is no longer crippled." He lay back on the grass and stared up at the clear sky. "I have need of him. I am glad he has come." He turned his head, looked at me and smiled. I knew what he was thinking; another face had been filled in on the wall painting. Almost there, if Mary was to be believed and I had no reason to think otherwise.

Then, with seemingly boundless energy, he was on his feet. "Come, let us be on the move. What are you all doing, lazing around in the sunshine? There is work to be done!"

We struggled to get up and picked up our possessions, smiling. It was good to know we were almost, almost there. A group needs to know its boundaries, its defined members, so it can work together and be as one. We were not far from being that group.

Joanna came over to me as we shouldered our packs and began to walk.

"I would walk with you a while, Judas, if that is all right?"

"Of course. We were interrupted in our conversation, perhaps now we can continue it."

"I hope so. I wanted to know what you felt when you saw John the Baptist."

I saw serious intent in her eyes, knowing this was no trivial question, it was something she had a deep longing to discover. I wondered afresh at her connection with the Baptist but could not ask.

"I felt – as if I were in the presence of someone outstanding and powerful. The way he could, with a word, silence a crowd of hundreds of people, the way he defied the river itself by standing in the current like a rock. He never swayed, no matter how fast the waters swirled around him. He defied the authorities who came, looked and left again, even if they did mutter threats against him at the time."

"Were you there-"

"No. To my regret, no. I went on three consecutive days. I wanted, so much, to step into the water and be baptised by him but he looked at me across the crowd and shook his head, such a small movement I doubt anyone saw it but I did. It said no, it was not for me. Somehow I knew this, even as part of me fought the other part of me which longed to go into the cool water and be – changed."

I was aware of laughter and talk from those walking in front of us, jokes were being passed around or some gentle teasing was going on. I heard the high melodic tones of Mary's giggle, an infectious sound. I smiled. Joanna was taking no notice, she was thinking on my words, it seemed.

"And so you did not go back. Of course not, you had no need to go back."

"No. If I was not to be baptised, why trek to the river and watch others going through their immersion? How I regret it now, though!"

"It doesn't matter, does it, Judas? You are here anyway."

"Yes. And tonight we might sleep in beds and eat from plates, if we are fortunate in finding friendly people in the village I see ahead of us."

The houses, clustered together seemingly for security, were not far away. Joanna brightened up at the sight.

"I shall be glad of that. I like sleeping outside, the stars are incredible, but oh the ground is so hard at times."

"Ask someone to sell you a thin mattress. I will carry it for you."

"Judas, would you do that for me?"

"Didn't I just make the suggestion? Of course I will."

"Thank you!" In an impulsive gesture she put her arms round my neck and kissed me. I felt myself flush and also felt a surge of love such as I had never experienced before. It shook me considerably.

"I will tell you about John the Baptist before too long." She had turned serious again and that gave me time to come to terms with my feelings.

"I would like that."

She turned her gaze, cool, liquid eyes that had depths I never realised, onto me. "I know. You want to know

92

more about him but you have been too polite to ask. So I will tell you. When we move on, I will tell you."

When we move on, I thought, we will have others with us, but surely none so startling, so complex and enchanting as Joanna.

It was then I realised I had, for the first time in my life, fallen in love.

Chapter 11
Miracles of Healing

It was a strange day in every sense of the word. First I had my new emotion to deal with; love came strange to me. It conflicted with my sense of myself, of being a single man in complete control of his thoughts and feelings. Second, there was a sense of expectancy running through everyone, as if something momentous was going to happen but no one knew what it was. We all seemed to be in high spirits and even the haranguing of the village Pharisee – there always seems to be one – about us picking ears of corn as we walked past a cornfield was quashed when Jesus quoted a religious text at him.

We were welcomed in the village, invited to stay, to eat, to preach, to talk and to heal. We all were given lodgings in different houses, but gathered together in one place to eat. While we were there, a man, obviously wealthy, came to Jesus and bowed to him. "My daughter has died, Master." It was all he could do to speak through his grief. "Come and raise her up for me. I cannot bear to lose her."

"I will come." He looked round at those who had honoured him with their hospitality. "I will return," he told them. "I have this task to perform for the glory of God."

I wondered at his words, it was the first time he had spoken that way. I also wondered what he would do with someone who had died.

We walked in a group with the man, who was leading us to his home. The villagers crowded round us, as interested as we were, if not more so, for Jesus was new to them, although they knew of his reputation.

Suddenly he stopped and looked round.

"Someone touched me."

Peter began to laugh. "Everyone has, we are such a crowd here!"

"No, someone touched me for a reason. Who is it?"

A poor shrunken woman edged forward. "Forgive me, Master." She went down on her knees in the dust before him. "I have been ill these twelve years and knew if I just touched your robe, I would be healed." We looked at one another, wondering at the faith which had brought her to do this simple thing. Equally, we wondered at how Jesus knew she had done that, did he feel a small draining of his energy, did he feel the healing flowing out of him? Until he spoke to us of the way it worked, we would not know.

"You are healed." He put out his hands and helped her up. "Your faith healed you. Go in peace."

Her smile was radiant. The villagers who had heard the exchange looked shocked and surprised. I could sense their thoughts: Maybe this man was all they said he was. Nothing was said but the looks were as expressive as any words. Some approached the woman and began to talk to her, but she didn't say much, only that she was radiantly happy at being cured. We walked on and began to hear the funeral dirges before we reached the house. Jesus became impatient then, hurrying forward, pushing them all aside.

"The child sleeps," he told them. "Stop the noise, you do no good at all!"

Sarcastic laughter followed him as he went into the house. I saw the girl's father rushing after him, shouting: "Wait! You know not which room it is!" But he did, he knew the way and before any of us knew what was happening, he was standing in the doorway, holding the girl's hand.

When you throw a pebble into a pool, the pebble disappears but the ripples spread outwards and ever onward. The pebble was Jesus and the child, the ripples were the villagers. At first there was a stunned silence and then they spread out, shouting the news to all whom would hear it. 'This man raises people from the dead!'

I went cold from head to foot. Cold to my core with the thought of what he had just done. Or perhaps the child did only sleep, perhaps – but I knew my in my heart, which was warm still, that the child had been dead. And he, Jesus, had brought her back to life.

Jesus brushed aside the thanks of the parents, who were totally overwhelmed and almost incoherent as they tried to speak, and walked back down the road to the house where he was staying, as if he had done nothing more than leave a message.

In truth he had left a message. I understood then his words, 'I have this task to perform for the glory of God.'

Joanna walked back to the house with me. We were both silent, trying to absorb what we had just seen.

Finally Joanna said, "I wonder if he will tell us what happened."

"Was the child unconscious, do you think?" I felt guilty, treasonable, in saying it, for I knew that she had been dead. Knew it even though I had not seen her for myself.

"Are you doubting, Judas?"

"Always." That was not a lie. Even as I knew what had happened, part of me disbelieved it, part of me, perhaps the rational part, declared it to be false. The two sides of me fought for acceptance. It was good to know I was not alone in that feeling.

"Good. I know others do, from time to time. It seems unbelievable to us, what else can we do but doubt? We only have the father's word that the child was dead. It should be enough. But…"

"You wanted proof. You would have liked to have checked the child yourself before he touched her."

"Yes."

"It feels wrong to question."

"Always question. Jesus doesn't mind. I've spoken with him at length, questioned him on many things and received wonderful wisdom. I know he likes to talk with you, take your chance to ask, Judas. We are being asked to do the work with him, we need to be sure of what we are doing, thinking and feeling. Most of all, we need to be sure of what we're seeing."

What we were seeing were miracles, one after the other. Two blind men came and were given their sight, children with deformed limbs stood straight, a woman losing blood and in danger of losing the child she carried was healed. An elderly man, crippled with the condition which turns the hands into claws and gives untold agony regained the use of his limbs. Devils were driven out, those who could not speak sang praises, those who could not hear put their hands over their ears until they became used to sound.

It seemed almost as if every person in the village had an affliction of some kind and Jesus patiently, lovingly, healed everyone.

By the time the sun began to set, he was clearly tired and the family firmly and lovingly sent everyone away who had gathered with gifts as a thank you. Food and wine, bedding and clothing were left for us. Quietly he distributed it among those of us who had need of it, the food and wine he gave to the households who were taking care of us. No one was forgotten.

We left him there, in the care of Mary of Magdala and Susanna, and went to the houses who had agreed to take us in.

For the first time in a long time, or so it felt, I slept in a bed. Oddly, it felt confining. I wanted to see the stars, hear the night wind and the night life, smell the freshness of vegetation resting from the heat of the sun. I wanted to feel the dust under my fingers and the taste of cool water on my tongue.

But my body said, make the most of the softness of the bed. You know not how long it will be before you find such comforts again even though I knew well other villages would take us in and care for us in the same way. The mind is a strange thing, it plays games. Mine was saying; this bed is empty with just one person in it. Logic was saying, one kiss does not make a loving relationship. I found it hard to accept.

Some time in the cool of the night I woke, seeking the outside to relieve my body and my thoughts. I crept through the house and went outside, breathing deep of the chill and the scents. I dealt with my relief and turned to go back in when I heard his voice.

"Judas."

Then I knew why I had been roused from sleep. Jesus stood close by, beckoning to me. "Walk with me a while, if you can stand to be away from your soft bed."

"I can do that. It is not a hardship."

We began to walk slowly, matching our steps, comfortable with one another in a way that usually only comes after a long period of knowing the other person. I did not pressure him to speak, I knew he often needed time to think things through.

"I have been at prayer this night," he said eventually. I nodded. I did not want to admit I knew of his night prayer sessions but he obviously knew otherwise.

"You know I do this? Why do I ask, of course you know. Why do I doubt myself this night? Because much has been taken from me today. Healing is good but it is draining in its own way."

"Is that how you knew the woman had touched you?"

"Yes. To be jostled or touched or even held is one thing, but someone seeking healing from you is a different feeling, you can almost sense the energy leaving you. I knew someone had been healed, I just wanted them to stand up and say why. I need the witnesses. Although I tell each one not to talk of it, I know they will. I need the witnesses because it is the healing which will bring them to me to listen to the words I need to say. They need a reason to come. Healing gives them that reason."

"Was the child dead?" I did not mean to ask, I had no intention of asking, but the question burst out of me. He smiled.

"Yes. Oh, some will say she was unconscious and I revived her, others will find some other condition from which she suffered which rendered her as dead but she was not truly so. They will say everything, those who wish to discredit God's hand in all we do, but I tell you, Judas, she was dead. But, newly dead. Her spirit was close by and I was able to restore the spirit to the body. She does not have a long life ahead of her but she has fulfilled her role right now. She was chosen as an example to prove to the many that the few, us, can do miracles – if we believe."

"You knew this before the father came. You knew the room she was in, you knew how long she had been dead."

"Yes. Of course. How else could I go with such certainty and know with surety which room she was lying in? It was a bright flame in my lantern, Judas, and it was as I saw."

We walked on a way, slowly pacing through the night breeze and the dust of the road. Before long we would have to turn and walk back, if we were to make it to our beds before dawn.

Jesus stopped and looked at me. "Judas, may I ask a very personal question of you?"

"Ask what you will. I will answer as best I can."

"Thank you. Have you ever hungered, truly hungered, for a woman?"

The question took me completely by surprise. It was truly the last thing I ever dreamed he would ask of me.

"Yes," I said after a long pause to put my thoughts in order. "I saw once the comely wife of an associate. I saw no more of her than a look, before she covered her head and turned away. It was enough. In that moment I yearned for her in a way I could never believe possible."

"But since then-"

"No woman, no hunger, no nothing."

"Until today."

We were of equal height, we looked in each other's eyes without having to strain or look down. We were of equal stature, slender but strong. We were, in that moment, almost brothers in the intensity of the emotion between us. I did not know whether to be shocked he had seen, or detected it, or pleased that someone else knew.

"Until today," I agreed finally.

"Two things, Judas. First, the hunger you felt back then is the kind of hunger I feel every hour of the day and night to be in contact with God, to do his work and his will. No matter what he asks of me, I will do it. I have no other reason to live. I have no wife, my family I left behind in Nazareth to come and do this work. I know it will be unpopular with many who are in authority, many who should know better but who cling to the old ways without seeing there is a new clear pathway to the Kingdom of Heaven. I know I may not become old, that is always a possibility. It has been brought home to me with the execution, no, the murder, of John the Baptist. It matters not. The word must be spread, the glory of God must be revealed to all.

"Second, Joanna is a beautiful woman of great strength and devotion. All I ask is, you do not break her heart."

"I have never loved anyone before. I am afraid of it, afraid of hurting her, afraid of rejection. I will walk soft with her. Everything else will be her choice, not mine."

"That is all I wanted to hear and all I knew I would hear from you. Judas, you are a true friend. I thank you for walking with me this night, when you could have been resting in a soft bed. May I ask; will you do this again? I have a need at times to talk about things, past, present and as much of the future as I think I can see clearly."

"You need to ask? Just call and I will be there."

"There are not enough words to thank you. It is strange, is it not, that I love every person we walk with, some more than others, I will admit but that is a natural thing for anyone to do. I love them and would do anything for them, but when it comes to something deeply personal and meaningful, I turn to you. Forgive me, there are bound to be times ahead when you would wish you could just sleep and I will want to talk."

"I said, just call and I will be there. I do not say anything lightly."

"This I know, this I rely on. Come, we must be getting back. Maybe there is time for a little more sleep before the cock crows and the day begins."

I detected a lightness around the horizon and doubted there was much time for a little more sleep, but I knew even if there was, my thoughts would keep me awake.

We had one quick embrace and then we went to our beds. Just as I knew would happen, I found no sleep. The thoughts were tumbling round in my head. How did he know about Joanna and myself? We were at the back of the group, no one saw us, because if they had, they would have made comments in the way a group of friends always do. We had been circumspect in our way of being with one another when we were in everyone's company and had avoided one another since we arrived in the village. And still he knew.

As always, Jesus remained an enigma and an outstandingly perceptive man. It would be a fool who tried to deceive him.

Chapter 12
Ministry

The miracles of healing continued. The man who stood up in the middle of the synagogue when Jesus was preaching, holding up a deformed much shrivelled arm which Jesus healed without touching him. This brought down the wrath of the elders, who said it was work on the Sabbath. They were confounded by his argument in response and, I detected, consumed with jealousy that their prayers were ineffective. Jesus said later it was because they prayed without faith, without the deep burning faith that consumed him and, he believed, all of us.

There was the child who could not walk, the young woman who was barren and about to be discarded by her husband, lepers, those outcasts of society, all healed and restored to full life. But mostly it was the possessed. These people came, fighting that which had overtaken them, throwing themselves on the ground before him, rolling around in wild fits until he named the demon and sent it hence. Many times it was overheard that he cast out the demons with the help of the Prince of Darkness and many times he retorted that a nation divided cannot stand. Why would the Prince of Darkness allow his servants to be cast out when they had much work to do in the person they had taken over? Many times they slunk away, muttering into their beards that this was surely evil without seeing that the work of healing was pure love.

And still the crowds came. In what seemed like despair he turned to Peter one day and said: "The harvest is great, the reapers are few. It is time."

He turned his back on the crowd which had gathered, much to their bitter disappointment, asking the group as a whole to tell everyone he could not work that day as he was unwell. He walked away alone, gesturing to anyone who tried to follow. It was clear he wanted to be on his own and we let him go. We had enough to do placating the crowd anyway.

We sat quietly together, saying little, tending a small fire, eating a few figs, dates and a little bread, putting some aside for his return. Joanna sat on the other side of the fire to me. I tried not to look at her too often, although her beautiful face drew my gaze like a strong magnet.

Miriam went to get water. When she came back, she knelt down next to me.

"Judas, if I did not know better, I would swear you were smitten with the lovely Joanna." It was said with great love and I could not do anything but smile at her.

"You would be right, Miriam, but then, when are you not right? You are like a mother to us all and nothing gets past you."

"In that you are right, my dear one. Joanna is a beautiful soul. If you had to choose anyone here, then you picked the right one for you. Susanna is a lovely person but she is looking for something which she has yet to find. Mary has found her vocation, she is almost a bride of God and has found the man to walk with. I seek a husband, but know he is not yet in my life. You and Joanna will make a lovely couple."

"Thank you." I put my hand on hers where it rested on the grass. "You are wise beyond your years, Miriam. I do not think the man you need is far away, a few more miles, a few more nights and a lot more of your tender care for us all and you will leave us."

Her eyes filled with tears for a moment. She blinked them away. "I would want to stay with him for the rest of his life but he has already told me that which you just said, Judas. I thank you for that. There is a sadness in me that I must leave him at some time, but gladness that the man I seek is out there. You have others to take my place and Mary says more are to come, too."

"Mary sees a lot. Some she does not speak of."

"Yes. That tells me how much you see, too, Judas."

I looked around. "Will he be gone long, do you think?"

"Judging by the way he looked when he left, yes. I don't expect him back until morning."

"Is this usual, then?"

"Oh yes. Jesus has been doing this since I first started to walk with him. He needs this time, this meditation and the prayers to find out where he's going and what he has to do. It's an awesome responsibility." The kindly face looked sad for a moment. "He has all of us in his care as well as all those who come for healing and his words. Then there is the ever present threat from the authorities, Roman or otherwise. I would not trade places with him for anything."

She got up and moved away, busying herself with tasks, sorting and packing. I watched her without really seeing, thinking on her words. Yes, his task was immense and I wondered how any of us could help.

She was right. He did not return until dawn, looking drained, weary, almost haggard. In that moment he looked like a much older man. I was awake and got up to greet him.

"Water?" he asked as he sat down. I went to get some for him. As he drank, I also fetched the food we had put to one side to await his return.

His smile was a bit weak and I asked no questions as he began to eat with obvious hunger. "Your patience is commendable, Judas," he said, between mouthfuls of figs.

"I have your welfare to consider before my curiosity can be satisfied."

The others were slowly getting up, attending to their needs and acting as if Jesus had been there all along, not that he had suddenly appeared after half a day and an entire night away.

He waited until everyone had returned and then held out his hands, his usual signal that he wished to speak and it was serious.

"I spent the night in prayer with God," he began. "I know now I have called the right people to me. You are the start of the ministry. More are to come; more will join us as we work, as we get the word of God to people. Peter, Andrew, Matthew, young James, John, Nathanael, Philip, Thaddeus, Thomas, Mary, Susanna, Joanna, what I am going to ask of you now is this: I need you to go out, in pairs if you wish, alone if you wish, to take the healing and the word of God to as many places as you can. Cast out the devils from those who are possessed, do it in God's name and they will go. Take no criticism from anyone for your actions. Tell them you come from me and from God, tell them your mission is to bring peace, not conflict. Take nothing with you but your clothes and maybe a staff to walk with. Take no food. Live on that which is offered to you and be sure to pray for all who help you on your way. If a village refuses to accept you, shake the dust of their streets from your feet as you leave but ensure you leave a blessing behind you. They will, in time, want you to return. Who has questions?"

They all did, it seemed, by the look on their faces, shocked, surprised and in some instances, pleased. It was a little while before anyone spoke, then Peter asked: "how can we do this?"

"Through faith, my rock, my friend. Through faith. Believe and it will happen. Those you touch will receive the love of God and that will heal them, or cast out their demons, whatever it is you are asked to do."

"What about those you have not named?" This was from young James, who looked scared at the prospect of going out into the wider world.

"They are to remain with me, for I have much work to do here whilst you are gone. I will not be idle! I need people to help me with that. You have all been chosen for different reasons to do different tasks. If you are worried, James, then link up with someone to go with you, someone you can learn from, but I know well you will be more than capable of doing this task."

I saw James look round, saw Thomas's nod and knew that would be all right. A good companion for the young man.

"How long do you want us to be away?" This came from Philip, who was frowning.

"As long as you want to be gone. You may stay away for a week, a month, several months. One by one you will return and when you do, you will be filled with God's grace and love and will be ready to carry his word into every part of the world, should that be your calling. You need the experience. Does this seem right to you?"

There was a general consensus that it did, although there were still a few worried faces.

"Be not afraid. God is with you. God will always be with you, as he is with me. I have not led you astray by following his words, his will, and you will be safe if you do the same. Observe the Sabbath, try not to offend the authorities and return to me safe and well and experienced."

"Where will you be?" Peter asked, with a touch of anger in his voice. He was not happy at being sent out into the world, that was quite clear.

"Here and there and around this area. I have work to do even as you do. I have others to call. The group will be much larger by the time you return. I have the three women to come Mary has spoken of, for a start! There are others, too. Peter, I love you dearly, you are my rock. On you I will build my church. Believe me, I trust you and am entrusting you with this mission. If you wish to take several people with you, then that is good, the more hands there are, the more healing and preaching can be done. Do what you feel is right, my dear friend, go with your own feelings."

Peter subsided then, his anger obviously fading. I sat very still, wondering if I was honoured to be chosen to stay or whether I would have been honoured to be sent out with the others. I knew I would miss Joanna but it was not a bad thing, she had made no move toward me and I did not wish to jeopardise any chance of happiness with her. Maybe her time away would make her realise how much she cared about me. Foolish hope, perhaps, but then we all live on foolish hope, sometimes it is needed to give us the strength to go on.

All morning discussions were going on, who would walk with whom and where they would go. They appeared to sort themselves out and one by one they came to say goodbye. When they had all gone, walking away in different directions, I looked at Simon, James and Miriam, trying to assess their reaction to being seemingly left behind.

Jesus must have seen my look. "Now we are five, but see how soon that five will become fifteen and then fifty and then five hundred. It will not take long. Are you disappointed I asked you to stay?" He looked at each of us as he said that.

"Yes – and no." James looked a little puzzled, though. "I would have expected you to keep young James with you."

"He has need of the experience of the wider world. He will be all right, he has chosen to walk with Thomas, one of the wisest people we have in the group when it comes to common sense. The decision was not mine, James, but that of God. I struggled long with this throughout the night, who to send, who was to stay. I have work and I needed the right people to remain with me. Simon, are you content to be asked to stay?"

Simon was older than Jesus, a middle-aged man much on a par with Matthew, a man of great feeling and compassion. He did not hesitate in his response.

"I would as soon be with you as out there with the others. The work is the same. I feel I am better used here than out in the larger world."

"And you are right. You were named first as being one to stay with me, my friend. I am glad you feel that way. Miriam?"

"I am glad to stay. I know the person I seek is not far away and if I had gone, I would have missed the chance to meet him. Thank you for that."

"This I know, for it was shown to me. You won't be the sole woman for long. I know well that Mary's prediction is right, there will be others coming very soon."

He turned to me. "Judas, my friend…"

"There is no need to ask. As I told you the other night, you only have to call and I will be there. You have chosen me to stay."

"Apart from anything else, you hold the money, Judas. I might want to stay in an inn somewhere or need something. Yes, I know people would be kind and give me what I need, but right now I need my disciples, those chosen by God, to have the kindness of others shown to them. They need to learn to rely on people and on faith and on God himself. This they will do. When they return they will be wiser and better workers for him. Now, forgive me, it has been a long night."

He was asleep almost the moment he stretched out on the grass. Quietly, Simon, James and I rigged a canopy over him. Then we sat down to wait.

Chapter 13
Testing Times

As the sun made its ordained journey across the sky, I sat in the quiet and went deep within myself to contemplate all that had happened. It had occurred to me that despite time to think, I had not taken in all that had happened since the moment Jesus' face had appeared in the vision which drew me to him. I needed some time like this to walk through my thoughts. I wondered if he knew this.

My first thought was, why was I more surprised at the fact he knew of my love for Joanna than I was by his assertion the child he raised was actually dead when he got there? Logic would dictate I would be more surprised by the latter than the former but then, I had become used to his miracles of healing and perhaps that was why it did not come as a shock. But his knowledge of my innermost thoughts did, for I was sure they were sacrosanct. Obviously not.

Fact: I had given up a home, a career, a family, to walk with this man who now slept in peace by my side. He was deeply asleep, his chest hardly rose and fell with his breathing, he did not stir and his face had fallen into the familiar lines of the young man I knew – and loved – not the ageing haggard man who had all but staggered back into our midst earlier that day. Whatever he had been through during the night of prayer, it had been extremely taxing. Choosing who to send out into the world and who to keep with him must have been very hard indeed, for he loved us all and to part with friends, even for a short time, is never easy. But, I thought, he had chosen well. Simon was a big man; he could help with crowd control. James was wise, full of common sense and dry humour, which we could do with at times. I knew I had little in the way of humour to offer and we needed to laugh. Miriam was the mother figure, the right person to welcome the newcomers we had been told were coming to join us. Everything fitted well. Peter would do well in the big world, the one beyond the group. He had a temper; he was quick to anger but equally quick to quieten it down. Working on his own would be good for him. I knew Andrew had chosen to go with him, they were shadows anyway, but essentially Peter was the leader and he would have his way in most things. The shyer ones among them would be filled with confidence to teach and heal, the more extrovert ones would preach and convert. When they returned, we would find them to be very different people. Would I have been glad to go? I asked myself the question again and knew I was grateful he chose me to stay.

Fact: although I had given up so much, changed my entire way of life, not for a single moment had I regretted anything. I thought of my home, my work, my family, from time to time as anyone would but not with longing to return there, go back to doing the same things I did every day. It would be good to see my family but not to return to the old life. It held nothing for me. This companionship, this new way of seeing life and the pathway to God was so revealing, so satisfying in its completeness, I could not imagine doing anything else.

I thought back over his teachings, some to the crowds, some to us. His words when we were sitting around in a tight silent almost solemn group on the hillside resonated with me through the dark times.

"The poor are fortunate," he said, "for they know the Kingdom of Heaven is theirs." He saw some sceptical looks and added, "riches, wealth, property and possessions become more important than seeing the way forward, the way to work for and worship God. Those who are rich see no further than their fortune.

"The sad people are fortunate, for they can and do find consolation in turning to God. He does not frown on those who are happy and content but those who are sad and lonely are the seekers after truth. If you are content with your life, you do not seek God or any kind of spiritual progression. Would you not agree?"

I did. I knew it well. In my black days I sought God through the teachings of the Law and finally found it here, listening to the man I walked with.

"The gentle people are blessed by God. Why? Because there is no answer in violence and evil thought against others. Violence breeds violence, in truth, those who live by the sword die by the sword. No man who takes power by force can be truly content with his position, for others, equally ambitious and ruthless, will conquer him by force. I tell you that the Romans, who think they have conquered this land, will find their empire falling into dust and they will not understand why it has happened. It is because they do not rule by consent but by force. Eventually it must fail.

"Those who seek righteousness will overcome all, eventually. It will take time, everything takes time. In truth, my friends, things take time is a saying you should hold close to your hearts. Rush into nothing; consider all before you make a decision, wait before hoping something will happen to you. You seek spiritual awakening, it will come. In God's time it will come. Believe me when I say you will all be as powerful as I am, preach as I do, heal as I do, but only when you, your heart, soul and mind, are ready. God cannot give you talents to use until you are able to receive them.

"God will smile upon those who show mercy. Stand back from the harsh words, the harsh actions, even those who use you and hurt you and shout insults at you and shower you with stones and hurtful things. Be merciful to them in your heart and you will be shown mercy in return, when you are reunited with your God in the Kingdom of Heaven. Man, of his own nature, is not a merciful being but by being merciful you can begin the

111

task of spreading kindness and mercy to all. People learn by example. You must counteract the harshness of the regime under which we all live and you can do this by example. Be merciful. It will not be easy. Some of you, I know well, are quick to anger and that is not good. Control your anger, it will damage you.

"God's smile is turned on those who are pure of heart. These people are rare, like gemstones among pebbles they shine brightly and are treasured by some and coveted by others. One such was the man you know as John the Baptist. A man of fire, a man of principles, a man of courage and conviction. Yes, they cut him down, that proud fine man, but before they took his life, did he not baptise many and bring them to the understanding of repentance and walking the righteous pathway?"

He smiled at Joanna as he spoke. "Dear one, I know well of your service to my kinsman. I know of your devotion and so does God. You will be rewarded."

He looked back at us then and went on: "God does smile on those who work for peace. The authorities who control this land should also smile on those people but instead they perceive them as a threat. I don't understand why and it's not given to me to understand why, although I've asked. My thinking is they dislike anyone or anything that is different, they perceive it as a threat to their rule. They are foolish and misguided but we cannot change that. We can only continue to work for peace.

"I must again mention John the Baptist. God has a special blessing for those who are persecuted in his name, who fight for his way to be shown to the world, the way of righteousness, the way of redemption, the way of peace. John paid for his passage to heaven by losing his head. God knows some of you may be called upon to pay the ultimate price some time in the future, even as I may well be called. Our deaths will be but a small step to glory.

112

"You are the light of the world. Each of you has been chosen to walk the pathway with me to help light the world, to show everyone the way forward. Walk with me. Work with me. Together we will help build a new understanding."

I recalled there was more, much more, but not all of it stayed with me. I knew, though, by the faces around me that others had absorbed Jesus' words and I had to hope they would remember them in the future. Maybe even as they walked out into the world now, they would recall his words and preach them to those they met.

There were many lessons spoken to the crowds who came to hear, stories which expressed his teachings in a way they could understand. I was often astonished at the simplicity of his words and wondered why the synagogues did not put their teachings in such a simplistic way. It would be better for everyone if they did. No wonder the people flocked to hear this special man preach, he spoke to them on a level they could understand but without patronising them by simplifying everything so much they felt like children.

And the healing had gone on, the centurion's son, the lepers, the possessed, all healed, all restored to full life and vitality, all going out to tell everyone of the miracle of healing they had received. So his fame spread and more came, and yet more.

The evening hour approached, we had been sitting, resting, for some time whilst Jesus slept. He stirred, flung out one arm and struck me with it. In doing that he woke, sat up and apologised.

"It matters not," I told him. "You were in a dream of some kind and woke suddenly. Did something disturb you?"

"Ah, yes." He rubbed a hand over his face as if to remove the memory. "I was… no, it matters not. It was just a dream."

Miriam handed him a flagon of wine. "I have food here, but you need something to drink. You have slept for a long time."

"It seems I have, the sun was high when I went to sleep and now I see it is beginning its journey into the darkness."

"It was a long night of prayer," Simon observed with a small smile.

"It was. I had a long fight with my conscience and my heart, deciding who was to stay, who was to go."

"How did you decide?" I asked, knowing there was more to the answer than just his conscience and his heart.

He smiled and it was radiant, as if he had seen something wonderful. "I was in the darkness for a long time, through the afternoon, into the evening, nothing but darkness. I fought my way through, blindly, step by step, my hands out to avoid crashing into obstacles. The obstacles were the sins of Need, of Security, of Fear, of Uncertainty. I had to get past them, I had to let go my need for everyone to stay with me, to break down the security which you all gave me, to conquer my fear of the pathway ahead and the uncertainty of what is to come. As I fought my way through, step by step, I realised the darkness was becoming brighter, the pathway clearer. I saw an angel, with a blazing sword, standing on the pathway, beckoning to me. I walked up to him, for it was definitely a man, albeit with all the glory of heaven radiating from him, and he held out a scroll for me to read. On it were inscribed the names of those who were to go and then, beneath a line of fire, those who were to stay. When I read it, I was content for the names made sense. Those who were to go needed

114

the experience, those who were to stay were the ones I needed to work with me here. It was all so simple."

"So why the test?" Miriam asked. "You have enough tests in your waking times without enduring them in your prayer and silent times!"

"Why the test? Miriam, dear one, we are all tested time and time again, to be sure that we're fit for the work. Does not the blade for the sword have to be thrust into the fire time and again before being beaten into shape by the smith, to make something which will withstand all comers, fight off all other blades, be victorious? And so we are tested and tested again, through ordeals of fire, as it were, to make us strong enough to go on."

It made perfect sense. But then, everything he said made perfect sense. Inviting us to leave our families, our homes, our secure way of life, was the first test. Not everyone could do it, not everyone could renounce everything and walk away to start a new life.

"Tomorrow there will be new arrivals," he told us. "When they are here with us, we can move on. Right now our group members are finding their way through unknown paths, talking to unknown people, taking the light of God into new places. I could almost wish I was with them but I have to wait, even as you have to wait, for the right moment for us to move on. Come, let us eat! Miriam has once again wrought her own miracle with the food we have available. Miriam, I will miss you and your cooking when your lucky man comes to claim you!"

With laughter ringing in my ears, I sat back to try and absorb yet more of this amazing man's teachings. I decided it would need a lifetime of study to understand all the implications of all his words. Did I have a sufficiently long lifetime in which to do it?

Chapter 14
A New Group Forms

"What family did you leave behind, Judas?"

As so often happened, Jesus' question took me by surprise. We had been awaiting the arrival of the women Mary had said were coming and were discussing the next day's travel, what Miriam might be cooking for our evening meal, anything and everything but family.

"Four brothers, their wives and assorted children, one father."

"I just wondered. I was remembering the time I went to a wedding in Cana. It was a member of Peter's family, as I recall, sister or someone close. I was invited because Peter was close to me, I suppose. I'm not entirely comfortable with such gatherings, because everyone is making a show, they come in their finest clothes as if trying to outdo the bride and groom."

I grinned. I knew that feeling well. Each time one of my brothers had married, my mother had gone to amazing lengths to create some outfit that was guaranteed to outshine everyone else.

He continued, "On this occasion, the host underestimated the amount the guests could drink and he ran out of wine."

"Not a wise thing to do."

"No, not at all. It shows disrespect to the guests, among other things. Peter was frantically waving at me, a 'Do Something' action, not that anyone else would have interpreted it that way."

"What happened?"

"He changed the water in the huge amphoras into wine." James broke into the conversation, smiling as he did so. "Everyone praised the host for keeping the best wine to serve last, rather than first."

I was speechless. There really was no end to his abilities. Then I wondered why he had told me, but again he read the thought.

"Any of us can do anything, if we believe sufficiently in what we are doing."

Another quietly expressed lesson for me.

"All of us have left family behind, if you think about it. We all belong to someone, as wife, daughter, sister, cousin, aunt and so on. Change that for the men. Peter left a wife and son, James here left a betrothed, Andrew was courting someone and left with just a word and so it goes on. All are committed to the cause, spreading the word of the Kingdom of Heaven. I know at times you think you have no special talent to offer, Judas, but believe me you do. I would not have called you if I did not have need of you, apart from the linked destiny, that is."

I saw James look up with sudden interest at that but Jesus quietened the moment. "We know, I know, that Judas and I are linked in some way but what it is has yet to be revealed to me and to him. When we know, you will know. We are not keeping anything from anyone!"

"I didn't think you were." But the look belied the words. Jesus went to him and put an arm round his shoulders. "James, you're important to me, too. Why else did I hold you back? Simon is as well, he who sits so silent and doesn't miss a word or a movement. Simon is on guard every hour of every day, aren't you, my dear friend? I need you, all of you I chose to stay I chose for a reason. Never doubt it."

"We don't," Miriam said firmly. "James hates to think he's being left out of something. If you would rather have been out there, struggling with non-believers and argumentative elders, James, feel free to go!"

"No." He looked a bit despondent for a moment and I wondered why. "I'm sure you have reasons for me to be here, Jesus. My apologies. I didn't mean to question you, or Judas, come to that."

Then I realised what the problem was. A sense of being left out. He had been part of the group before I arrived and there I was, being mentioned in connection with a shared destiny. The words could be interpreted several ways, it was not necessarily all good and I had the distinct feeling at times it was not going to be good. Not that I could do anything about it, no matter what it was. The pathway was set and I had to walk it. I had no idea where that conviction came from either, but it was there and I went along with it.

"So, what else have I missed?" I asked, trying to lighten the moment.

"Oh lots!" James grinned. "Like the time our beloved leader stormed into the temple grounds and overturned all the money changers' tables."

"What?" I think it was the first time I had been shocked by anything anyone had said.

Jesus grinned and looked a little shamefaced, even. "I did get a bit carried away, I have to admit. But at the time it was – well, almost fun. I was so angry it was untrue. They were charging such high rates to change the money that some people were being ruined by it. I went in, told them they had turned the house of God into a house of thieves and overthrew their tables. The sight of them scrabbling in the dust for their precious coins is something that I think of some nights with great amusement."

"That it is not the way to conduct a quiet, peaceful mission," Miriam said sternly, but with a light in her eyes which said she was joking.

"Start as you mean to go on," Jesus told her. "That's what I planned to do, anyway. That particular happening got people listening to me, if nothing else."

"Is there any more?" I asked.

Simon laughed. "Probably. Keep asking, Judas, I'm catching up as well!"

"Not much more, lots of preaching, teaching, healing, oh and telling some woman in Samaria she had already been through five husbands and the man she had at that time was not married to her. She was a bit shocked."

"I imagine she was." I wondered at the depth of Jesus' abilities. He noticed, as usual, and smiled.

"Bit of far-seeing, Judas. Anyone can do it if they set their mind to it. Look, let's see how well you do. Who is coming to join us and when?"

"What do I do?"

"What did you do when I called you?"

"Cleared my mind… oh, I see. I do the same thing."

"To start with. When you get used to using your mind in that way, you won't have to do the clearing part. James is able to do this but refuses, says it hurts his head. Miriam doesn't want to try. Simon has yet to try. Simon, do you want to try?"

He shook his head. "No, I leave that kind of thing to you."

I sat quietly, pushing all thoughts aside as best I could, visualising an empty road and then allowing someone to walk along that road.

I saw a pretty woman, her head covered so I could not see the colour of her hair, walking proud and tall toward us.

"A young woman comes," I said slowly and carefully, unsure of myself. "I think her name is Rebecca, I think she's a widow or a betrothed who has no man, for some reason."

"We shall see." He was so calm, so accepting of my words, I began to think there was a possibility I was right and that in itself held an excitement. Could I do this, could I farsee as he did?

We talked of other things for a while, wondering how the others were getting on out there on their own, dealing with demons, sick people, hatred from Pharisees and Sadducees and just outright condemnation from any who perceived them to be a threat.

As we talked, a small cloud of dust began to show on the road. After a time it became more distinct, a young woman, her head covered against the sun and the dust, walking proudly toward us. She carried a small bundle on her back. Jesus cast one look in my direction and turned back to watch the woman approach. She slowed down when she saw us, held out her hands in a gesture of peace and then came and stood within speaking distance.

"Master, may I walk with you and learn to serve God?"

"You may. Come closer, welcome to the group, Rebecca."

Her shocked look told me everything. "How did you…"

"We have been waiting for you," Miriam told her. "Come, sit, have some wine. I'll be serving food very soon."

"Thank you." She looked at Jesus with love and longing. "I can really walk with you?"

"Of course. There are two more to come and then we move on, to fulfil our mission in life, to preach the coming of the Kingdom of Heaven to those who would hear and to heal those who are sick."

"Oh yes!" Her eyes lit up. "I want to help with the sick ones."

"Yes. Your role is with the sick people, Rebecca. I am pleased you are with us."

She visibly relaxed then and looked round at the rest of us.

"Judas," I told her, "of Kerioth."

"Simon." He held out a hand and she took it, almost timidly. I wondered if she had been hurt by someone large like Simon, she seemed afraid of him.

"Miriam." The two women hugged for a moment and then Rebecca looked at James.

"James."

She nodded. "You already know somehow, I know not how. I am Rebecca. My husband succumbed to a fever and I am alone. I see no way forward for me but to seek a new pathway. I've heard of your preaching, Master and the fact you always take in those who want to serve. So here I am."

"As I said, I am pleased you are with us. Now we are six and there are more to come. The group rebuilds itself, just as I thought it would." He looked at Rebecca who seemed a bit puzzled. "We were a large group but many have gone out into the world to preach, heal and teach the people. Until they return, we are a small group which is slowly getting larger."

"I was surprised to see so few of you here," she admitted. "I thought there were a lot of you, at least, that's what I was told."

"Some got to go, some got to stay," I said.

"Good job too." Miriam began handing round food. "Someone has to look after the Master."

Jesus smiled. "I can look after myself, Miriam, but I have to say it's very pleasant when others do it." He turned to me. "Judas, do we have enough money in the pouch for us to sleep in luxury tonight?"

"We do."

"Good, then that is what we'll do. I think that our other arrivals will find us if we move on to the next village and find lodgings. Rebecca, is that the place you left?"

"No, Master, I came from a village some distance away."

"That's even better. Sometimes it's not good to return home. Having said that..." he looked weary for a moment. "I do want to return to Nazareth and see my family. Perhaps I can preach in the synagogue there, if they will permit me. Somehow I doubt it will go well but I have to try. No one could then say I turned my back on my home." It was said with sadness and I knew it was not going to be good.

We moved on after our excellent meal and found lodgings in the village, just as he said. That evening he preached and healed outside the elder's home, opening the eyes of a blind man, unstopping the ears of another man, helping a child regain his strength so he could run and hop and skip like the other children. The joy that radiated from the people was so intense it could be felt deep inside us.

I knew too that he would call me in the night and he did. I woke to hear his voice in my head, rather than my ears. I dressed quickly and went down to find him outside, pacing up and down the road.

"Judas," he began. "This night my mind is sore troubled. Walk with me."

And we walked for the rest of the night, back and forth through the village, then making a complete circuit and then back to walk through it again.

We talked through his fears for those who had gone from us, whether they would be hurt, or even killed, for the preaching they were to do and the healing they were to do was beyond the imagination of those who ruled the country and those appointed to rule the country by them.

I argued that the choice was made by each of them to go, knowing the risks, for there were risks in every part of life when living under an occupying force. This he accepted. "I know not where these fears have come from," he confessed at one point. "I suddenly became plagued with sadness and regrets that I sent them away."

"Are you not human?" I asked him. "Do we not all have regrets, worries and cares? Do you think yourself different from the rest of us in that regard? Do you not think I have thought often of my family and wondered what they would make of my new life, were I to see them? We all have our thoughts, Jesus! We are all plagued with doubts. I didn't believe I would see anything when you asked me to look into the future but there she was. If you had then asked me if I believed in what I saw, I would have said no."

"You're right, of course. I must put these thoughts aside. I tell everyone to have faith and then I have doubts. I look into the future and I see no problems."

"Then put that demon aside, the one that is insinuating these doubts into your mind. We look to you to be the strong leader."

"I think that's the problem. I am the leader, you all rely on me. Am I strong enough to keep going, am I wise enough to choose well which direction to go, am I the right vessel for God to pour his wisdom into and out of? I think I must be or he would not have asked me to take on this task, but still I doubt."

He straightened up then, as if throwing off a burden he had carried for some time.

"You help so much, do you know that? Just the fact I can talk with you freely in this way helps so much. I know what I have to do. Stay with me, Judas, help me do it."

"Here's my hand on it. And my heart and my life."

"Thank you. I know I can rely on you, my dear friend."

"You can. No matter what you ask of me, I will do it."

He stared at me for a long moonlit moment and then shook his head. "I – hope you don't regret that promise."

"I won't," I insisted but again he shook his head.

"That's not what I feel, but never mind. What has to be has to be. Come; let's end this wandering. I feel better and that's all that matters right now."

I felt a touch of coldness deep inside, wondering what he meant and what I would have to do in the future. Then, as he had done, I put it to one side and went back to my bed.

But there was no sleep for me for the remainder of the night. There were too many thoughts, too many strange worries, somehow even though I had reassured him, I had not reassured myself. The darkness held many doubts and fears and only with the coming of the day did I finally dismiss them.

Chapter 15
Nazareth

Nazareth was a surprise.

I'm not sure what I expected, busy place, lots of people, activity, I don't know. I thought on it a lot and came to no conclusion. It was a relatively small place, a few homes, the usual industries, if you could call them that: baker, blacksmith, carpenter, apothecary and a synagogue. Every place had one, no matter how small. We walked along the main street, with Jesus looking at everyone and everything as if he would devour it with his eyes, such was the intensity of his gaze. I thought, this is a man looking at a place as if he will never see it again, he wants to store every brick, every doorway, every doorstep firmly in his memory. A few people were about, they looked but did not seem to recognise him.

I had not realised the carpenters' shop was where Jesus grew up, or that he learned the trade of working with wood, for he had never said. When we stopped there, I was surprised. James knew, though, and he turned to me.

"He's home."

It took a few moments for the meaning to penetrate, when it did I understood why Jesus was just standing, staring at the door, the window, the roof.

Suddenly the door was flung open and the most beautiful person I had ever seen in my life raced out and threw herself into his arms.

"My son!"

"Mother." The tenderness with which he said the word was unbelievable. I had heard him speak with tenderness to the women who walked with him, but never like that. Never with such overwhelming love and consideration all wrapped into one small word.

"Are you home to visit or to stay?" She had tears of happiness rolling unchecked down her face as she looked up at him.

"First, may I introduce my friends?" He turned to us. "This is Judas, my friend, someone who hears all my woes. Here is Simon, who is my strong man, silent and loyal. Here is Miriam, who mothers all the friends who walk with me and takes care of our meals. This is Rebecca, who joined us very recently and who is learning everything she needs to help me spread the word. Friends, this is my mother, known as Mary."

Jesus' mother looked flustered and embarrassed for a moment, then she collected her thoughts and smiled at each of us in turn.

"Do forgive me! I should have greeted you. Welcome to my home. I am so sorry, I only saw my beloved son."

We smiled as one, instant forgiveness, for we had seen the depth of her love in that small demonstration and knew we would be the last ones to criticise her for that.

"I am here for a visit and perhaps to preach, if permitted, come Sabbath."

I saw a fleeting look pass over her face, as if in denial, but she was wise enough to say nothing and it went. I could almost convince myself I hadn't seen it.

"Come in, all of you. It is too hot out here, come and sit in the shade and let me bring refreshments. James is in the workshop, my son, if you wish to go and see him."

"Father?"

"Out at market this day, with some smaller items to sell. It has not been good lately, we are doing our best to make a living."

"I know that well," he murmured as he went inside.

We followed him in to the small, clean, sparsely furnished home. I thought it was a good thing that we were not the large group we had been, no way would we have all fitted inside. Jesus must have thought the same, for he said,

"I have a load of friends, Mother, all out spreading the word at the moment. This is the small group I have kept with me for companionship and to help me work. More are coming, but right now this is where we are. If the others had been with me, we would have had to remain outside."

"Then I thank the Lord God that you are with just these few people, my son, for I would not wish to see you outside your own home! Come, sit, rest, let me get you something. I'll tell James you're here, if you don't wish to go out and see him right now."

He caught hold of her hand and pulled her close to him. "Mother, let me see James in my own time. You know well he resented my leaving, he will not be happy to see me return and disrupt the household. Or so he will think."

She nodded. "As usual, you're right. Let me get you refreshments at least."

"That will be good."

Being back in his home was good for Jesus, that was obvious. It was as if ten years had rolled away from him, he was a young man again, the lines were less obvious in his face and there was a certain ease in the way he sat in the chair and looked at us. *This is my home!* I picked up the thought as he looked at me and smiled back at him to let him know I knew. Another thought followed. *I will not see it again once we leave.* That came with acute sadness.

Mary came back with cups of lemon flavoured drink which was very pleasant. We chatted idly for a while about Jesus' ministry, we talked of the authorities who kept an eye on all he did which made Mary smile. "They try to stop every preacher, every person who claims to speak with God's authority. What is it they're afraid of?"

"Mother, you ask the question we ask all the time." Jesus got up. "I'll go and see my brother now."

No one moved as he walked out, knowing on this occasion he had to go alone.

"I hope my husband returns in time to meet you." Mary was obviously searching for a topic of conversation. I did my best to help out.

"Do you sell much at the market?"

"Oh, a few things, tools, utensils, small things which can be carried easily. The bigger items are made here and taken by donkey or cart. Jesus was a great help when he was here, he had an eye for the right wood for the different things we make. He was good at it."

"Jesus never told us he was a carpenter."

She smiled and the gentleness of it was something to behold. "He wouldn't. I imagine he has told you very little about himself."

I thought about that and knew she was right. Always he said things to draw us out. The only time I saw the real man was when he was in distress and then it was feelings, not facts, which emerged. He told me about turning the water into wine as an anecdote, not as a fact of his life. He constantly amazed me and it looked as if he was going to go on doing just that.

Miriam stood up. "Thank you for your hospitality," she said with obvious affection. "Judas, if you think we can afford it, I will seek out lodgings for us for the night. I assume Jesus will want to stay here but the rest of us…"

"We can afford it."

"Good. Then I will bid you farewell, lovely lady and hope to see you tomorrow."

"Miriam, it has been a pleasure to have you here. All of you, come to that. I wish I had room for you all."

"It doesn't matter. Come, Simon, Rebecca, let's go. Judas, would you be good enough to wait for Jesus and tell him what we are doing? I'll send a message to let you know where we are lodging."

"Of course."

The wisdom behind Miriam's seemingly innocuous errand was clear to me, if not to anyone else. We had overwhelmed this quiet serene soul by appearing in her home as a group, rather than individuals. She was removing a good part of the group. I admired her for the tactful delicate way she had handled it.

When we were on our own, Mary seemed to relax, to take charge of her home again. It was an indefinable reaction, hardly noticeable, but since I had been walking with her son, I had learned to read more into people's actions and reactions than I had ever done before. It was as if he had opened my eyes and my mind to many different aspects of humanity.

"I know Jesus grew up here," I told her, more to hear her voice than anything, "but he did tell me he was born in Bethlehem. Is that far from here?"

"Where are you from, Judas?"

"Hebron. This is the furthest I have travelled, being held down by work and family living close by up to now."

"What do you do?"

"It's more like, what did I do. Since I met your son, all thoughts of what I did have somehow vanished. I was an actuary."

"Oh. You gave up a lot, then."

"No more than the others. We all seem to have given up a lot to walk with him."

That smile again, the one that touched the deepest recesses of my heart and soul.

"He does that to people, he has that attraction. It's partly the man he is and partly the message he preaches."

"I have heard his preaching but what stays in my mind is the conversations we have, often in the middle of the night, when we walk and talk. Or rather he talks and

I listen. Then he tells me things which go deep into my being."

"He would. That is typical of him. He has never slept that well; he often went walking through the night. He told me he spoke with God during that time."

"I think it was the one time he found an element of peace."

I felt comfortable with Mary, she had a quiet presence and a gentle way about her which made conversation, now we were the only two people in the room, easy and – I have to say it – truthful.

"You're probably right. I hadn't thought of it that way. Yes, he was born in Bethlehem. It's a fair distance from here. We had to go there for some census or other that the Romans had ordained had to be carried out. My family is from Bethlehem, so we had to return there. I was heavily pregnant at the time, so ... he was born there. It happens that it fulfilled the ancient prophesies and so some believe he is the Messiah we have all been promised."

I had to ask. "Do you think he is?"

A smile dimpled her cheeks, a different one, a knowing one. "That, my dear friend, is between God and me. I cannot commit myself to an answer when I am not entirely sure. I just know his power and his depth of knowledge outshines all the learned people I have ever listened to."

At that moment Jesus came back in, looking weary again but with a smile for us.

"Where is everyone?"

Mary stood up and held him to her. "How did you get on with James?"

"Difficult. But you knew it would be, Mother, didn't you? He has no real idea of the force that drives me to go out and spread the word. He only sees the lack of my strength and skills in the workshop. But if I was here, I would be another mouth to feed."

"Did you reach any understanding?" She looked anxious as she waited on his reply.

"I think so. He made no promises, neither did I." He looked over her head at me. "So, where is everyone?"

"Miriam has gone to find lodgings for us for the night. She thought you would stay here, but the rest of us need somewhere to sleep. I am waiting on a message to tell me where that will be. Meantime, your beautiful mother and I have been talking."

"Yes," she looked up at Jesus. "Did you know Judas was an actuary?"

"No." He laughed. "I never thought to ask him what he did before he became a part of the group! Sorry about that, Judas!"

I smiled back. "Does it matter what I did? That is very much in the past."

A young woman stood at the door, looking in with trepidation.

"Forgive me, is there someone here called Judas?"

I stood up. "Yes, that's me."

"Miriam asked me to show you where we're lodging tonight."

"We?"

"Oh yes – I'm Rachel. I joined the group this afternoon, if the Master will accept me, that is."

Jesus went over to her and put his hands on her shoulders. "Rachel, you are most welcome. I know you will be a valuable member."

Her radiant face told me everything. Another convert and another part of Mary of Magdala's prophesy come true.

I said my farewells and walked with Rachel, who chattered endlessly about the group, Miriam and now the Master, what power he had, as we went to the lodgings Miriam had secured. They were comfortable and clean, but I knew, with certainty, I would be called that night to walk and talk.

131

I was right. I was.

Chapter 16
Moving On

Jesus stood with his arms around his mother. He looked sad and determined at the same time.

"Listen," he murmured to the top of her head, he being so much taller than her, "when I sent my group out to preach the word and heal, I told them if any place rejected them they were to shake the dust of that place from their sandals and walk on. Nazareth has rejected me. It is time I did the same thing. I need to do that which I preach, after all."

"But they don't understand…"

"They don't understand because they do not want to listen to the word of God, Mother. Forgive me for this, but the people here are blinded by the fact they know me. You heard them, 'how could someone from the village know so much?' They could know as much, if they were but to open their hearts to God."

"I don't want you to go." But she stood back as she said it, knowing the determination in him to move on, to continue his work.

"Son." His father, Joseph, moved closer and took Jesus' hand. "I would wish you could stay but I understand. For as long as I can remember you have been the one with faith, the one with complete trust in God, far more than any elder or scholar ever was or will be, as far as I am concerned. Go to your work. I know it calls you."

"Father, I thank you. Take care of Mother, take care of James, take care of – well, everything. I'll send word of what I'm doing and where I'm going. Perhaps you can come and see me later on. I would dear love you to meet my other friends, the ones who are out doing God's will at this time."

We stood in a small huddle outside the carpenter's shop, Rachel, Rebecca, Miriam, Simon and myself. There was sadness resting over us like a thick cloud. Jesus had held such high hopes of preaching to those he knew. To be rejected, to be shouted down in his home synagogue, had hurt very deeply. We knew that and we had deliberately not spoken of it to him. I knew he would speak of it himself, when the time was right. If that time was never, so be it.

After final farewell hugs, we began to walk out of Nazareth, watched by suspicious eyes but no words were shouted at us.

As we moved down the road, Jesus gave a huge, sad sigh and said; "No one is a prophet in their own home town. Men down the ages have known that, men will find it the same in the ages to come, too. But we have other people to see, other work to do. Let's move on. It was a lesson and we have learned it well."

It was not spoken of again for a very long time.

We travelled back to Capernaum. It seemed a good base for us, somewhere the others would know and return to when the time was right. It was close to the water, which he seemed to love and above all, he was not rejected there. People came to see him all the time, some to consult, some for healing, some just to listen.

We had lodgings, the people of Capernaum were very generous with their hospitality and we were grateful for it, our money went just so far. But, after an evening meal, we would go off on our own, build a small fire and sit around and talk, or listen to Jesus who had much to teach us. We would talk far into the evening and heard him say things, quite casually, that were surprising. For example, he said that he could walk on water, he had done so several times; he could quieten storms, he had done that too, he could heal from a distance, this we knew, we had seen it and believed it. He told us this not to boast, for there was not a moment that I was with him he boasted about anything, but as examples to us of what we could do if we had his unconditional, total, all-consuming faith. In some ways it was hard to believe, in other ways we had seen so much, heard so much and done so much ourselves we had to believe it. Had I not healed the woman I helped that time? It was true I had not done any healing after that but I had no doubt that my time would come. The point was fast approaching when we would all need to work, to help Jesus, because the crowds were too big and the demands too great for one person to cope with it all.

The synagogue in Capernaum welcomed him, even after a demon possessed madman disrupted the service with shouts and insults. Jesus ordered the demons to be gone and the man was cured in that moment. This raised his standing with the community who came in even greater numbers to see him and then we were, all of us, involved in the healing.

It's impossible to explain what it felt like, to have the power flowing through my hands into the body of the sick person, sensing what was wrong with them, setting it right. What it felt like to order out demons and see them depart, see their evil blackness melting into the ground or into the air like a thin puff of smoke. Where they went I have no idea but I did not care. All that mattered was the whole person left to walk freely in the future, without their devilish evil mutterings disrupting their peace of mind. What it felt like to see people pushing forward, seeking the help you could give them, to release them from their torment of pain and suffering.

One night Jesus spoke of the healing as we sat around the fire, rebuilding our energies for the next day.

"Not all can be healed," he told us, repeating an earlier lesson. "You think you're healing everyone but for some, what you've done is ease the pain they're suffering and so will ease their passing. It's not given to

135

us to extend someone's life beyond the time which God has allocated to them. What we are doing is healing those who still have life to live, so they may live it without the pain they are going through. They have, by enduring it this far, learned what it is to suffer, it is their time to know what it is not to suffer. Remember, everyone is here in this life to learn. When they return to God in heaven, they take with them the knowledge they have acquired in this life. It is for their soul to learn the lessons. But telling someone who cannot stand straight this is a lesson is something they could not accept."

I thought on this for a while and found it made perfect sense to me. We were healing bodies, the bodies housed the spirit, the soul, which was here to learn.

"Then we have all lived before," I said finally, having suddenly seen the vision Jesus was giving us.

"Yes, of course. We have all lived before. We all return again and again to learn more. But – for some there has to come a last time they will return. Every one of you chosen by me will not return again. Your reward will be in Heaven."

"You need to tell the others that when they return," commented James.

"And I will. When they come back, they will have learned a lot and I will add to their knowledge. They are experiencing much, just as you are, by being here with me."

There was another silence while we all thought about his words. He looked at each of us, as if waiting for a further comment. Finally Rachel spoke.

"Master, if what you are saying is clear in my mind, we none of us truly die."

"No. The body dies, the spirit does not."

"You do not preach this," Simon said quietly. It was not a criticism, just a comment. Jesus looked at him.

"Simon, my friend, you are right. I do not preach on this for right now the people are not ready for this kind of teaching. But the time will come when all will be revealed. It is not yet and it is not for me to say anything yet but let me assure you, the time will come when the truth of the spirit living on after death will be shown to you all."

Miriam asked further questions about this, but he refused to be drawn on his enigmatic statement. I felt as if I ought to know what he meant but it escaped me. I had to wait, knowing all would be revealed in time.

He spoke of the Pharisees and Sadducees, who tried to live by the letter of the law instead of the law itself. "Those who ignore God and concentrate only on what is written, those who are afraid of offending one single tenet in the scriptures, will not necessarily go to Heaven, for in their observance they ignore those who are in need. How many come to us for healing of their minds as well as their bodies? How many are hungry for the preaching which they hear? How many go away radiant with the knowledge that the Kingdom of Heaven is within their reach, even if they do not have rich possessions, fine homes and money to make endless sacrifices in the Temple? Do they really believe God is pleased only with the smell of burning animal flesh? I tell you that Heaven rejoices when one sinner turns from the pathway he is on and seeks the righteous pathway instead. That pleases God far more, for that person has found redemption in his soul, rather than through the intermediary of another, a person who doubtless has to be paid for the privilege. No, my friends, seek your own pathway to God, the one I have spoken of so many times. A meek heart, showing of mercy, loving one another, not returning violence with violence but with gentleness, this will reap its own rewards.

"And now," he got to his feet as he spoke, "it is time we went to those comfortable beds the good people of Capernaum have for us."

Simon put out the fire, Miriam and Rachel walked off together, arm in arm, heads close together, no doubt discussing his words, James held out his hand and helped me up. I had grown stiff from sitting in the one position for too long. Jesus smiled when he saw that.

"This night I might let you sleep through, Judas."

"I am there if you need me."

"That I know but I am weary myself and should sleep tonight, God willing. Come, let us go to our rest."

But even then there was no rest; word had come that Peter's mother-in-law was sick of the fever and Jesus went to her home to heal her. It seemed there was no end to the calls made on him. I wondered how long it would be before he was completely drained of energy and needed time away from it all.

And whether he would get that time.

Chapter 17
Coming Back Together

It seemed as if we had travelled miles, seen hundreds of people, spoken thousands of words and spent a lifetime in service to God, but in reality it was not that long, maybe a few months, no more. It felt like years, because my being longed for Joanna's return. I knew, from comments made during the dark hours when only the moon and I heard, that Jesus too was waiting on the return of his friends.

"I miss them," he confided one night, when the moon was new and cast no light on us. "I miss them and worry about them. I shall be glad when they come back, one by one, two by two, however they arrive. I know it won't be much longer, for I feel them coming close. I had to send them out, they had to learn. There will be much for them to do in the future and they need that confidence, that experience. But oh Judas, I need my friends!"

And they did return. First Peter and Andrew came back, full of confidence and bursting with stories and news, then Joanna and John. I held her a little too long and I saw Jesus holding John in a hug that went on forever, too. Then the others came and before long we were one large group, exchanging talk and greetings for the new arrivals.

I could hardly bear to let Joanna out of my sight but there was much to do. With so many of us gathered together, there was food to buy, lodgings to find, talk to exchange – my head was reeling at the end of each day and I was glad to get to my bed where I could send my thoughts and prayers to Heaven that the good feelings we had and the good results we were having, both in healing and converting the people, would continue for a good long time.

The crowds continued to come. I wondered where they came from, how far they had travelled, what word got to them that we were there, were healing and preaching, for none of us were sending out messengers to say 'here we are'. Did God's angels, his messengers, do the job for us?

It was a question I asked one night, when we were gathered as usual to listen to his words.

I recall the smile, one of great tenderness and almost with a humble voice, he said: "my birth was signalled to shepherds by angels, they tell me. Working men, tending flocks, were told I had arrived and they came down into Bethlehem where my mother was nursing me. They said angelic messengers had told them to come. Do I believe it? Would my mother lie to me? I doubt it. She also told me of the astrologers who came, bearing what she thought were incredibly expensive gifts, frankincense, myrrh, gold. They said they had followed a star which was even that night hanging over Bethlehem. They said they had come to worship a king." He laughed at that point. "King! Look at me, a travelling preacher with no money to my name. But I cannot dispute the fact those men arrived. I also have to tell you that they had asked Herod where they could find the child born to be king and he, in his fear of being usurped, had every first born son killed by his men."

There were nods and murmurs, the killing of the babies was known by some, if not all, of those present. It was news to me and I was horrified.

"They missed me, as you can see, because my parents went home another way to avoid them. My mother never told me how she knew, but once again, were the angels the messengers? I know this, I do God's will and only he could have warned everyone to save my life so I could do his work. Whether or not I am supposed to be a king of some kind is immaterial, my dear friends. My work is here with you, with the poor and the sick and the

140

heartsore and the lonely. If I were a true king, in terms of being royal with a palace and money, I would be removed from this level and that would mean I could not speak with the people who come, those who need us."

The emphasis had changed and I knew everyone had noted it. 'Us' not 'me.'

"Now, tell me of your journeying."

One by one each of those who had been away spoke of their preaching, their healing and their reception everywhere they had gone. No village had turned them away, no authorities had challenged their work. Jesus nodded and smiled.

"It was as I hoped it would be. You did well, all of you. I will find out in the next day or so just how much you have learned, how much faith you have in yourselves, how much further you can go."

They looked at one another, as if astonished there could be yet more to learn. He noticed it and laughed. "There is a way to go yet! I need you to do the things I do so you can carry on when I am not here."

A sudden silence fell across the whole group. Peter finally broke it. "Jesus, what are you trying to say? Are you going to leave us?"

"Not in the way you think, Peter, not in the way you think. I will be with you as long as I can, as long as God permits me to be, but my time is not infinite. I know this well. I have spoken with the others whilst you have been gone and this is a good time to repeat it.

"First I need to repeat something I spoke of a while ago, the healing. Not everyone can be healed, for it is not their life path to be healed of all that troubles them. What you are doing is healing those who still have a life to live and easing the passing of those who are destined to go to Heaven. Does this make sense to you?"

Philip looked thoughtful and then nodded. "Yes. I did wonder why, even though I did healing on some people, I knew they had died."

141

"You helped their passing. You see, God knows when each person has to return to the heavenly realms, God knows the heart of each person and what they have to do in this life to experience all that they have to learn before going back to Heaven."

He spent the evening talking of all that he had said to us, how each soul comes back to earth to learn and then goes back, how none of us truly die and how, in time, this would be revealed to them. I saw Peter adding all this together in his mind and wondered when he would make the connection I had already made, that Jesus knew somehow he would die before too long and that he would find a way to let us know his spirit lived on. It came just as Jesus was winding down the evening and bidding everyone go to their lodgings.

"Am I right..." Peter began slowly, almost reluctantly, "am I right that you think you are going to die before your ministry is done and you will show us life continues after death?"

"You are right, my friend. It will not be easy for any of you, I am sorry to say, but what you will learn between now and that time will help you carry on the work I have begun."

"Does that mean you have an illness that will take you from us?" Rebecca asked, with infinite sadness.

"Dear ones, I do not know when or how I will pass to the heavenly realms, it has not yet been shown to me. I just know, from all I have been shown in my prayers and meditations, that this is what will happen. I need you to know it, so you will not be surprised when it does. I need you all to be strong in the faith which I know you have. Now, let us be gone to our beds. Tomorrow looks as if it will be a busy day."

He was not wrong. How he knew I do not know but the next day the crowd was greater than ever. I tried to count heads but gave up, guessing there was at least one thousand people gathered, patiently waiting, some singing psalms, others offering prayers to God. The whole mass was one joyous gathering which was wonderful. Jesus greeted them and the whole lot fell silent, just as I had seen the crowds fall silent when John the Baptist spoke.

He talked to them of the Kingdom of Heaven, going over much that he had given to us, the meek, the peacemakers and so on. It seemed to be well received. All of us were directed to go amongst the people, healing where it was needed, doing what we could.

"Is there any food?" one elderly lady asked. She had not come for healing, she said, just to hear this wonderful man speak of that which touched her heart. Now she was hungry for physical food, having had her spiritual nourishment.

I looked around. The whole crowd sat waiting for us. None seemed to be eating or drinking anything. I walked back to Jesus just as Nathanael approached him. Together we said: "is there any food?" and laughed at the synchronicity of it.

"How many are there, do you think?" Jesus asked.

"About a thousand," was my guess. "Maybe two thousand or more," Nathanael suggested.

"And what food do we have?"

Peter came back to us at that moment. "Everyone seems to be getting hungry," he reported. "We should send them home now so they can eat."

"No, we can't do that. Some have travelled a very long distance, some have young children. We cannot send them away with hunger and thirst in their material bodies. Find out what food there is, would you?"

He seemed calm, with a quiet inner certainty I had come to associate with either one of his miraculous happenings or teachings for us, or both.

The sum total of available food was a few small fishes and a couple of loaves.

I looked at the vast crowd and the small portion of food. There was not enough there to feed a single person, let alone that many. But Jesus did not seem bothered. He took the fish and the bread and began to hand it out to each of us who were around him.

And went on handing it out.

I was given twelve fish and twelve loaves. Peter was given about the same. Philip had an armful of bread; Nathanael followed him with a basket he had picked up which was full to bursting with cooked fish.

Where had it all come from? We looked at one another in total astonishment and silently went on distributing the food. It was just – there. In our hands. In their hands. Being eaten without anyone asking 'from whence comes the food, friend?' It was as if they *knew* and in the knowing, they accepted, as we did, that a miracle was taking place before our eyes.

We went through the crowd, all of us, handing out fish and bread. Handing out God's gifts to his people. Containers were 'found' I know not from where. Everyone laughed and talked and smiled, the whole crowd was joyous and that added to the wonder of the day.

Water was poured for every person so they could drink as well as eat. Where did the water come from? There was no spring in the area. And yet, pure clear water was available for everyone. I touched it, it was real. I drank some of it, it filled me with joy. I saw children wandering about clutching portions of bread and pieces of fish, smiling as they ate. I realised the food was not 'just' fish and bread, it was so much more than that. It was imbued with the grace of God himself. The miracle was that so much could come from so little and in the giving of it, each person there received a tiny portion of God's grace.

Do not ask me how I know this, for even now I do not know where the knowledge came from.

When we were done, when every person had received a portion, Jesus directed us to sit with him and take what we wanted from his hands. And still the food came, more than enough for every person who walked with him. We sat silent and ate and drank the clear fresh water and marvelled yet again at the ability he had to astonish us.

When the crowd dispersed, we silently collected baskets full of bones, scraps of fish and crusts which we threw to the ever present gulls who swarmed around us to grab the free meal. I wondered if they too experienced the feeling of God's grace. I am not one who believes animals and birds have no sentient soul. Are they not of God's kingdom too?

We sat long into the twilight, none of us speaking. Jesus sat with us, saying nothing. I felt he was waiting for someone to broach the subject. Eventually Andrew spoke.

"How-" He stopped, looked around at us, looked at Jesus and began again. "How did you do that?"

"Wrong question, Andrew," Jesus said quietly. "It should have been, why did you do that? I did it for two reasons. One is that I could not see the patient starving people go home unfed. The other is that you, all of you, were ready to send them home unfed, when we had something with which to feed them."

"But so few..." Peter objected. "How could we..."

"Through faith, Peter, my dear friend. Did I not send you out into the world to experience healing and preaching and to gain faith? I did not mention that word before you left, I hoped you would find it, all of you. Where did you think the healing came from? Where did you think the preaching came from? You reached into yourselves and found that part of you which is connected to God. All I did was reach into myself and find that part of me which is connected to God. He provided for his people. I did not. It was his doing. And so the people were fed.

"For each of you, this is another lesson. Provided there is something, no matter how small that something might be, to work with, you can do miracles. You heal with the small amount of faith with which that person comes to you for healing. You take that small amount of faith and build on it with your own and through that combination comes the healing that person needs. If someone comes but has no faith at all, is nothing but a block of stone, no healing will take place. There has to be something, no matter how small, for the faith within you to connect with. I hope this is making sense, for today's lesson was rather exhausting."

In truth, he looked totally drained. We all looked at one another and as one we nodded. The lesson had been driven home. We should never ever turn anyone anyway if there was the slightest chance we could help them.

"Look within," he told us. "Look within to your own heart, your own soul, your own faith. There will be the ability to do miracles. If you have but a mustard seed of faith you could demand that mountain to move, and it would." He smiled. "You're not quite ready to move mountains just yet but given time you will do more miracles than you have already done. Do you not count your healing as miraculous?

"Come. It has been a long day and I am in sore need of rest. I am sure you are too. Tomorrow anything could happen."

He got up and began to walk toward the village where we were lodging. We scrambled to follow him, wondering where and how he had such knowledge, such ability, such assurance and wondering too if we were really fit to follow in his footsteps.

Chapter 18
Heartbreak

Moving on, moving on, seemed to become a way of life. Sleep somewhere, eat at first light, be on the road and heading for the next village, the next town, the next place where the crowds would be waiting for us. I said before, how they knew I don't know, some kind of message seemed to go out that we were coming and there they were. I still didn't know.

There was one particularly large gathering where more people were fed and this time we almost took it for granted that he would hand out more and more food and we would gather up basket loads afterwards which we fed to the ever present gulls. Somehow it seemed natural that so much bounty came from his hands and we even thought we might have a part in it. There was no pride involved; it wasn't 'aren't we clever?' but more 'look what can be done with faith.'

I recall that after that particular meeting, he spoke with us on a very different topic, one he had not mentioned before.

In the light of the fire he looked alternately young and old, the shadows and flickering flames altered his appearance quite dramatically. I was watching this as much as listening to his words, catching a glimpse of the young man he was before he began this travelling way of life and also catching a glimpse of the older man he might become, if he lived. I had in mind always the authorities who were out to entrap him in some way. Why they considered him a threat I do not know, but it was clear that they did.

"God has ways of working with people which many do not understand. What I have to say is this: what you give out you get back. The facts are that simple. If you give out hatred, that is what you will get back. If you give out love, you will receive love and compassion in return. If you give your last piece of food to someone who needs it more than you, then food will be given to you in abundance. If you hand your cloak to someone who is shivering in the cold, you will find someone gives you a cloak in return. Have I not proved this to you time and again? I gave out food to the people and food was generated to give to them. I give out love to you and receive love in return. I give compassion and healing to the people who come and they in return give back their compassion and even their healing to us, to me, for the combined power they create by being together gives me more power to work with and heal more people. When that power begins to diminish, as it must after a while, you will see me tire and become drained of energy."

He looked at us all in turn.

"I have to say something else, too. The Pharisees put great store on what a man does before he eats. I say this: what you put into your mouth to eat is processed by your body and passes through. What comes out of your mouth comes from your heart and mind. That is where it can go wrong, for you cannot always stop the words which fly from your mouth and, once said, they cannot be taken back. Your hearts and minds need to be pure so that the words which come out are the right ones. You should never have to be sorry for words you said."

Peter asked, "what about the woman who came to us for healing for her daughter and you said you had come for the lost sheep of Israel, not for others?"

"What about her?"

"I wondered why you did not immediately grant her wish, that's all."

He gave one of his soft musical laughs that said he was amused.

"It was a test. A small one, but a test for all that. How much faith did she have that I could heal her daughter? What did I say to you about working with the

148

small amount of faith in someone's heart? By testing her in that way, I knew she had sufficient faith for me to heal her daughter without going anywhere near her. Tests, small tests, but they work and they reveal the depths of someone's faith. You will try that in future and you will find some people lacking in their faith and you will not be able to heal. Remember that. It will save you disappointment and more than that, save others from pointing a finger and saying the healing does not work. I have explained to you that it will not always be as you would wish it to be, for God knows when people are to return to Heaven and even, I have to say, to live on here with an affliction, for even in that there are lessons for that soul and for others who have to tend them."

John threw more wood onto the fire and then looked up.

"We were asked if you had ever travelled outside this land."

"An odd question." He smiled. "No, I have never travelled outside this land and I do not intend to – in this life anyway."

"What do you mean, in this life?" Joanna was on her knees before him, staring into his eyes. "Does that mean you plan to leave us?"

"Joanna, my dear one, my fate and that of all of you is known only to God. All I am saying is, I will not leave this land in this life. What I do in the next life is in God's hands."

In that moment I knew two things: one was that Joanna loved Jesus more than she had ever loved anyone in her life and the other was that she would never love me. I had watched and waited every moment since she had returned, hoping she would favour me with confidences, or words that said 'I missed you whilst I was gone' and they didn't happen. None of that happened. My heart had grown heavier and sadder by the day but I had fought it off, telling myself she was newly confident in her role as follower and worker and would turn to me later. She didn't.

As slowly as I could manage, I got up and began to wander away, for all the world as if seeking a place for privacy to relieve myself. I was going to, but not in the way they would think. I walked some distance from the group, walked until they were no more than shadows and shapes around the glow and then gave way to the tears which had been threatening for some time. I was sure they could hear me, the sobs were so loud, so painful and heart-breaking, but I could not stop them. I never knew the meaning of heartbreak before that moment. Another lesson for Judas Iskariot. I was on my knees in the dust, head all but touching the ground, tears watering the sparse grasses and plants beneath me. No one was to blame, no one could be held culpable for this feeling. I had fallen in love and so had she, but not with each other.

When the storm had passed, I strolled back, sat down and tried to act as if all was well. It was, until I tried to speak and my voice cracked.

"Too much dust and sun," said Miriam, in her usual authoritative way. "Here." She handed me a flagon of wine. I drank more than I should, but I needed it. Jesus was looking at me with his penetrating gaze and I knew he had seen through my charade, even if the others hadn't.

They talked a little more but the tiredness was apparent. Jesus stirred, looked around and commented: "time we went to our beds. Well, you can, I want to sit here just a little longer and say my prayers with the glow of the fire to warm me."

He looked at me and made a tiny gesture, indicating I was to stay. I got up, saying, "I'll just see to-"

No one took any notice; they were all too busy getting themselves together for the walk to their lodgings. I went part way with Nathanael and Philip and then turned back, saying I had forgotten something. I don't think they even noticed my going, they were that deep in conversation.

By the time I returned, Jesus was half dozing by the fire. I felt sorry that I had to disturb him but it was his idea I returned, or stayed.

As I sat down, he woke and looked at me.

"I would have let you sleep," I began but he made that small dismissive gesture I knew so well.

"Judas, we have to talk. Your heart is breaking and this I cannot leave this to the passing of time to ease. Tell me."

"You know."

"Yes, I do, but I need you to say it, to voice it so that it is clear between us what the problem is."

"I love Joanna and she does not love me. Since she went away to preach and heal, I have not spoken with her in private. She promised to tell me of her service to John the Baptist but I have had nothing. And then…"

"And then she knelt in front of me with love in her eyes and you knew you would not have her for your own."

I looked down at the embers and nodded.

"And in that your heart broke and you needed the release of tears. Judas, tell me one thing before we go any further."

"Anything."

"Have you known any woman at any time?"

"No."

"Like me, you are pure. It makes it harder in some ways. Listen…" He stirred the embers with a branch, then threw it into the flames to burn. "Those of us who have not known a woman tend to view them differently from those who have known them and take it for granted. Your love for Joanna is pure, this I know. The sadness is, whilst she might have had feelings for you, the confidence she gained by going out into the world and learning how to heal and preach has removed all that from her mind. She knows now she is connected with God himself and as such sees her mission in a different light. I am the catalyst for that mission. She does not love me as much as what she sees in me, my connection with God."

"Then there is no hope for me."

"There may well be, there may well be not. I cannot say. But Judas, my friend, stay pure. It is better for you that way. By not involving yourself with a woman you will keep your thoughts on the course I need you to walk, the one which is linked to me."

"If that is my destiny, then I will accept it and I will walk it."

"Thank you, with all my heart I thank you. Now, as Joanna has not told you, let me fill in the story. Joanna did all she could for John, cared for him, took food to him and when he was executed, murdered she would say, she took it upon herself to dig through a dung heap to rescue his head and bury it. She would not leave part of him to rot in such a place."

I was speechless. Jesus smiled and leaned back on one elbow. "That woman is amazing, Judas, which is why she is one of the chosen group I have to walk with me. Mary of Magdala is another, Susanna is yet another. Exceptional women. Love them all equally for they are of equal value and standing in this group."

I felt a touch of shame then for desiring Joanna so much but quenched it. I was, after all, only a male.

He got up and stretched his back as if he had been lifting a heavy burden for some time. "Now let us be gone to our beds. We travel on tomorrow. I wish to cross the sea and walk a different part of this land."

"Thank you for your understanding."

"Thank you for understanding, Judas. It is not an easy burden but you will carry it. The bigger burden will come later, that will be a lot more difficult for you."

"Can you tell me more?"

He shook his head and then I realised how long his hair had grown since we had been travelling. It was time someone cut it for him. I wondered if mine was overlong too. Foolish irrelevant thoughts which crashed in to avoid the bigger ones I was thinking.

"I cannot say anything because the pathway is still in darkness. When the lantern lights it, I will tell you. Until then, trust me, there are things you do not need to know."

I had to be satisfied with that.

Chapter 19
Travels

The next day we were divided again. We could not all go to Magadan, the boat was not big enough. There were people waiting for healing and help where we were at that time, so decisions had to be made, who was to go, who was to stay.

In the end, as we could not decide, Jesus decided for us. He chose Peter, Andrew, John, James, Matthew and myself, asking everyone else to carry on the work whilst we were gone.

The journey was an experience for me; I had never been in a boat before. From the shore the sea looked enormous, from the water itself it was even more enormous and a little frightening, although the fishermen among us would no doubt have dismissed such thoughts had I expressed them. I recalled my arrival in Galilee, watching the fishermen working on their boats, wondering at their skills. I saw the same thing whilst sailing, they revealed many skills of a kind I had never seen before. It brought home to me yet again how different we all were but how we needed one another, I could not have sailed the boat, I needed them to do it. Quite what they needed me for was another matter entirely. I did not wish to go down that pathway of thought and backed away from it.

We were not sailing for very long, it seemed, or was I just enchanted with being on the water? I don't know. It stopped being frightening, the movement was gentle and we travelled at a pace that meant we were brushed by the breeze, not battered by it. As we sailed, Peter reminisced about the time he was out on the sea in a raging storm, fighting for stability, when he saw Jesus walking across the water to him.

"I thought he was a ghost, didn't I say that to you, Jesus? It seemed impossible, but what did you do but tell me to get out of the boat and walk toward you!"

"Did you?" I asked, wondering if I would have had that level of faith.

"Of course. And I walked on the water for a good way too, before I lost my faith and fell in. Jesus rescued me." There was a roar of laughter from Andrew, who obviously loved the story.

"I let him get out and walk," he said through his chuckles. "I stayed right where I was! It was impressive, though, he got some way before he fell in."

Jesus looked round at me. "I've done my share of miracles, you see. That was just another of them. Anyone can do it, truthfully, it's all in the mind."

No, I thought, it's more than that. Much more than that.

"Peter, drop the sail, let's just be here for a short while. It's so rare I get the chance to be away from everyone during the day."

"Yes, a good thing to do."

The boat rocked gently on a slight swell, the sky was a perfect blue and the landscape rich with colours. I don't think I had ever been so aware of colour as I was during that time, everything from the peeling paint on the boat to the shades in the water as the ripples moved around us. I don't think I have known such peace, either. All of us were silent, just looking, feeling, being. It seems strange that such a simple thing could give so much pleasure. It was another lesson. I recalled my times of peace alone in my home, with my scrolls and books, with wine and fruits, with a soft bed awaiting me. Now peace was sitting on board a small fishing vessel with close friends and an uncertain future.

The breeze was in turn cool and then hot, then ruffling the surface of the water as if impatient with us for being still. At last Jesus looked up. "It's time we moved on. A crowd awaits us."

I could see them gathering on the shore, looking out at us, some waving, some seemed to be calling but if they were, we were just too far away to hear their voices.

"You can stay a bit longer if you wish." Peter had both hands on the rope as he spoke, ready to drop it again if Jesus decided to stay. He shook his head.

"No. I've been selfish enough to claim that small amount of time for myself. It's been good and helped me a lot. Now we have to move on."

They could hardly wait for us to disembark. Hands reached out to touch us, to touch Jesus, to put a finger on his robe, to hold his hand for a second. I heard with my physical ears and I believe my mind too, their words and thoughts which mirrored that of the woman who wanted to touch his robe. 'Just let me touch and I will be healed.' I found my arms being touched, my hands, someone put a hand on my back, someone else cried out for help and I reached for them. When I looked, we were all doing the same thing and the people we touched were doing the same thing, falling to their knees in joyful thanks.

I had never felt so humbled by anything in my life. The sheer overwhelming faith of the people was incredible. So was the healing.

Even as we tried to make our way through the crowd, we saw the Sadducees and Pharisees coming.

"More tests," muttered John, with obvious annoyance. Jesus saw them and carried on healing, ignoring their calls to be given a sign from Heaven.

"What do they think this is?" asked Matthew.

"They want more than that," Jesus turned to us. "They want an angel to descend and speak with them or they want a beam of light to transfix them to the earth, one they can climb and see the glory of Heaven for themselves. Unfortunately all of this is denied them for they walk in darkness created by their own rigid rules."

I watched the Sadducees and Pharisees walk away, obviously disgusted that they did not get what they came for. I felt sorry for them, the peace and the tranquillity of true faith was beyond their vision and understanding, they could not see there was life beyond their rules.

At last the people cleared a pathway for us and we were able to sit and rest. Jesus found a large piece of stone which he used to raise himself up a little so he could preach to the gathering. He talked until the sun began its homeward journey and the crowd heaved a collective sigh, knowing the time with Jesus was over. Slowly they began to drift away, leaving us food and water as they went, small gifts which we appreciated.

As we had done so many times before, we lit a small fire and sat talking.

"Take no notice of the teachings of the Sadducees and Pharisees," he told us. "They are rigidly bound by their own teachings and can see no glory in the world that belongs to God. They had every sign from heaven this day that any person could want and still they asked for it. Maybe they disbelieved the healing. If they did, they are more foolish than I thought."

He spoke to us for some time about the two sects, comparing them and disparaging them, telling us many things which we stored in our hearts.

We moved on the next day, finding more people coming to us with gifts and with needs. We did all we could for them before once again night overtook them – and us.

"Judas has money," Jesus said that night. "If you would prefer to sleep in a bed I am sure it can be arranged."

"Save the money!" Peter dismissed the thought with a wave of his strong arm. "I am just as content to sleep out under God's sky, until the rains come."

Everyone agreed, so it was done, we slept under the stars once again. The night was warm enough that we did not need anything to cover us. Jesus must have been tired, that night he did not want to walk and talk. I have to admit I was grateful for that, I needed sleep, too.

The next night, as we sat with our food and a flagon of wine which had been donated to us, Jesus asked a surprising question.

"Who do they say I am?"

"By 'they' you must mean the people," Andrew responded. "Some say you are John the Baptist come back to life, others that you are the prophet Elijah."

"Who do you say I am?"

That silenced us all for a while. Who do we say he is? A preacher with extraordinary talents, a man of God, a true prophet, one who…

"I say you are the Messiah, the son of God." Peter said it with such reverence we could not speak for a moment or two.

Then Jesus smiled. "You're right, Peter. You see clearly. I tell you now; on you will I build my church for you are truly my rock. You will hold the keys to Heaven. But before then, we have a long way to go and much to endure."

Peter was silent, taken aback by the fact his words were accepted, if the look on his face was anything to go by.

Jesus seemed to drift into a semi-trance, his eyes glazed over, his voice became almost ethereal.

"I have to warn you now, and I will have to warn the others when we return, too, that the time is not far off when I will be delivered into the hands of the authorities, to suffer and to die."

We stifled our comments, not wanting to disturb the trance-like state.

"But you see, it has to be for I will rise again from the dead and prove to all that there is everlasting life. This is only a body, the spirit lives on."

It was too much for Peter who grabbed Jesus' arm. "Heaven forbid!" he said loudly. "This cannot happen to you!"

Still in his semi-trance, Jesus pulled his arm away. "Be gone, Satan, for I will not give in to your temptation. You tried it once and failed. You will not win a second time!"

He seemed to come back to himself then and smiled at us.

"The lantern glowed a little brighter tonight, it seems. Now you know. My time is limited; I have to fill it as best I can with the work God wants me to do. Are you prepared to go with me right to the end?"

As if there could be any other answer but 'yes'.

We sat in silence for a long time. Jesus, being handed over to the authorities, to die. And to come back. Could this be? Even after all the miracles we had seen and taken part in ourselves, it still seemed – beyond comprehension. I studied the faces of the others; they all bore the same shocked look. They were no doubt thinking the same thoughts as I, how could we go on without him, where would his message, his ministry, go without him to lead us ever onward, what would we do without his teachings, his power, his charismatic personality?

Then my thoughts took a turn I did not like. They sent a cold chill shuddering through me, which he noticed and made that small gesture. It was odd, it was the same thing every time but it said different things to me. This time it said, say nothing.

He looked at the others, one by one. "There is time to absorb this revelation, my dear friends. There is time to think on it and work it through in your minds. You will know more nearer the end, for I have yet to tell you all that I know, all that I have in my mind, all that God wants preached to the world. For now, you need to know that it will end, long before I would wish it to, but that is God's will, not mine. We are not able to question his wisdom, he knows what he has planned for us and how it fits into the great scheme of mankind."

"But you are the son of God!" Matthew protested. "Surely he would not allow his son to suffer and die so soon, when there is still so much to do?"

"Matthew, in this life I am a mortal man. As such I am subject to his laws, his will, not mine. When I return to the glory that is his heaven, then I will be able to do great things, for I will lose the restraints that the human body imposes on a spirit. I cannot go to other lands from here, there is too much to do and too much depending on me. But free to roam where I wish, I can visit those other sheep." He smiled a little diffidently. "I see myself as a good shepherd, taking care of his sheep, seeking out the ones who get lost and bringing them back into the fold."

"It's a parable you've used in your preaching," Andrew observed.

"Yes. It works well, people understand it."

I suddenly realised John was crying, silently, almost unmoving, just huge tears rolling down his face. Jesus realised it at the same moment. He leapt up, all but jumped across the fire and took John into his arms.

"My friend, my beloved one, come! This will not do! There is work ahead, there is time, I already told you that."

"I cannot bear to lose you." The words were choked and muffled. I felt my eyes filling with tears at his emotion, because it mirrored mine. In that moment he revealed how much he loved Jesus, how much we all did.

Jesus looked round at us, all trying hard to control our emotions.

"This is why I told you first," he said with the utmost gentleness and feeling. "You are part of my chosen twelve. I was told to choose twelve fine men to walk with me, to carry on the work, to do the tasks they were best able to do. I was told who would do what and so far you have all done just as I asked and expected. I am grateful for your friendship and devotion, each of you, to a greater degree than I can tell you. Sometimes mere words seem inadequate when I try to express my feelings to you all."

John was quieter by then, his tears had stopped flowing and he looked less gaunt, less haunted than he had.

James spoke quietly, as if he did not want to say the words but had to. "The authorities cannot allow you to live, can they?"

"No. You're right." Jesus spoke over John's head. He had slumped down and had his head on Jesus' chest, his eyes closed. "But my work and my words will live on. The end will not be the end."

"Then we can accept what is to happen," Matthew said, so slowly and carefully it was obvious he had given it a good deal of thought already.

"Thank you, Matthew, thank you, all of you. I thought I would begin by speaking with you to see what reaction you had, it will help me when I speak with the others, when we return. Now, we should think about sleep."

Sleep? I knew well we would talk half the night away. His quick smile at me confirmed my belief. I was learning to live without sleep. Just.

Chapter 20
Destiny Revealed

Peter had the ability to sleep the moment his head hit the ground, no matter where he was or what he was sleeping on. He needed no pillow, no comfort, just – lie down, go to sleep. Andrew wasn't far behind him. Matthew found it more difficult, he being used to a bed and comfort but I soon heard his distinctive snores and knew he was safely asleep. James and John spoke for some time together, then their voices went quiet and they were asleep.

I sat quietly, waiting, thinking, feeling a sense of doom slide over me. I had some idea of the destiny Jesus had spoken of and wondered if I could go through with it. Foolish thought, had I not already committed myself to go through with it?

"Come." It was as much a command as a request; somehow he had the ability to do that. We walked away for some distance, so we could not be overheard and there we sat side by side in the cold moonlight and said nothing for a while.

Finally he spoke in a calm quiet voice, all but devoid of emotion. "Judas, what I am instructed to ask you to do for me is something beyond most people's abilities. I know now why I had to choose you, why you mean so much to me, why of all the chosen twelve, you are the one who has to do this – for me."

"I have some idea."

"I know. I would not have spoken of it this early but your abilities have developed considerably since you have been working with God and his angels to minister to the people. I realised you had some idea, you probably know the whole thing, so we need to talk about it before we move on and certainly before we return to the others."

"It was a surprise and yet not a surprise."

"I can understand that. I gave you the idea I would die and left you to work out the destiny part once I mentioned the authorities. I know you worked it out, I saw it in your eyes." He turned then and looked me full in the face. "Judas, this cannot go wrong. The intention is that I am turned over to the authorities, I suffer and I die. I then return to show people, physically show people, that there is no death. On this my work, my teachings, my whole ministry, is based. It cannot go wrong. So ... I need someone to literally betray me. It has to be you. It is why you are here, why you were chosen, why you were called long before you saw me calling you. What I am asking is an enormous thing, far bigger than you maybe appreciate right now. It will possibly mean your name reverberating throughout the land as a traitor. You see; I can tell no one else about this, or they would make sure it went wrong. They would stop you doing it. Am I right? You saw the reaction this night when I talked of dying. Can you imagine them letting you go ahead? So it has to be a secret between us two, now and always."

"What of..." What did I want to say? What could I say when someone hands you the most horrendous task imaginable? It was the equivalent of saying, 'kill me. I am fit, healthy and have many years of life ahead but I want you to kill me because-"

He was asking me to be executioner. Oh yes, it might be in the hands of others, it might be their ultimate responsibility but the instigator would be me.

Two thoughts came in close together. One was, I had to do this out of love. There was no other basis for it, no other reason for it, no other way to look at it.

The other was; I could say no.

To block the thoughts, for I needed time to think about this in great detail, from every angle, I asked: "What of the teachings you give to people, about the
163

pathway to the Kingdom of Heaven? What part does that have in your death and resurrection?"

He smiled and looked away, across the rolling landscape to the sea which moved endlessly under its own currents and rhythms. The trees were dark shadows against an almost black sky, there were night scurrying animals living their lives in total innocence of the momentous words which had just been spoken. All around us life went on normally. The other men were sleeping, lost in their dreams and deep thoughts. Their bodies were functioning normally. I felt as if mine had slowed down, as if the heartbeats were spaced out and the breath which came and went was slower and deeper than before. My words seemed forced but once uttered they sounded normal to my ultra-sensitive ears. All my senses were fired up; I was a complete receptor of sound, sight, touch and emotion.

It seemed an age before he spoke. I wondered how much time he was giving me to settle my mind.

"I need the people to see the simple pathway," he said eventually. "I need them to understand that making a life building money and possessions and making that their aim before all else, before worship of God, before care for his neighbour and fellow citizen, is not the right way to go. Believe me when I tell you this, Judas. There is judgement in Heaven for all deeds we do in this life, for those we scorn, for those we ignore, for those we hate and abuse and hurt. But that judgement is done by ourselves. We are confronted with our lives and are shown all we have done. When we accept we were at fault on this and this and this, we decide whether to come back and live a new life and try and put right all that we did wrong last time, or whether we will stay in Heaven and work from there to right all wrongs. If the people live a good life, with few hatreds – man will always hate, it is part of his character – and little violence and other sins, it will be better for them when they have to review the life they have just left. Does this make sense to you?"

"It does." And it did. I could see where his preaching was going, this insistence on taking care of others, of trusting God to provide instead of stamping on your fellow man to get what you wanted. I could see it clearly. It was simplistic in a way, for greed and hatred were natural products of a man's mind. It needed a great step of faith to walk away from what was inbred, as it were. I recalled the young man who had come asking how he could get to the Kingdom of Heaven and Jesus telling him to sell all he had and give it to the poor. He walked away with shoulders bowed, knowing he could not do it. Jesus said later if the man had given half his possessions away it would have helped him on his pathway. The problem was, he could not bear to part with a single coin. His possessions, his wealth, were everything to him. God was excluded. Material possessions were his god.

"Is it really necessary for you to die?" I asked after a while. I had hesitated to ask but it had to be voiced.

"Yes." The answer was immediate.

"Have not many died and returned before now, to tell us there is life after death?"

"If they have, they have not been accepted. Judas, I know what you're saying. Listen to me for a moment. Those who have returned have been called ghosts, have been vilified and disbelieved. They have not had the ability to speak, to talk to the people they have visited, in a physical sense. Mind to mind they have spoken but not out loud. What I have been called to do is simple. I have had to live a life where I would become well known, which is why I have the skill and the ability to do what you call 'miracles' and I call 'using my mind.' My fame has spread. You agree with this?"

"Yes, of course."

"And so, this highly regarded person who can do miracles of healing and other things dies – and returns from the dead to speak, to teach and to encourage those who are left to carry on the work. Is that not the best way to spread the word that life is everlasting? And if before then and after then, even, I can encourage people to live better, fuller lives, caring for others, not only for themselves, encourage them to seek the service and the word of God in their lives, encourage them to become better people, to cast out all hate, scorn, envy, greed and all the other sins from their hearts, would this not be a better land?"

"It would."

"And – given my freedom from this body which confines me and holds me and which I regard as nothing but a shell housing my eternal spirit – can I not then travel to other lands to speak with people, to give them the message of love and life and freedom? For that, any sacrifice is worthwhile."

He looked at me with the piercing gaze I remembered from my vision. "Judas, I need you. Think on the others I have chosen. Do you think any of them could do what I have asked you to do for me? I know it will tear the heart out of you. I know it will bring such condemnation to you as no man should ever carry. I say to you, from God himself, your reward will come and the time will come when you can tell the truth of this night, of the words we have spoken, of the commitment we made to one another. Before then, it will not be easy and you will suffer as much as I. I am asking you to walk the pathway of sorrow and pain with me, even though we will walk different pathways."

"Can I ask-"

"You 'can.' More than you 'may,' Judas, you can, for this night is ours, the time we will spend talking here will affect both our lives, so ask."

166

"What did you mean when you said to Peter, 'Be gone, Satan, for I will not give in to your temptation. You tried it once and failed. You will not win a second time!' I did not understand."

"Nor did Peter and in time I will explain it to him. You know, I am sure, that I went to the River Jordan and was baptised by John the Baptist."

"Yes. I endlessly curse myself for not going that day. I had gone for several days but – the Baptist shook his head when he saw me. It was not for me, was in that gesture. I did not go the next day – but you did. I missed my chance to see you."

"It was meant. Everything we do is meant to be. We are where we are because we have to be there at that time. From that baptism I was shown the work I had to do but before then, I had a battle to fight with evil, with Satan himself, for he came immediately to tempt me, to show me glory and luxury and infinite power, if I would but turn my back on the chosen pathway. I stayed in the wilderness for many days, alone apart from the angels I know were guarding me. Why else did no wild animals attack me, why else could I find sufficient water, seeds and other small fruits to keep me alive? I fought long, though, for the visions of power and wealth were very strong. I knew I had that power if I decided to follow him instead, I knew I could lead people and generate sufficient following to ensure I lived in luxury. The people would come and they would receive my words and my healing and they would pay me. I could see that all so clearly. I knew too that it would be false, that Satan's healing would turn against them and reduce them to untold misery and pain. I knew that the wealth would be tainted. So I dismissed him and his minions, sent him howling into the darkness he created when he left the Kingdom of Heaven where he could not be God, could not do as he wished, so he created his own world where he was the supreme ruler. A dark, savage world

167

that holds great attraction for some people. Not for me. I looked into it and turned away. I spent the rest of the time coming to terms with having to give up my life as I knew it, leave my family and friends, leave the place where I had grown up, go out into the world with nothing but faith to see me through."

I sat mesmerised by his words. He spoke with such conviction and with such love that despite my reservations, which were plenty, I knew already what my answer had to be when he asked me again, as I knew he would.

"I walked my own wilderness at the same time."

"I know. God spoke to me of one, a special one, who was walking his own wilderness as he fought through his problems, his desires and his needs. God spoke to me of this even as I walked through that barren landscape. I knew you were out there, Judas. I just needed the time and the ability to call you. And you had to be ready when I did."

"I was more than ready. I have no desire to return to that life, that home, that way of thinking."

"But are you ready to agree?"

"I had been anticipating you would ask again. I have one answer, Jesus my beloved friend. Yes."

His eyes filled with tears, which I did not expect. Then he held me in a fierce hug that seemed to last an age, before he let me go and went back to staring at the landscape.

"You do me the greatest service any man could do for another, Judas. You are fulfilling my destiny – and yours. Great will be your reward in Heaven."

The reward might be great in Heaven, but at that moment I felt as if I had torn out my own heart, thrown it into the Sea of Galilee and was watching it sink, never to be put back in its place again. I had no tears. I was cold, completely incredibly cold. I had committed

168

myself to an act so unbelievable it was hard to believe I had done it.

"When I am dead, I will come back and find you, my dear friend. I will come back and embrace you and thank you for all you have done. This I promise. Be somewhere I can find you, be close to Capernaum or Nazareth or – anywhere I know well. Even if you are being hunted by the others and in danger of your life, be somewhere I can come and thank you."

"I will." Would I? I had no way of knowing what I would do when the time came, whether the others would allow me to live. On the other hand, if I was dead, we could be together in the Kingdom of Heaven. It might be a mercy if I was.

I knew one thing. I would do it, no matter what, simply because he asked me to. The power of the man was beyond belief. I could only say in my heart, this truly is the Son of God.

Chapter 21
Transfiguration and Work

The day after our talk, Jesus took James, Peter and John and climbed a mountain nearby. I think he needed their protection as much as anything. I am only guessing, he said nothing other than he would be gone for a short time.

When they returned, the three men were full of emotion, talking of the moment when Jesus became filled with light, his body and his clothes and that he seemed to be talking with Moses and Elijah. They spoke with deep humility of hearing the voice of God saying Jesus was his beloved son and that they should listen to him.

The rest of us sat, looking at Jesus with awe but he laughed and told us not to be intimidated. "All I did was find a high place where I could speak with God," he told us. "It was his decision to send Moses and Elijah to talk to me. I am deeply honoured by their presence."

"Did you not hear the voice of God?" Peter asked. "I know I did."

"No. I heard only the prophets who were with me. My future is clear, my fate is clear, for they have told me what I need to know."

"Which is?" Matthew was determined to find out.

"I will tell all of you before too long. It is not something I wish to speak of right now, forgive me for that. I need to be quiet and think about this." He glanced at me and I knew there was much more to talk about. He had received a very vivid vision during that moment. "But I would ask you this, do not speak of what you have seen this day until I come back from the dead."

I saw each of the men look round at each other, mystified. Jesus smiled at them. "I will explain when we are all together. It is better if I speak to everyone at the same time. Do you not agree?"

There were nods but unhappy faces. The word 'dead' had been mentioned and that must have struck cold chills into their hearts. They found it hard to accept 'come back from' in front of the word. I knew this without anyone saying it, probably because I felt the same way.

Jesus got up then and shook the dust from his robe. "I think it is time we returned to the others. Then I can speak of all that is troubling you right now and direct all of you where you need to go and what you need to do. We have done all we can here; it is time to move on. There are still many people who need us."

We set sail once more, back across the sea, this time with a stiffer breeze to move us onward, as if the weather itself was impatient to return us to the familiar shore. I felt a little queasy but put that down to all I had experienced during our time on the other side. It was not a vast distance and yet I felt as if I had been in another land with alien people and strange experiences to relate. I felt as if I carried the weight of a mountain on my back, as if my shoulders were so bowed under the burden I could scarcely stand up straight and yet I was. I wondered why I had been chosen to take on the unbelievable task of betrayal. I wondered how he could look me in the eyes and know I was to be the one to condemn him to death. I wondered all this and yet knew the answer even as I thought it – because God willed it so. Because I could be trusted to carry it out. Because he loved me enough to trust me. My thoughts were trapped in a circle of sorrow, endlessly turning underneath the mundane thoughts, I am seasick, I am anxious to return to Capernaum, I want to see Joanna, I want to be with the others, I want to eat – no I don't for I feel seasick – I want to drink myself into oblivion – no I don't for fear of giving away the secret. Who knew what

I might say in the depths of drink? I would have to limit myself strictly to very small amounts of wine in the future. I could not, must not, under any circumstances reveal what I had to do. His trust was not only that I would carry out his will but that I would not speak of it, either.

I wondered if he knew how hard it would be.

Then I rejected that thought. Of course he did. That's why I was chosen. The strong-minded man among them. The one who would do his bidding without hesitation. No matter how hard it was.

Sorrow. Deep churning sorrow. Grief before the event. Bereavement before being bereaved. Sickness, not from the sea but from the intensity of my thoughts and feelings. I thought I would never eat again.

Selfishness. Why was I mourning all that I felt when it was he who would suffer and die? No matter what emotions I had, was it equal to his facing up to a horrific death? I had no doubt what that death would be; had we not all seen it often enough, bodies hung on crosses, suffering wrought deep into the faces and the distorted muscles as they died? I shuddered and pretended I had a chill from the breeze. I could not do it. I could not condemn him to that. I had agreed to condemn him to that. I needed to talk to him more, make sure he knew what he was asking, what he was walking into – and again rejected the thoughts. Of course he knew, hadn't he been seen with Moses and Elijah, hadn't he said they had told him of his fate? The strength of the man was amazing. I had to equal that strength and do as he asked, no more, no less.

A crowd awaited us when we beached the boat. A man rushed forward, carrying a boy.

"Master! Help my son from the fits he has, please! I asked your followers but they could not heal him."

For a moment I saw Jesus look exasperated, almost angry but then he controlled it and reached out to the child, who was instantly healed. Then he turned to those of our group who had come to greet us.

"Why couldn't we do that?" asked Philip, a little uncertain, as if afraid of being lectured.

"Faith, my dear friend." Jesus sounded a little weary then, but patient and understanding as always. "What have I said to you about having a mustard seed of faith? If you had that you can remove mountains? You need faith, absolute trust in God, to reach out and heal someone. To reach out and do anything. I have much to talk of later, but for now…" he gestured to the crowd. "I have to work and so do you. Let us attend to these people before the evening comes."

And so we spent the next few hours healing and talking and comforting and preaching where we could of the Kingdom of Heaven and all that it meant. It helped me a lot, being able to work. I was glad of it and grateful for it, for healing meant a connection with God and that in turn brought its own balm to my troubled heart and mind. Those who heal are healed themselves and by the time the sky darkened and the stars appeared, I could once again consider eating without my stomach rebelling at the thought. It was true, as someone had said once, the real emotions lie in the stomach, not in the heart.

Miriam had worked her usual wonders with the available food. Joanna found a way to sit beside Jesus, trying hard not to keep looking up into his face when he spoke. It hurt, deeply, but not as much as it had before we sailed away into destiny – and sailed back again into what was real life, the preaching, healing, travelling commitment to God.

"Tell me how it has been whilst we were away," he requested. Several people spoke at once, laughed and then gestured to one another to be the first.

Nathanael began. "We have been healing, casting out demons and talking to people of the kingdom to come," he said in his soft melodious voice. I thought, anyone speaking to me in that voice could convince me of anything. "We know we were watched, we know too that we were tested at times, but nothing happened. No one tried to break up the crowds or interfere. They asked for you, the people that is, but were content to accept us when we said you were not here."

"That's good." Jesus nodded and looked round at the others. "How did it feel, doing the work? I know you have been working, when I sent you out to work you had to fend for yourselves, but I know now the crowds are larger and the presence of the authorities is more obvious."

"Intimidating," Simon admitted, "but challenging. I found I healed better when I thought someone was watching and all but taking notes. I know too one Pharisee came to me in disguise - he had left off his official robes – to ask for healing and got it. I knew who he was, I had seen him observing us. He looked surprised, shocked and was speechless when he left, cured of his affliction. I doubt he will be one who will speak against us in the future."

"Even better," Jesus observed. "Simon, that is good. You are determined to do your best for God and for the people."

Others spoke of their experiences and then Jesus leaned forward. "Now I know you can work without me, I have to tell you of what I have learned and what is to happen, in more detail. Whilst we were away I had a vision. I was told of my fate. It is this. At a time quite soon I will go to Jerusalem and there be handed over to the authorities. I will suffer and I will die." He held up his hand to prevent anyone speaking. "This is ordained. I cannot go against my destiny, my friends. I know my time is short. But – I will rise from the dead and prove to everyone that there is life after death, that the grave holds no fears for any of us. I know you will feel leaderless and lost for a while but God will ensure you are empowered to carry on the work. I need to return to God and be empowered in a different way to visit other lands, other people. I liken myself to a shepherd, as you know, and I have other sheep in other lands. I cannot reach them from this land in this body in this life. Freed from the restraints of this body, I can travel and speak and pass on the message of the Kingdom of Heaven, even as you will. Understand this and think on it well, it may seem like a disaster to you, it may be filling you with grief -" in truth I saw tears in many eyes at this point, "but you can see how it has to be, if the word is to go on being given out. This sinful world needs to turn its back on its ways of material possessions and rigid rules, we must persuade people to look at life in a simple way. Love the Lord your God with all your heart and soul and love your neighbour as yourself."

"Who is my neighbour?" asked Peter.

"Anyone who is in need. Think of it like this, whatever you do for someone in need, you do it for me. Did I not come as a stranger among you, did you not welcome me, accept me, follow me when I asked? Did you stop to think of what you were giving up or doing? No. Then when you see someone in need, help them. They are your neighbour, they are your fellow citizen.

"On the subject of giving everything up, I know you gave up everything to walk with me. Now you think you are going to lose everything because I say I am not going to be with you much longer. Believe me, you do not need me to walk with you. Each of you is strong enough to walk alone, to take the message to wherever your feet lead you, to whatever land you are directed to go.

"I wish for no arguments, please, no denials of what must happen. Know that this has come from God. Ask

Peter to tell you what happened on the mountain over the other side. He will tell you of what he saw and heard."

Peter coughed, shifted a little, as usual uncomfortable at being the centre of attention as all eyes turned his way and waited on his words. He was fine when speaking spontaneously but something like this was always difficult for him.

"Jesus went up the mountain, James, John and I went with him. He prayed for a short time, then he stood up and it was as if a beam of light came from Heaven and filled him. He – glowed, is all I can say. We, all three of us, saw two figures with him, one on each side. We knew them as Elijah and Moses but I don't know now how we knew who they were. As they talked, we heard a voice, as if from God himself, saying 'this is my beloved son, listen to him.' I cannot tell you how it felt."

"Overwhelming," said James quietly.

"Humbled," said John, looking around at everyone. "Can you imagine this? Jesus transfigured by light and with the two great prophets of God standing with him? And we were permitted to hear the voice from heaven? I don't think I've recovered from it yet. So, it is easier now to accept that our friend here has to die, just as ordained. I believe he has much to do that cannot be done in this life. But dear God, it hurts."

The women were crying softly, unashamedly letting the tears pour down their faces.

"Come," Jesus said softly to them and to all of us. "I have to do this. I have seen my future clearly; the prophets showed me what is to come. I am afraid of it, no sensible man would be other than afraid of it, but knowing what is to follow on from that time, which is finite, it is worth it, for my time then will be infinite and I can do God's will for eternity. Now, you will need peace in which to think on this and sleep to rebuild your energies for the morrow. I bid you, get some rest, please."

Some of the women went to kiss him and hold him for a moment. He accepted this as patiently as he did everything else in his life, watching as they went to find a place to sleep. Then he nodded to me and I got up and walked away, knowing he would follow when he could.

I stood in the darkness, only just able to see the flicker of the flames as the fire began to die back. I stood and felt my emotions boiling up inside me. I could not do it. I had to do it. I could not do it. I had to do it. I did not want to do it. What I wanted was irrelevant. He wanted me to do it. God wanted me to do it. How could I condemn someone I loved to something he feared? But I had to. I stood, eyes squeezed tight shut, hearing his footsteps on the hard packed ground, hearing the softness of his feet within the sandals, the swish of his robe. Then his arms were around me and I was being held in a tight hug.

"Judas, I know this is-"

"Do you?" I could not help the outburst, but kept my voice as quiet as I could. "This is killing me!"

"Judas, it is killing me, too. And I am the one who will die. Come, sit and let me tell of you of my vision."

We moved a little further away to a grassy mound and sat down, the entire display of God's stars arrayed on the blackness for us to look at. We both ignored it.

"I am to be crucified. You know that, don't you?"

"I do. I have seen it and I detest it and I fear it for you."

"Don't. What Elijah showed me was this – the cross, at the moment a symbol of barbaric death and dishonour, will become a shining symbol to the whole world, a symbol of everlasting life and promise of the Kingdom of Heaven, for those who believe. Is that not reward enough for dying on it?"

"No. Well, yes, it is." The concept was hard to absorb but if Elijah had shown it, then it had to be true. "The whole world?"

"Yes. I looked into the future. I saw the word spreading from land to land by people who had seen the truth of the Kingdom of Heaven and who believed enough to take it upon themselves to preach and heal. Provided they do it in God's name, they will succeed. I saw them wearing a cross, a symbol of all they stood for. Judas, this has to be! Can you not see that?"

"I can see it – I just don't want to accept it! In the name of love, why me?"

"You know why. You know full well why. You have been over and over it in your mind. Your thoughts have hardly stopped turning since I asked you. Will it help if I tell you that my death will be swift? I will not hang there for hours, as some poor wretches do. Moses showed me that. I will hang there for a while; sufficient to please the authorities who need their blood tribute, then I will die, for God will take me home. Does that help?"

I thought about it and admitted, reluctantly, that it did. "I confess I had visions of you hanging in screaming agony for hours, a day, a night, however long it took, for you are a strong man and would not die quickly."

"This I know but this is what has been promised by the great prophet of God, the one who led our people out of captivity and into freedom. So he will lead me out of the captivity of this body and into freedom so I can go where I will to who I want – and need - to make sure my work goes on."

I felt some of the mountain I carried break away, as in a landslip, leaving me a bit lighter than I had been. I reached out for him, gripping his shoulder in friendship.

"I will not let you down."

"This I know. This is why I have entrusted you with so much. For me, be strong, my dear friend. Know that God is with you."

Then we did study the array of stars; both lost in our thoughts. Finally he spoke again.

"How great is God that he can put those far distant stars in the Universe for us to see, ordain their movement across the sky, affix the moon so that it is there to give us light at night and affix the sun so that it gives us heat and light during the day. If he can do all that, think what he can do for you. Ask him for strength, Judas, be sure you will get it."

Almost immediately he had spoken he lay down and was fast asleep before I could even draw breath. I had not realised how tired he was until that moment.

I wished for sleep myself but it would not come.

Chapter 22
Spreading the Word

Next morning I walked away from the group to find somewhere to wash and tend to my needs. I heard the rustle of clothes and click of sandals and turned to see Joanna hurrying after me.

"Judas, a moment." I stopped and waited for her to catch up. "Forgive me, I know you are leaving to wash and everything but I wanted to speak with you alone."

"I am more than glad to stop and listen, Joanna."

"Thank you. I have not had time since we returned..." Her eyes belied the words, she knew she lied but it was one of convenience, of diplomacy. We both knew she had been avoiding me. "I wanted to ask if there is anything wrong. You look exhausted, ill almost. Is something troubling you? Can I help?"

It was almost impossible not to say "I am to betray the man you love" but I bit the words back, hard, swallowed them along with my heartbreak and decided on honesty anyway.

"Joanna, there is nothing you can do. The truth is this: I love you. I have loved you from the moment you arrived but I know you love Jesus to the exclusion of all others. I am finding it hard to live with that knowledge at the moment. That's what's wrong."

She drew back as if in fear of me, hand to her mouth, eyes wide with shock. "Oh Judas, I didn't... oh I am so sorry! I didn't..."

"I know you didn't know. I was hoping we would build a relationship, slowly, as people do, walking together, eating together, being together, talking but you were sent away and when you came back you were different."

She nodded. "It changed all of us who went. We were scared stiff at first, afraid of our own shadows and even of each other, but we were welcomed and feted and listened to and asked for help and in that our confidence grew. I felt myself change, felt myself become the sort of person I thought Jesus would love. I never dreamed…"

No, but you came back and you did not speak with me, I thought with a touch of burning bitterness. You came back to him, not to me. In that time your perceptions changed and I, staying behind as I did, was not part of it. A surge of something that felt suspiciously like rage tore through me and as suddenly departed. I was left with a sense of peace, far deeper than when I had sobbed my heartbreak into the welcoming earth. But the pain remained, which was odd. It seemed to sit there alongside the peace. Acceptance did not always alleviate the heartache, it would seem.

She put a hand on my arm and for a moment I did not feel it. "Judas? Can we stay friends?"

"Of course." I managed to find a smile from somewhere, a place where the great burden of pain was not crushing everything. I could not decide which was worse, my love for her and the fact I would never have her for my own or my love for him and what I had to. In that moment they were equal in their weight and their suppression of any kind of joy.

"That's good. Judas, I am sorry, truly I am. There is no one but Jesus."

"I know. I saw the way you looked at him. He knows it, too."

"This … talk of dying, it is true, isn't it? He has seen it, hasn't he?"

"He has. It is real. We have talked about it at length; it is a vision he has been given several times. Each time it gets a little clearer and he understands a bit more. It has to be, much as I would wish, hope and pray it could be otherwise. God has ordained it - there is nothing we can do."

Her eyes filled with tears and her mouth drooped. In that moment she looked very much like the woman she would become in later life, still beautiful for her bone structure would keep her beauty in place for many long years but one haunted with overwhelming sadness. I knew the sadness would never lift, would linger in her eyes forever, for her love was deep and very real. She had lost one man she loved, someone for whom she had done the unspeakable, rescued his head from dung. Even to contemplate such an act took strength and willpower beyond that which most people had. To carry it through took even more strength and willpower. Then she turned her love onto the man who took John the Baptist's place in the world, bringing the message of redemption and the pathway to the Kingdom of Heaven, only to find she was to lose him, too. I longed to hold her, to tell her I would be there at her side, if she wanted me, whilst knowing she didn't want me and I could not utter a word.

We stood looking at one another, both full of questions. She wanted to know what I had spoken of with Jesus. I knew that and in turn I wanted to know why she had approached me that morning. Neither of us spoke. The moment passed and the questions would never be asked, for the time would not come again when we would be that honest with one another.

"You were on your way … I should not detain you any longer." She turned to go.

"I am glad we had a chance to speak, Joanna. I am sorry if I hurt you with my words."

"You paid me a great compliment, Judas. I will never forget it."

Then we did both turn and walk away, in opposite directions.

We were heading for Jerusalem, he said, via Samaria. No one asked why we weren't going straight there, Jesus always had his reasons for everything he did. We were not aware of all the visions, all the instructions or advice he received from God and his servants. Sometimes he had a faraway look and we had learned not to speak to him or even touch him during that time, we knew he was communicating with a higher authority and we had to wait until he returned to this plane. This often happened in the evenings, when we were gathered together and he had perhaps been passing on more of his teachings and philosophy, exchanging anecdotes with those who had been with him from the start mainly to enlighten us, who came later, about some of the teachings and happenings. They were evenings of true companionship, for we laughed together, had sympathy for the painful lives people led before they approached him for healing – this when he spoke of some of the healing he had done – and knew ourselves to be one group. It felt as if we were one organic group, each person having a part to play in it in some way.

But before we began our travel to Jerusalem, Miriam left us. In one of her visits to a town to buy food for our meal, she had met the man she knew she had been waiting for. We were sad, for she was an integral part, not only a good cook but a comforter and stalwart protector of those who were troubled in any way. Jesus just smiled when she told him.

"Did I not say this would happen? Go in peace, Miriam. Enjoy your life which from now on will be rich in everything you want. I thank you with all my heart for everything you have done for us, all of us, myself most of all. You have been a wonderful companion."

She was full of tears, both of sadness at leaving us and happiness that she had found the man she sought. She cooked us one last meal, shared an amphora with us and then walked away into the twilight, head high and bounce in her step.

"Miriam was intended only to be with us for a while," he said when she was far enough away not to hear. "She has been invaluable. Her work will continue, although she does not realise it at the moment. She has the power to heal and people will go to her for healing and for the comfort and wisdom she brings to all who sorrow.

"The way is open for any of you who feel you cannot continue the journey with me. I will not condemn anyone who feels they cannot go on, or they meet someone to share their life." He nodded at the other women as he said this. "I know Joanna is committed, as is Mary and Susanna but Rebecca, Rachel, do not feel tied to me. When the time is right, if you feel you need to go, then don't look back. As with Miriam, you will take the work and the word with you.

"I say the same to all of you men, too. I know some of you yearn for your families. Matthew, if it ever becomes too much, tell me and return to Sarah. Philip, Nathanael, please do not feel bound to me."

There was total silence after this, as everyone retreated into thoughts. I saw indecision on one or two faces, but then resolution returned and determination took its place.

"I'll know when I've had enough walking," Matthew joked, breaking the uncomfortable silence which had enveloped us. "When the blisters become so numerous I can't get my sandals on!" There was a good deal of laughter, forced at first and then it became real. I saw Rachel wipe away a tear and put on a smile. I knew she would be next to leave, having a brief vision of her walking away with a handsome young man who would be good for her.

"I think Peter's happier on the water than on land, but for all, he does cover the miles well," observed Andrew.

"I am that," Peter agreed. "You don't do so bad yourself, brother."

Jesus smiled and looked at me. The thought came; they understand and are all here because they want to be – for now.

We talked far into the evening until, one by one they sought sleep and relief in dreams from the worries and cares of the day. I waited until they were breathing steadily and then got up and moved away. Nothing had been said, no sign had been given but I knew he wanted to speak with me.

Soon he quietly got up and walked toward me where I stood in the darkness, looking at not very much.

"I saw Joanna with you this morn, Judas. Did you resolve your difficulties with her?"

"She asked if I was ill, if I had a burden and if she could help. I told her the truth, that I loved her but she loved you and there was no hope. That the burden was my heartache but I would live with it. We agreed to remain friends."

"Good. It is enough for now. She knows you carry a burden and that heartache is big enough to cover it. Judas, I am concerned that I asked you too soon and gave you too long to carry this. I am sorry; it just worked out that way. Everything was happening, being revealed, you had guessed and it was only fair to you to tell you it all."

"There can never be 'too soon' for something as big as that," I told him. "I need time to get used to the idea. Everything tells me we are on the final journey anyway."

"Yes." The word came flat, devoid of any expression, something Jesus never did. It revealed something of his torment to me. "I will not keep you from your sleep this night. We are to be on the move again and will need our strength. Samaria will not be good for me but I know I have to go there. They will reject me, just as I was rejected, twice, in Nazareth." He glanced at me. "I know how rejection hurts, Judas. You have been rejected by Joanna. It hurts. We cannot win every battle, every heart, every mind. Remember that when the days are weary and the nights are long. We can win some, but not all. As long as we win more than we lose, we can still call ourselves victors."

We went back to the fire and our sleep without speaking further on anything. He knew my heart, I knew his. It was all I needed.

Samaria was bleak at that time. No rain had fallen in an age and the ground was parched. We were not as welcome as we had been before; we fell back on our own resources, using our own supply of money to ensure we could get food and water when we needed it. We were all used to sleeping outside which was good, it conserved the small amount of coinage we had left in the pouch.

As we left one village and were heading for another, we were approached by a group of lepers. They were pathetic creatures, the disease – and the people around that area - having dealt harshly with them to the point when they were like walking skeletons. They called out for help and they got it, immediately. They stood and stared at their bodies which had become whole.

Jesus instructed them to show themselves to the authorities and be declared clean, so they could re-join their families, something he did every time he healed a leper. The group as a whole turned and began hurrying away to do just that. One man stopped, looked at himself again and came back.

"Lord, I thank you."

"Go in peace," Jesus told him. "Your faith will radiate to others and tell them of the goodness of the Lord God who healed you."

As if nothing had happened, we walked on.

The next village rejected us totally. We were not welcome, we could not buy supplies, we were outcasts.

We walked on, mostly in silence. A sense of foreboding seemed to hang over us, no amount of jests and comments from Matthew and a couple of the others helped any. I had my personal burdens to carry and Jesus had the burdens of us all on his shoulders.

He spoke once, when we stopped for a brief meal and ate the last of our figs, dates and dried meat.

"Jerusalem awaits. There lies my ultimate fate, my friends, but not on this visit. This is just a preliminary to the main event. Walk on with a good heart with me, please. I know you are all carrying sorrows of different kinds, but we are not near the end yet. There is a time to go before that. Come, speak with me as we walk, help me not notice the miles and you will do the same."

There were hesitant smiles and then Mary got up, walked over and kissed him. "We're sorry. We are all worrying about the terrible words you gave us and wondering when it is to be."

He smiled. "Now you know. It is not yet. There are still miracles to perform and people to talk to and the word to be spread. Nothing is over yet."

The relief was almost physical. We packed up the few things we had used, got to our feet and prepared to walk on. Mary took Jesus' arm, very gently, looking up into his face and again I was struck by the purity of her features and the gentleness of her nature. If only I did not love Joanna to the exclusion of all other women, she would have been someone I would have been attracted to.

As we walked on, I wondered why we fell in love with the wrong people. Was it God's way of testing us?

Chapter 23
Feast of the Tabernacles

I had lost track of the days, the feasts, the festivals and occasions Jews followed with rigid devotion. For some time I had not considered myself a Jew, a strange thought after being born into and raised in the Jewish way and observing all the rites. I realised I had been thinking differently since spending nights walking under the light of the moon with Jesus, discussing the laws and the scriptures and seeing them in a completely different way. It was only when Thaddeus asked if we were going to Jerusalem to celebrate the Feast of the Tabernacles that I found out yet another festival was upon us.

Jesus said, "No. You can go, feel free to go, please. For me the time is not right. They are seeking to kill me. I would not be safe."

"We would protect you!" protested Simon and some of the others. I watched his face as he spoke, wondering how much he wanted to go and why he felt he couldn't.

"They seek to kill me," he insisted. "It matters not, only this is not the right time."

That cowed everyone for a moment or two, it brought back the thoughts they had all suppressed and managed to forget for a while.

"If we go, what will you do?" asked Matthew.

"Stay here with whoever wants to stay with me," he replied. Everyone began looking at everyone else. The desire to go was written clear on their faces. Jesus laughed.

"I know one who will stay with me, our friend Judas. If you want to go, all of you, then go. I will have someone here, I won't be alone."

"I'll stay." Mary spoke quietly but firmly enough that we looked at her in surprise. "I have no desire to go to the Feast of the Tabernacles. I am afraid my family will be there and will make a scene if they see me. I am not considered by them to be clear of the demons that possessed me."

"Now there are two staying." Jesus looked round. "Anyone else?"

"I'll stay." Thomas edged forward. "I have no need or desire to go."

"Now there are three staying with me, which makes us four. That is enough of a group to deter robbers and thieves, not that we have anything worth taking! The rest of you, please feel free to go if you wish."

Rachel looked up. "I would like to stay but-"

"Rachel, dear friend, you need to go. The person you seek is in the crowd you will find at the temple." She blushed a bright red, no doubt wondering how he could see so clearly into her thoughts. I had experienced it enough times now not to even think about it. Then she giggled and said, "thank you. I really want to go."

"I know." He looked seriously at her. "Rachel, I am grateful for all you have done for us, but please don't feel bound to stay. I'm sorry to say the ending will not be particularly pleasant and for some, it would be better if they were not there to experience it. It is not your time for such horrors, sweet child."

She blushed again but did not argue with him. She probably knew, as we all did, that he was right. When wasn't he?

Everyone who wanted to go packed everything up they needed and headed out for Jerusalem. The four of us stayed where we were, in a comfortable place that had water, soft grasses and a supply of food. We had all we needed, for the time being.

We talked of many things that day, of healing, of redemption, of the giving up of oneself to become closer to God, how to find the right pathway through redemption and soul searching. "In truth," he said quietly, "we do not need fasting and days of contemplation and good works to ensure God writes our fate in the book in a good way. We need to work instead. What good does it do you to deprive the body of the fuel it needs just to impress God? He doesn't care if you eat, or doesn't eat. What he cares about is your heart, your mind, your purity of thought toward others. That is where the truth lies, not in outward appearances. And in what you give. The Sadducee who drops a single coin into the box for the poor and tells everyone he has done it. The widow drops in a single coin, all she has and tells no one. Which one does God favour the most?"

"Jesus." Mary was kneeling by his side as she spoke; looking into his face as Joanna had done that fateful time. It hurt. "When you cured the man who called himself Legion because of the many who had possessed him, did the devils really go into the swine?"

He laughed. "No, they didn't. No demon would do such a thing. What happened was, the great rush of demonic beings leaving the poor man created such a confusion of atmosphere the swine were sent mad and went head first off the cliff without realising they were doing such a thing."

"Would that man be able to live a normal life?" she persisted. He stared at her closely. "Mary, that was the real reason for the question, wasn't it? You fear you cannot live a normal life, even though I have cast out those who were possessing you."

She looked down at the ground, filtering the dust through her slender fingers. "Yes."

"Fear not. When I cast out your seven demons, I put an angelic barrier in place. They can never return. Not even if you invited them."

Her eyes filled with tears which spilled over and ran down her face in great rivulets. "Thank you. I wish I had asked before."

"You could not ask before because you did not wish to speak of your affliction in front of the others. This I know. Now you have and now you know the truth. They will never return and no others can come, either. You are healed, cured, dispossessed if you like, for the rest of your life."

She rested her head on his shoulder, one arm across his chest, weeping silently with pure joy. I felt my own eyes filling with tears and knew Thomas was the same. We all coughed and pretended we were all right. Mary looked round at us, her face shining with pure happiness.

"Is there nothing this man cannot do?" she asked.

Jesus smiled. "Oh yes, there is much I cannot do, dear one. I cannot change the hearts of the Romans who rule this land, I cannot change the thinking of the Pharisees and doctors of law who dictate what people can and cannot do. I cannot change what God has ordained for me, nor would I. But if I can heal a man who has been crippled for thirty eight years, longer than I have been alive, if I can raise a child from the dead and restore that child to their family for a while, if I can stop Satan from sending his many servants to possess the innocent, if I have turned but one person onto the path of righteousness, my life will have been of value."

It left us without words to utter, because they would have sounded trite in the face of such conviction. We sat for a long time, thinking our thoughts, saying nothing.

Then he got up. "I think it would be good to rest here for a day or two, for with everyone at the Festival, we will not be asked to heal and preach and we can rest and regain our energies. But then I want to appoint many more people to go out in my name, to do the work, to spread the word. Judas, when we have rested, will you help me find the right people?"

"Of course."

"Then you can go with Thomas and visit the local villages, see if anyone is prepared to walk with us, learn

191

the words, to go out and preach and heal. You will know who to choose. Bring them back for me to fill with the holy word of God and send them out. Not all will succeed, but many will."

He stood with his arms wide as if embracing the whole country. "I have many lands to go to, would that I were free to go to them now!"

That sent a chill down me, reminding me in that instant of the burden I carried. I could have done without the reminder.

We rested for two days, doing little, conserving energy but I felt the restlessness of him, knew that the rest was enforced, not welcomed, that he felt as if time was passing and he was not making the most of it. I spoke gently of this on the second night when the other two were sleeping.

"I know." He looked up at the full moon, which was looking back at us with its strangely marked face. "I know I need the rest but the days are limited in number, Judas. I know it as surely as I know the sun will rise tomorrow and the moon will go to its rest until tomorrow night."

"You will be of no use if you do not rest. The power you give out will not work. This you know. Now, be calm for the night. Tomorrow I will take Thomas and go to find new people for you."

"Tomorrow I am going into Jerusalem to see what they say about me."

I was shocked into silence.

"You don't think I should go, do you? Judas, I want to know what they say about me and the best way to do it is to go there, pretend to be part of the crowd, hear their words and then, and then – take the chance to preach the word of God and see what happens."

"You are out to provoke them, are you not?"

192

"In a way I suppose I am. I do want to know what people say about me, not from vanity but to see if the message we are preaching is getting through as it should. It could be distorted, it could even be wrong. You know how it is, one person says something, another hears it and passes it on and it becomes altered in the telling until it arrives back at the person who began it in a form he does not understand. I need to know God's word is reaching at least some people clearly. I can do this best by going there myself. I will be all right. I have protection."

It was as if a veil lifted for a moment and I saw the glowing figure of an angel standing behind him, wings outstretched, face a mass of pure white light. Then the veil dropped again and it was just Jesus, just a man again, albeit one with exceptional talents and a vast store of wisdom. There was nothing I could say.

Next morning we went our separate ways, Mary went to Jerusalem with Jesus and Thomas and I began the task of finding new people for the group.

I had not spoken much with Thomas, although I was very aware of him in the group, for he had a strong personality and an abrupt but friendly way of speaking that took some getting used to. At first some of the others thought him terse and offhand but it was just his way. As we walked, we talked of many things, he spoke of his great love for Jesus and belief in what he was doing, which told me he was a true member of the Twelve. It proved yet again Jesus knew exactly what he was doing when he called people and filled in the faces on the wall painting he had spoken of with me.

Finding people proved easier than I thought. Jesus' fame had spread sufficiently for everyone, well, virtually everyone, to know who we were and many responded to our request for new recruits. We visited several villages and by the end of the day we had some fifty or more people whom we led back to the place where we were staying. Jesus was already there; looking pleased, so everything must have gone well. He talked to the people who came with us, blessed them and empowered them with his touch. You could almost see each of them glowing as he spoke to them. When they left to return to their homes and then begin their ministry, it was as if a vast amount of energy went with them. I for one felt deflated for a while.

Mary was sitting by the fire, attending to our evening meal. She looked sad and I wondered at the different attitudes, Jesus looking pleased, she looking as if it had gone wrong in some way. I knew better than to ask, everyone would speak of what troubled them when they were ready.

Although the moon was full as it had been the night before, somehow the light it shed seemed weaker, as if diffused in some way. The breeze was cooler too. I noticed that Jesus wrapped his cloak around him a little tighter than usual. Mary was wearing a cloak, fastened at the throat with an ornate clasp I had not seen before, but then realised I had not seen her wearing a cloak before. She usually used a blanket. She saw me looking and smiled.

"Someone gave me their cloak in Jerusalem today, a stranger who said I looked cold and would I like something warm," she told me. "It was such a wonderful thing to do I am still thinking on it and asking myself, why me?"

"It is that level of concern for others that I want to instil in people," Jesus said. "A stranger took pity on her and gave her covering. If everyone took such pity on others, it would be a better world right now and there would be less poverty, hardship and misery."

"It suits you well," I told Mary, truthfully, for the softness of the material moulded itself to her body, where a blanket was bulky. She moved with easy grace within its folds and that made her even more attractive. But, as with Joanna, she only had eyes for Jesus.

"Thank you." She looked down, as if unwilling to accept a compliment. I remembered in that moment that she had been cast out, unclean through her possession and was probably still very sensitive when it came to being accepted as a person in her own right.

Thomas could not wait. Even as he took the bread in his hand to begin his meal, he asked, "how were things in Jerusalem?"

Jesus leaned back on one elbow, staring into the flames. "Busy with people doing – what? Hustling from place to place, acting as if they were important. Perhaps they were but – calm would have been better. It was worthwhile, though. I heard talk of me, some saying I was a man of God, others that I was good, yet more that I was leading the people astray. The confusion was very evident, but I wonder who had spread the word I was leading people astray. A shepherd never would do that."

"It was the temple, no doubt," Thomas asserted. "You know they don't like you."

"I know. I preached for a while, caused a bit of a sensation and they sent the temple police to arrest me, but they didn't. I just left and came back here."

Mary looked up. "He scares me, he really does! He goes there unobserved to see what the people say, then stands up and preaches! And they came for him!" She shuddered at the recollection.

"It was nothing." Jesus patted her arm. "It was not my time, I told you that."

"My love, you did not see the faces of some of them who approached you. They were ready to hurt and maim, to kill if necessary."

"It was not my time," he repeated. "You had nothing to fear." He sat up and took bread which he ate as if starving. "I will not go back until the last day of the Festival, Mary, when I have prophesies I have to deliver.

195

Then we will leave this place for a while, knowing the message is going out, thanks to Judas and Thomas who did such good work in bringing us these new people. By end of the last day of the Festival our missing members will be back with us and we can move on. Will that please you?"

"For a while." But her voice betrayed her words. Mary had seen something, heard something or sensed something in Jerusalem that had troubled her deeply. Or, was it that she had seen into the future and knew in startling detail what was to come?

Chapter 24
Travelling On

Everyone came back full of talk, bubbling excitement and energy from their time in Jerusalem. Several asked me if I had missed going there. I said no, there had been work to do and I had done it. No one asked what the work was; they were too full of their experiences. I did not begrudge them their enthusiasm; they had little enough of it in day to day life. Mostly we lived on the road, ever moving on, ever working and preaching and worrying about how we would cope if Jesus left us. We all replaced the 'when' with 'if' as if denial would stop it happening.

Joanna sat by me that night, even leaning against me at one point. It was fantastic and painful at the same time. She was treating me as a true friend; I wanted to treat her as the woman I loved – but couldn't.

When the chatter finally died down, Jesus told them what we had been doing whilst they were gone, how Thomas and I had recruited many new people for the cause, how he had gone into Jerusalem and what he had heard, felt and said. There was a shocked silence for no one knew he had been there, they had not heard him preach.

"We thought you would be here resting," James protested. "You should have been!"

"There will time enough for rest when the end is come," he said quietly. "Before then, there is much work. I wanted to find out for myself what the people said of me and test the reaction of the authorities to my preaching. At the moment it seems I can preach and the temple police will not touch me. This will not last but it was good to speak to those in Jerusalem for a short time. Now, I wish to move on to Judea, I have people there I wish to visit, there are many villages who need to hear the words we speak, there will be many who will need healing. We have work, my friends."

No one protested. One by one they fell asleep, Jesus too. I remained awake for a long time, working out the face on the moon, wondering if it were real or just an illusion. Why it mattered I didn't know, unless I was trying to decide what was real and what was an illusion in my day to day life. Did Joanna regret her words? Would she come to see me in a different light? Or was that one of my illusions, the fact she seemed to care for me just a little? I fell asleep seemingly about the time everyone was rising and preparing to move on.

Sometimes I felt Jesus was arranging confrontations. He healed a blind man on the Sabbath, knowing it would cause consternation, even uproar, and it did. He argued with the Pharisees, knowing they would hate it and they did. At one point they took up stones to throw but he evaded them. All of us gathered around him and more or less escorted him away. As we were not at fault, they could not stone us so they dropped them and walked away themselves.

I asked him about this thought of mine and he just laughed.

"They know well who I am, Judas. But yes, in some ways I am arranging it, everything at the moment is being done on my terms, not theirs. That situation will not continue but whilst it does, I will continue to puncture holes in their conceit and their learning with pinpricks of truth from God himself."

We talked of this as we travelled and again I wondered at his self-confidence, that he could talk so freely and with such wisdom to the most learned of men and confound them in their teachings. Men such as that could not stand to be put in place by someone who appeared to be of lower education and training than they were. If we told them what we knew they would not have believed us. If we had said in truth all teachings came direct from God and they were distorting and bending the teachings of God, we would have been thrown out.

Instead we took the word to the villages, working at preaching and healing. We were accepted everywhere we went, which made the rejection in Nazareth even more hurtful than it would have been otherwise. The rejection by the Samaritan village did not trouble us much, the welcome from the others more than compensated for that. As an example, I would cite the two sisters we met in Bethany, Mary and Martha, who took us into their home and their hearts, especially Jesus, of course. But then all women fell for him, it seemed. I still could not look at Joanna gazing at him with such adoration, it hurt too much.

We all grew in confidence; able to do far more than we could when we first began our walk with Jesus. It felt good to lift illnesses, to reverse crippling conditions, to restore sight, hearing or speech. It lifted our spirits considerably to be of service, to see their faces when they knew they were healed. I cannot begin to describe the feeling. The sense of unearthly power flowing through and into my hands, of seeing the face change from one of suffering to one of calm. To see the leprous condition driven away from the flesh, to see the flesh become whole. There is no way to express the emotions I went through.

Jesus explained to us, as he had to explain to others, that these people were living examples of the glory of God. Their role in life was to show that God could do anything, given faith on the part of the patient and the healer. The authorities did not like it. They could use the poor, the sick, the crippled as examples of people laden with sin when in truth that was not so. Sin did not cripple a man or make him blind. Sin crippled the mind and crushed the soul so that the person walked around with a perpetual black cloud hanging over them, rendering them unable to take any pleasure from life whatsoever. Whatever we did, we were arousing controversy and storing trouble for ourselves – and for Jesus. I began to see that my task, which I considered my burden, was part of a greater picture. The more we made our controversial moves, the more people sought us out and heard the word of God and the truth of the Kingdom of Heaven. I knew that in time the patience of the authorities, especially those who were in charge of the temple, would snap and everything would end. I knew that was my time, when I had to do that which he had asked me to do, to ensure the 'right' ending came, in accordance with the prophesies.

I knew that when the time came, my heart would break but there was no way I could refuse the commission he had laid upon me.

We returned to Jerusalem for Hanukkah, this time all of us travelling together. So it was I witnessed for myself the men who would seek to bring him down, standing holding stones to throw at him for what they called blasphemy. But even then he confounded them with his learning. He took their teachings and turned them back on them. Whilst they hesitated, he escaped by losing himself in the crowd of well-wishers and those who sought his aid. By putting up his hood and becoming one with the crowd, he could simply 'disappear' as they stood watching us all leave.

Later we talked of the incident as we sat around the fire, eating that which Rebecca had cooked for us. Jesus remarked that she was almost as good a cook as Miriam, to which she smiled, bobbed her head and said, "Miriam could conjure a feast out of nothing. That I cannot do." We all protested that she had done just that but she refused to believe us.

I cannot recall any one of us actually asking him about that incident in the Temple, but he knew of our thoughts and began to speak of it himself.

"I think some of you are wondering why they did not begin to throw their stones at me. Am I right?" There were nods and even a few murmurs from those of us who had obviously all been thinking the same thing. There was a sense of relief, each of us realising we were not alone in our thoughts.

"Remember – you should, it was not so long ago! – the woman taken in adultery who was to be stoned to death. I had two reasons for stopping that. The first is that it is an exceedingly brutal and callous way to die. If you have ever been hit with a stone, you will know how much it hurts. To be hit with stones time after time until your entire body is one enormous pain and still you live, is beyond my ability to begin to appreciate. Think on it; think on the sheer brutality of that kind of execution. The second was as I said, let the one without sin cast the first stone. It is not possible for most men to look at a woman without a flicker of desire for her, for it is the way of the human race. We were designed by God to be attracted to the opposite sex, to desire them, to lay with them, to bring forth children to carry on the human race. Not one of them could say their thoughts were pure. So they put down their stones. I forgave the woman her sin because there are those who are trapped in a loveless marriage who see another and desire them beyond all sense and reason. Are we to condemn them to death, such a horrific death at that, for a natural desire? I think not. I do not wish to advocate freedom within and without marriage, there has to be control of the emotions, or the world fall apart with relationships breaking down everywhere and children suffering as a result of it. But we must temper such condemnation with mercy. Stoning is not merciful. It never has been, it never will be."

We sat silently absorbing this teaching as he stirred the embers and created flames from the last of the wood.

"Those men who picked up stones were reverting to the basic instinct of the masses, this is different, let us kill it. Stones are an ancient weapon; we know this from David felling Goliath with a stone. The fact they reached for such an ancient weapon says to me that their instincts have not progressed. They are in the darkness of their own teachings and minds, the darkness of the past. I have come to bring light into that darkness but they do not want to see it. They shy away from it, they hide their eyes and deny the light is there.

"You, each of you in your own way, will bring light into this world. Each of you will, in some way, contribute to the spreading of the word and of the light that the word brings. For when man discovers the true simple pathway to God, there will be no stopping him. I believe, somewhere deep in their dark hearts, they know this and they are afraid of it. Then they will not be in control and that will mark the end of everything they believe in. That end is coming and they know it not.

"Tomorrow we move on. I want to work in Perea for a while. I need new places to go, new people to speak with, new recruits to continue to spread the word."

Jesus did not say 'time is short, I need to do all I can in the life I have left' but it was there, at least to me. None of us spoke of the ending of this time, of his life; it was as if we were afraid to say something. I had noticed people open their mouths and then shut them again and I knew they were about to mention it and thought better of it. At some point it would have to be talked about openly and freely, but perhaps with the experiences in Jerusalem so fresh in our minds, this was not a good time.

Once again I saw the tiny movement that said 'I want to talk' and once again I went through the pretence of settling down to sleep but watching to see when he walked away and going after him.

"It has been a time since I prayed all night," he told me when I caught up with him. "I wonder if I should start again."

"How do you feel about your connection with God?" I asked in return. "Is it strong, is it as it always was?"

He thought about it for a moment or two. "Stronger," he said eventually.

"In that case, God would not ask you to give up a whole night's sleep to speak with him. It seems to me that you have grown stronger in yourself, your connection with him is so clear, so uncluttered by earthly things, that you have no need for long prayer sessions. I know well you find time to pray and that seems to be enough."

"It just feels as if I am neglecting my duty."

"You are pushing yourself too hard. Is not the endless travelling, preaching, teaching and confounding the temple authorities enough for you – and for God - without whole nights of prayer, too?"

"He has not asked more of me," he admitted with a sound that was half a laugh, half a sigh.

"Then do not do it. What you are now is enough for him."

"You know this, do you?" His smile was one of pure humour. I smiled back.

"But of course. Has he not spoken to me with doves, white light and miracles?"

"Not that I've noticed… but no, you're right, Judas. I am pushing this body of mine to its limits but you know why."

"Yes. I know why but I also know if you go too far and wreck your health completely, then there will be no need for anyone to end your life, you will do it yourself. What will that prove?"

"Nothing." Another big sigh that was half a laugh. "I can rely on you to tell me the truth, Judas, for which I thank you. Now, are you ready to move on?"

"If that is your wish."

"You have not once asked about going to visit your family, friends, whoever you had in Hebron and Kerioth."

"In truth I have no desire to go and in truth I have no need to go there. My father will live his life quite well without me; he has my brothers, four of them, their wives, their offspring, to entertain his old age. My mother is already in Heaven and looking down on me. My place is with you."

"I miss my mother a lot." The admission surprised me. I thought him to be completely self-contained. "She is a human angel, my mother, pure and virtuous and the epitome of love. I would wish she were with me sometimes, but I would not ask her to have a life on the road. It would not be good for her."

"Does she…"

"Know of my fate? I have not spoken with her about it but it would not surprise me to know that she does. I believe she speaks with the angels, she seems to know things which are not of this earth. I am not sure if she is disappointed in me, that I did not stay in Nazareth, marry and settle down to give her offspring to fuss over, or whether she delights in my notoriety and work for God. Who can tell the mind of a woman?"

I thought of Joanna and of Mary and had to agree.

"Your death will be a sorrow difficult to bear."

"I know. I would wish I could take it from her. God's will must over ride mine at all times, though."

"Can I ask, what will be her status when she returns to Heaven? I mean, she gave birth to you, the son of God, the Messiah as we see it."

He looked closely at me and then smiled. "Judas, you have the ability to see through the fog of thought

204

and go to the heart of all matters. No one, not one single person, has questioned my mother's part in this mission – until now. She will be venerated in the Kingdom. She has been the perfect servant of God; she has done his will. She continues to serve him by being what she is, the loving, wise, comforting person most of the village turn to when they need help of any kind. Her service is amazing."

I recalled vividly the quiet, serene, beautiful woman who greeted us and made us welcome in her home and understood how the village would turn to her in their hour of need.

He looked unbearably sad for a moment. "I asked others to give up everything to walk with me. Little do they realise I gave up everything too – and am shortly to give up my life as well. I don't think God can ask anything more of me, can he?"

I had no words. I embraced him fiercely, trying to impress my deep love and caring on him without speaking. We seemed to stand that way for a long time but in reality it was probably no more than a few heartbeats. Then he stood back.

"Judas, I thank you. There is none other I can share such thoughts with, much as I love them all. They are, even now, concerned with who will sit at my right hand in glory and other such things which are of no real value to them. We are all equal in the sight of God, all who work for him and serve him and love him. I am grateful for your love, your work and your service, my dear friend. Now, shall we try for some sleep?"

I think we both knew it would be a long time coming.

Chapter 25
Life After Death

We packed everything up the next morning, rolled our possessions into bundles and set out for the Jordan river, where I paid ferrymen to take us across. The day was bright and unbelievably clear, we could see for miles. The river was calm, the currents seemingly benign, allowing the small boats to cut through the water and deposit us on the other side without any difficulties. For me, the non-sailor, this was a good omen for the days ahead.

Perea was new territory for us, but Jesus' fame had gone ahead of him. John the Baptist's reputation had gone ahead of Jesus, so they were more than ready for this visit. In the short time it took us to walk to the first village, a crowd had gathered and we were immediately involved in healing and preaching.

One afternoon, as the sun slanted across the land and shone on us as we worked, I turned and looked at Jesus who was sitting on a rock, a child by his side, preaching to the people.

My first thought was how children flocked to him everywhere we went. They seemed content just to be with him, to stand by him and listen to his voice. They were mostly too young to understand his talk of redemption, of forgiveness, of compassion and concern for others, but they stood with rapt attention anyway. He was like a magnet for them. I realised, in that moment, what he had given up, apart from his family; a chance to have children of his own love and to watch growing up, to teach them the ways of life. Did his heart ever ache for love of his own sons and daughters? Did his arms ever ache to hold his own child, not the offspring of strangers which he had to let go, watch them walking back to their parents? He had mentioned missing his mother, but what of his father, his brother James and the other brothers and sisters he never mentioned? Were they part of the 'missing' feeling too? There was so much he never spoke of. I felt that they were the things which went deep in his heart and he could not bring himself to talk about them. It was a rare moment, the admission of missing his mother but then she was an outstanding person.

It was odd but in that moment I experienced a deep longing to see my family, to embrace my father, to shake hands with my brothers, to see how the children had grown and indeed if the families had grown since I had been away. I had no doubt they had produced yet more children. The longing went in the time it took for me to recognise it but it left an ache behind. Again I wondered how much Jesus' heart ached at times. He had indeed given up everything. I just hoped the world would appreciate and accept his great sacrifice. He was a man driven by his vision of a better world, a place where God was venerated and loved and where men would live lives of compassion for others. A vision of a wonderful world. If it came true even in part it would be a miracle.

My thoughts ran wild. I hoped some of his teachings would live on. Perhaps Matthew would write down some of the words we had been given. He was an educated man; he could phrase it in such a way that others would understand Jesus' words. Someone had to record it or it would all be lost. I wondered why I didn't think I could do it.

My second thought was of how he had aged whilst we had been on the road. I had lost track of the time I had spent with him, two years? When he had called me, his face had been fresh, relatively unlined, marked only with weather and the natural toils of life. He had been comparatively young looking for his age. Now, even taking into account the longer hair and beard, he looked so much older. His mission was draining him; his need to communicate with God deprived him of sleep, which he needed. The constant travelling had taken its toll. Now his face was lined with what seemed like weariness, even sorrow. And he was thinner. His robe hung on him. I noticed he drew the girdle in tightly each morning, as if to deny the loss of weight. I knew the burden I carried, how much greater was his? Oh, he might talk to me of the freedom that death would bring him, freedom to travel, to preach and teach others, but before that moment came, he faced an unbelievable amount of suffering. We knew the Roman way well, we had seen it. To know what lie ahead, to be aware of it every moment of every day, to know that every step took you closer to that fate, is a burden no man should have to carry. But he did, together with the responsibility for us all. He spent time talking with us, helping us to become people who he could trust to carry on the work when he was no longer with us. He spent time with those who needed healing of the mind. The body he could heal with a touch. He spent time with people when he needed that time for himself.

I wanted, in that moment, to send everyone away and give him days of rest and peace. Days when no one made demands on him, days when he could just communicate with God as long and as often as he wanted and needed. Days when he did not have to think of the wellbeing of a disparate group of people who seemed endlessly to be saying 'Jesus, can we ... should we ... how do we ... what can we...' and he, with infinite patience, responding to every one of them in his quiet, emphatic way.

That seemed an odd word to think, emphatic, but it was the best way to sum up the manner of his speaking. He was gentle beyond belief with children, with those who were deep in sorrow and those who were possessed, especially after the demons had been banished, for then the person was weak and unless supported, likely to be possessed again. He was kindness itself to those who came for healing, the crippled, the blind and the deaf in particular. He was firm with those who came for healing but who were not likely to change their lives because of it. Some, we had found, came for healing but immediately became ill again because they lived on that illness, getting sympathy and help. Without it they would have to make their own way in the world. These people he knew, even before he touched them, and would often say aloud "accept this gift from God and amend your ways," even as he knew they would not, for it was an ingrained way of life for them and could not be changed without a supreme effort of will few were capable or willing to make.

He was emphatic; I come back to that word, with those who challenged his teachings and his authority to say such things. Then he became a true rabbi and no one who heard him could doubt his knowledge or his contact with God to preach such things. They hated him for it.

That bothered me. The hatred. Argue with him, yes, hate him, why? He brought nothing but peace to people who came to him, ease of body, ease of mind and soul. He cast out demons, he raised up the sick and the dead. What was there to fear, other than the fact he had greater talents than they did? Was simple jealousy at the back of the persecution? For that was the only word for it, persecution. Threatening him with stoning for preaching the word of God.

He turned and looked at me at that moment. He flashed me his dazzling smile, the one that melted every woman's heart who ever saw it and I knew he had sensed - if not actually read - my thoughts. He knew I had nothing but love for him.

It was a few days later when the messenger arrived with the news that Lazarus, brother of Mary, had died. Jesus looked sad for a moment and then his face cleared. "We will return to Bethany in a few days," he told us.

Peter objected immediately. "Martha and Mary will need you," he said, seemingly on the edge of anger. "Lazarus has already been dead some days."

"He is not dead but sleeping and his uprising will glorify God, Peter. Grant me the knowledge of what I am doing."

Peter subsided, but mumbled to himself. Jesus went over to him and put a hand on his shoulder. "Peter, if it would please you, go to Bethany and tell them I will be coming soon and not to grieve, for he only sleeps."

"I will do that." Peter began packing up his possessions. "Andrew, come with me?"

"If Jesus doesn't mind."

"I don't mind. There are enough of you here still to help with the work. Go, settle your minds and comfort them who sorrow, tell them I will be there soon."

The two men set off and Jesus turned to us. "Lazarus but sleeps. Everything is being done for the glory of God."

"That is all that matters," said Thaddeus. "But it will be good for Mary and Martha to know you are going to them."

We made our way to Bethany two days later. Martha was still distraught but Mary had the quiet certitude of faith and greeted Jesus as if he had come for a meal, rather than to raise her brother from the dead.

It was done so quietly and easily. We followed him to the tomb and he asked us to look in on the 'dead' man. There we saw Lazarus lying in his tomb, covered in a shroud. Jesus spoke quietly to him and the 'dead' body stirred, threw off the shroud and he was standing, completely healthy, colour restored to his face, movement to his limbs and breath in his lungs. His first words, "Thank you," were said in such heartfelt tones we knew he had been lying in his tomb waiting for his resurrection. Even though we knew of Jesus raising children from the dead but this, a grown man actually already in his tomb, some days after his 'passing', to see him walking and talking as if nothing had happened, stopped all the words in our mouths.

He and Jesus embraced and I noticed that Lazarus had tears in his eyes. Then they went back to his home, where the neighbours and what seemed like half the village were waiting. Some cried aloud when they saw what they considered to be a dead man walking amongst them. Others, realising what had happened, praised God for his great mercy. Many came to see Lazarus eating and drinking normally, as if to assure themselves this was not a passing moment, that he would not suddenly relapse into death again. In every way he seemed perfectly normal, the only problem he had was no memory of the few days between his death and his resurrection. That, he said, was not something he would worry about.

That evening as we sat round the fire, Philip asked, "Why can't we do that? Raise people from the dead?"

"Because sometimes it is not right to resurrect someone. Sometimes their earthly life is over and their task done. It is their destiny to return to the Kingdom of Heaven. As only God knows who needs to go back and who can go on living, it is not given to all to raise the dead."

We had developed a ritual of asking our questions after our meal, when we were quiet and there were no demanding people wanting healing, preaching or attention of any kind. It had developed naturally during our time of travelling together. It was in these times we learned much of what we were to preach in the future.

This night I had the strongest conviction I would not be one of the people going out and preaching after Jesus' death. It came as a cold wave that shook me from head to foot. Mary, who was sitting by me at the time, put her hand out to me.

"Judas, what happened then? Are you all right?"

I saw Jesus look anxiously in my direction. "I – had a cold shudder, as if someone had stepped on my grave."

"It was more than that," she insisted. "You shook for a moment. Are you sure you have no fever, or anything like that?"

"No, I'm all right, really I am. Look, it has gone now." I held out my hands, which were perfectly steady. Jesus was not fooled. I picked up his thought. *You had a premonition. I need to know, was it you or me? Tell me later.*

I nodded and he looked away, speaking to Philip again.

"Before you ask, Lazarus was an example to the authorities of what I could do. I know they will persecute me for it, but it was necessary. We will have to leave here very soon, for they will send the temple police after me for such a miracle." He laughed. "They can tolerate my preaching, just, they can tolerate my healing, just, but the so-called miracles, which are nothing more than God's will manifested on earth, are not acceptable. No wonder John the Baptist called them a 'brood of vipers' for their venom is such that it penetrates to the heart of every person who hears them and sadly believes them."

The talk became general after that. I sat back and tried to analyse the strange feeling I had, that I would not be someone who would carry on after his death. Did that mean I would walk away from all I had learned, experienced and seen? Did it mean that all his teaching was wasted on me? Did it mean… I ran out of variants.

Without stopping to consider my words, I sent him a thought *I am afraid.* Then I got up and walked away, feeling myself full of tears quite suddenly. Why I had no idea.

I heard Mary say, "Jesus, I fear there is something amiss with Judas. I am afraid he might be ill." I did not hear Jesus' reply; I had walked too far away by then.

He came after me, as I knew he would. He must have said something to the others, for when I turned and looked, they were preparing for sleep, damping the fire down a little, unrolling their cloaks, finding the best place to rest. I saw a face turned my way, Joanna I thought it was, and then all were in shadow as the flames fell back, leaving just a dull glow.

"Judas." He had an arm round my shoulders, pulling me close to his sinewy body. "What happened?"

"I don't know." I sounded miserable, even to myself. I took a deep breath and tried to overcome it. "I suddenly had a premonition I would not be there to preach and teach and heal after your death."

"And you are afraid of that."

"Yes."

"Why?"

"I want ... I thought... I believed..."

"Sit." A command as much as a request, accompanied by a tug on my shoulder. I sat, obedient as ever to his word. "Now, try again."

"You know already what I want to say."

"Of course I do. But if you don't put it into words, you won't know what you want to say."

It sounded like some convoluted logic but it made sense. I needed to formulate my thoughts, put them into words so I knew what was troubling me.

"I want to carry on the work I do now."

"Judas, listen to me. Do you think the others will accept you when they know it is you who betrayed me?"

"Well, no." I had not thought that far ahead.

"Did I not say to you it has to be our secret, for they will prevent you doing what you have to do?" I nodded.

213

"That goes for future work, too. My dear friend, you will not be able to go on working, for they will track you down and they will kill you. This is a fact and you have to face it."

"So what will I do? Where will I go?"

"Does it matter right now? There is time, not a great deal of time but enough for you to decide what you will do – afterwards. Can I counsel you for now to set those thoughts to one side and concentrate on one thing and one thing only – being my friend, the one I confide in, the one I moan to, the one who understands. Later you can do your soul searching and decide what to do. Oh that sounds so heartless of me! Utterly and completely heartless! You are worrying and I am asking you not to worry and to think only of me. But Judas, that is what I need you to do."

In that moment I realised he was not being heartless at all, but absolutely right. Why was I worrying so much about 'after' when there was much to do 'before'? If I died, or was killed or incapacitated after his death, what difference would it make? I had a task, a heavy, onerous task, and that was all that mattered. He had laid additional burdens on me by saying I was only to think of him, burdens I willingly accepted. I could look into the future knowing I had a role in his life, even if it was not a preaching teaching healing one, it was still essential. Did anything else matter right then?

"I asked you to give up everything for me, Judas, and you did. It might be that even more will be demanded of you before this life is done. I don't know, I have not seen that far ahead. But know this, your reward will be great in Heaven for you will have done God's bidding. About half of those we have appointed to work with us will leave the moment it is all over. None of the Twelve will leave, none of the chosen ones. I am referring to those we have recruited since. Only some of them have the faith to carry on. But they will be enough to spread the word. They will witness the raising up of the dead, they will have the truth of eternal life, they will be strong enough to withstand persecution, prosecution and death in my name and that of the lord God.   But you, my friend, your name will go down in history. It may not be the way you would have wished it or would even like it but the truth is, this is your role in my life. No one, no one person, has a role with greater importance than yours. We have talked this through, have we not? Stand by me, Judas, I need you. Forget the work after, that is immaterial to you. I need you now."

"I am here. I will be here for as long as you need me. For as long as you are capable of needing me."

"Until the bitter end, Judas, until the bitter end. Then you will be released from your commitment to God and to me. Then it will be your choice of where to go and what to do. Until then…"

We gripped each other's hands in a silent covenant, one that went far deeper than our spoken words.

His words lingered into the dark hours. Was my life measured by the day, as his was? If it was, then I had no reason to fret about tomorrow.

Chapter 26
Perea – and Jerusalem

For a while we took refuge in Ephraim, a small town some distance from Jerusalem, as word came that there were those who were plotting Jesus' death. "The time is not right." he told us. "I have more to do." He hoped that by going out of the area for a while, everything would quieten down. No one had referred to his prophesy of dying and coming back to life again. I think everyone wanted to forget he had ever said it. He spoke of it freely and often, so that the subject and the thought never went away completely, but no one ever answered him when he spoke about it. I saw the wry smile he gave when this happened; he knew well their thoughts and feelings.

Next day something wonderful happened. A crowd gathered, bringing children with them, more than we had seen before. Jesus immediately organised us – and them – arranging for the children to sit around him in a circle and the adults to go to one side for healing. Then he began a story telling session, sliding teaching into the stories as he did so. The children loved it. They sat in complete silence, with rapt attention, taking in every word. I watched in amazement, his ability to switch from deep philosophy based on the scriptures to simple stories children could understand and appreciate was incredible. Because, the same teachings were in both, living a good life, being kind to everyone, respecting others' way of life, the rights of others to live their life without interference, the rights of animals to live their lives without being starved or beaten or neglected. It all came into his teachings and in the simple stories he told.

Before we knew what was happening, an entire afternoon had gone by and the children had to go home. One by one they went over to Jesus and either took his hand, kissed his cheek or hugged him. When the last child had left, he sat with tears pouring down his face. I knew what he was thinking, but some of the others were astonished and rushed to his side to find out what had gone wrong, was he in pain, did he need anything?

"I had the most wonderful afternoon," he said quietly. "I love the children."

Then they began to understand.

When I heard the words from Rebecca, "are you in pain?" it hit me, hard, that at no time had I ever heard him complain of such a thing. Surely at some time food would sit uncomfortably, his feet would hurt and his legs would ache from the walking, a stone would dig into his hip as he slept and cause a problem next morning or his head would ache from too much sun, too many people and so many pressures. He never complained. I would have to watch him closely during the next few weeks, I told myself, to ensure he did not suffer pain – foolish thought for his death would be nothing but suffering, but then, he need not endure it before that time. I think the reason I had not noticed it was because the others often moaned about something, 'my legs ache' was a regular one, 'my feet are sore' was another and at times someone would eat something that upset them and we would have to adjust our travelling to take account of their frequent stops and consequent weakness. My head ached terribly from time to time, a peculiar one-sided headache that also disturbed my vision. I never spoke of it, for he had enough to cope with without my complaining of a headache. I could have asked for healing but did not want to admit to being unwell. Instead I contrived to rest a hand on his shoulder, find an excuse to shake hands, brush past him, anything like that and relief would come, just from touching him.

That night his words to us centred on the children he had talked to all afternoon.

"The simplest way to explain to any newcomer or disbeliever how to enter the Kingdom of Heaven is to tell him they need to be as a child again, to be reborn. Not to re-enter the womb, for that is impossible, but to put aside all earthly things. To think like a child with the clarity of a child. The boys I spoke with today will grow up to be fine young men, with clear minds and a perfect grasp of logic and understanding. The girls I spoke with today will become fine mothers who will pass on to their children all they know in the way of how to be good citizens. Between the logic of the father and the instinctive goodness of the mother, the children will grow in God's favour. Each person who seeks to enter the Kingdom of Heaven must be as a child, baptised not to take away sin, for that is something they themselves must do, in their own hearts, fight with their own consciences, make their own decision that they will forgive, forget and desist from all future sinful actions, but baptised as a token, a sign of starting a new life.

"When you are out in the world, working in my name and that of the great all-seeing God, baptise those who come to you. It will give them a sense of starting again. It is needed. It is not something that can be easily forgotten. As they stand, wet and perhaps chilled, they will receive the glory of God in their hearts. They will witness his greatness, they will be examples of his great love."

It made perfect sense. My heart ached because I could not see that I would be able to do that work. I longed to, with all my being.

Once again I had the feeling he had read my thoughts, for he turned and smiled at me, then looked back at the group.

"Not all are called to do the work I am asking of you. Not all have the same pathway to walk. Sometimes the pathway takes the person in a different direction but whatever it is, if it is in God's name, it is right."

He let them all think about that for a few moments, and then he started to talk again.

"The time is coming close when I will be handed over to the authorities, I will suffer and die. And then I will return to show you the truth of eternal life. The Passover is close, we must think about returning to Jerusalem for our Passover meal."

The silence was complete. He smiled. "You will not speak of it with me, you are in denial. It will happen, I assure you. I cannot change God's will. Much as it hurts me inside to know I have to go through this, I cannot go against his wishes, his plan, his destiny for me. Believe me, I have prayed long and hard over this and will no doubt do it again and again before the time, but the answer is always the same. This is my will. This is what must happen. This will fulfil the prophesy. This will be the start of something new and wonderful. When you see me alive again after my death, then you can go out and preach the word of God from your own knowledge, that which you will have seen with your own eyes."

Still no one spoke. At last we all prepared for sleep, still not having spoken. I heard the sound of crying and wondered which of the women was in tears that night. I wished I could go and comfort whoever it was, but unless they came to me, I could not do it.

That night we slept. That night Jesus did not want to talk.

Next morning, in a sombre mood, we packed up ready to move on. Jesus worked at trying to lift the atmosphere, but it didn't work. We all knew where we were going and why. It was a blackness resting on our heads, our hearts and our minds and even though I could detect no forced humour on his part, he must have known he could not change our mood at that moment.

We walked in pairs. Jesus was ahead with John, who seemed totally bowed down by the knowledge he was carrying. I somehow managed to be last, with Joanna walking with me.

We had been travelling for some time before she spoke. I didn't want to be the first to say anything, for fear of it sounding trite.

"I saw Jesus go straight to you that night when we thought you were ill. Did you find relief in his words?"

"I always do."

"Do you want to talk about it?"

"No. I hope that doesn't sound harsh, Joanna, I would not be harsh with you if I could avoid it but the problem – and the resolution – is between Jesus and me and I cannot, would not, break that confidence and tell even you."

"It is something very big, then."

"Yes."

"Something that concerns him."

"Yes."

"I-" She shook her head. "I could go on asking questions all day and not get the answer, so I won't. Forgive me for asking."

"No need for forgiveness, there is no question of that between any of us who walk with him."

But my heart was aching with an intensity I did not believe possible. I wanted to hold her, talk to her, share my heartbreak with her and I couldn't. I even had to swallow the word 'love' when I spoke with her.

"What do you think is going to happen when we get to Jerusalem?"

"Just what he said would happen. He will be arrested, he will be executed."

Tears began flowing silently down her face as she walked, head down, so they dampened her robe. "I cannot stand to see him die."

220

"Then, my dear one, you will need to leave the group before this happens."

"I cannot walk out on him, either."

"You have the same problem we all have. None of us want to see him die; none of us want to walk out on him. I know we all have to stay there until the end, regardless of how we feel."

"How can he remain so cheerful?" she demanded suddenly, with a spurt of anger.

"He knows his destiny. He has known it for a long time, he has had time to accept it and he also knows what he will do – afterwards. His freedom from this body, this time, will let him visit other places, other people, to teach them so they can in turn pass on his words. In that he finds the comfort and the strength to face up to that which is to come."

"Would that we had the same strength!"

After that we walked in silence.

In Jericho the crowds came out in their hundreds. As always, I wondered how they knew Jesus was coming, what kind of message flashed through the place to let them know we were on our way. As always, he stopped to speak, to heal and to comfort. The blind, the crippled, the sick, all were healed. Our healing, those of us who walked with him, seemed stronger than ever, the merest touch and we had done the task and were able to move on to the next. "Glory to God!" was heard all the time and Jesus seemed to gain strength and energy from that, he was everywhere at once, or so it appeared to us, who stood back and watched as he went through the crowd, touching, smiling, bestowing a blessing here, a word there and we watched the faces light up with happiness, joy, relief, a mixture of emotions which we could not begin to record.

As he moved down the road, with us following like the sheep we were, in the care of the Good Shepherd, the crowd grew even thicker. Ahead of us I noticed a tree shaking wildly, even though there was no wind or even a breeze to move the leaves. Jesus seemed to ignore it until he got to the tree, when he looked up and laughed.

"Zaccheus, come down!" he said, smiling. "I would like to have a meal with you this night."

A short man scrambled down the trunk and came over to Jesus, holding out both his hands.

"I could think of no other way to see you, Master!"

"Very clever of you, my friend. Now, is it possible for us to eat with you this night? There are a lot of us."

"For you, Master, anything is possible! I will go and arrange it now!"

With great delight he began to trot down the road, pushing his way through the people who were laughing at the incident.

"You see what faith some have?" Jesus turned to us and began one of his short teachings, something we were well used to by now. "He would risk his limbs and his life by climbing a tree at his age just to see me. His faith is rewarded. We will eat at his home tonight and he will receive the blessing of God and will join us."

Then he turned back and continued his healing as if nothing extraordinary had happened.

But we stood and looked at one another. He had known the man's name. He knew where the man lived without being told. I had no doubt he would lead us directly to Zaccheus' home later that day. He knew the man would join us. All this from a few words. No, from the depth of his knowledge and his amazing ability to see into the future.

Whatever else Zaccheus may do for us, I thought, he had managed to lift our spirits from the gloom which had enveloped us, for the first time that day we were all smiling.

Chapter 27
Fulfilling the Prophesy

Zaccheus was fun to have around. We needed a true joker in the group and we had one with him. Ever laughing, making fun in a kind way, he had us all laughing or smiling in no time. Much, much needed. As always, Jesus had found the right person at the right time.

As we neared a place called Bethpage, Jesus called Philip and Thaddeus to him. "I would ask you to do something for me, something you might find strange. If you go to the next village, you will find an ass tied to a wall, her foal alongside her. Untie her and bring her and the foal to me. If anyone asks what you are doing, tell them I am borrowing the animal for a short time. There will be no problem."

We were standing around, looking a little bemused at this. Zaccheus asked, "tired of walking, Jesus?"

He smiled. "I have been walking this land for the past three years, my friend. It is time I rode in style, for a change." Then he became solemn. "This is to fulfil the prophesies. The circumstances of my birth apparently did some of it, it is now for me to complete the rest, if I am to persuade the authorities to take me, and my teachings, seriously."

We stood around waiting, unsure of how to answer this, what to say, how to react even to this odd happening. But, if that is what he wanted, we would go along with it.

"Now it gets serious," I heard someone say, one of the women, it might have been Susanna. She was right. We had been able to push away the thoughts of what was to come, with an effort, but Jesus' precise arrangements to fulfil the prophesy of the coming of the Messiah. We were in awe and so we were silent.

The two men came back, leading the docile animals. "It happened as you said," Philip reported. "There was no difficulty."

Jesus nodded. Peter unrolled his cloak and laid it on the animal's back. Jesus mounted it and with us following, we began our journey into Jerusalem.

Something, someone, must have told the people we were coming. There were cloaks laid in the street for the ass to walk on, branches were cut down and scattered in our pathway. Shouts echoed from the city walls, ringing in our ears, shouts of acclamation, of hosannas and cheers. We were all smiling, it was like a festival but it was just Jesus arriving – seemingly to claim the city for himself. I heard voices, 'who is he?' and the answer 'the prophet, Jesus of Nazareth!'

He walked into the temple as if he owned the place, his robe shining in the sunshine as if it were spun from silver, not from wool. He stood, staring at the money changers with a look of pure anger such as I had never seen before.

"I threw you all out of here once!" His voice took on a note of ultimate authority and they shrank back from him. "And you put it all back and carry on your trade!" He grabbed the nearest table and overthrew it, sending the money flying in all directions. It was a signal. Before we knew what was happening, the crowd had joined in and the tables were quickly thrown to one side, the coins carpeting the floor. No one stole anything; they took advantage of the moment to show their contempt for the men who robbed them just to change their money. The temple police quickly appeared but stood back and did nothing.

Instead the blind, the sick and the lame came to him, as they did everywhere he went and in the middle of the temple grounds he healed them all and blessed them.

Then he argued with the chief priests and lawyers who came to try and trick him with complicated points of law which were too esoteric even for me, who had studied much. They lost the argument. They always did.

Jesus looked round at us. "Come," he said curtly, "I have no need of further words with people whose ears are stopped with the dust of ages and whose eyes see no further than the scrolls on which the past is inscribed."

We went back the way we came. Philip and Thaddeus returned the animals he had borrowed for that triumphant journey whilst we made our way to Mary and Martha's home. It would be good to be with friends for a while.

It was a day of strange things. I had the what can only be called a triumphant arrival in Jerusalem to think on, then the reaction of the crowd in the temple, the ineffectual arguments of the priests when Jesus confronted them with their own teachings, the fact we could 'borrow' an animal without even seeing the person ourselves … it all made for a day of the most unbelievable happenings.

Then something else happened which almost threw all the other thoughts out of my mind.

We were relaxing after our meal, Mary and Martha were bustling about, clearing up, making us feel comfortable and at ease in their home, when Mary of Magdala walked over to Jesus, holding a small bottle in her hand. She didn't speak, but uncapped it and poured something over his head. It was spikenard, I recognised the smell immediately. It was spikenard which was in itself prophetic. She reached out and touched the oil as it ran down his face, wiping it away with such tenderness it was heart-breaking to see.

"That could have been sold and the money given to the poor."

The voice crashed into the solemn moment and shattered it. Jesus looked over to Lazarus, who was standing in the doorway.

"My friend," he spoke with great sadness. "It is true the oil could have been sold and the money given to the poor, as you say, but this beloved one knows my destiny. She has embalmed me before the event, so I know of it and I thank her for it." He took her hands, slippery with the oil, into his. "You know, don't you?" he said softly. She nodded, unable to speak. "You know because you have seen and because you have seen, you will be able to go through it with me." He looked round at us and then back at Lazarus. "Is that enough for you, my friend?"

Lazarus looked shamed for a moment. "I apologise. I had not realised…"

"There is no need. We, this group, are very close, we know what is ahead. We are dealing with it on our own very different ways. This is Mary of Magdala's way. I cannot find fault with her, she understands because - like me - she sees into the future."

I do not know if any of us slept that night. I know I didn't. If Jesus was awake and wondering or worrying about his immediate future, he did not call to me to walk and talk. I wondered if he had gone away to pray all night, as he had done in the past.

The morning light told me I was right, for he was weary, dark rings under his eyes and an abnormal irritation about him. On our way to Jerusalem he reached for a fig but the tree had none to offer. In what was – for him – an unusual burst of temper, he cursed the tree and it immediately shrivelled up and died. He seized on that as another example for us, how we could do anything, if we had the faith to do it.

Then he spent the entire day arguing with the priests and lawyers, confounding every point they raised, teaching the people with his stories which contained morals, shocking the authorities and pleasing the crowd, who spoke of him with high praise all around us.

That night he did call for me and we walked in the moonlight. He walked like an older man, his weariness showing in every line of his body. With me he did not have to put on a pretence of being strong, with me he could be himself, be the person he was underneath, a man on a pathway to a destiny that no one, not one single person in Jerusalem, would wish on anyone, unless of course they were the chief priest and his acolytes.

"Judas, tomorrow I need you to go to the chief priest and offer to betray me. I need you to do this, or it will not happen as it should."

"I had not…"

"I know. Your mind cannot go further than the act itself, but these are the practicalities of it. I have thought it through and had it in a vision as well, so please, for my sake, do as I ask. Go to the chief priest and offer to betray me. They will offer you silver, take it. It seals the bargain. Whatever you do with it afterward is for you to decide; put it in the communal purse, give it to the temple, give it to the poor, it does not matter. It has to be done to seal the bargain. You understand this?"

I nodded, unable to speak, suffering intense pain that stifled every word I might utter in protest.

"At the Passover meal, I will give you a signal to go. Then you must go and do just what I have asked you to do." He turned and looked into my face with those intense blazing eyes I had seen on a few occasions. "Judas, whatever you feel, do this for me."

"I made a promise."

"I know, but you and I – well, it will be hard, if not all but impossible, for you to go through with this because of our closeness. I need you to be sure."

"I am. My heart is breaking but I am sure. It is your wish and God's command. What more do I need?"

He smiled. "A touch of hatred, perhaps, disappointment that I am not here to rouse the people to a revolution against the oppressors? Either of those would make it easier for you to do this for me. Am I right?"

"Of course. You always are."

"Instead I ask you to do it from the highest motive of all – love."

He sat down very suddenly, as if all the strength had gone from his legs in a moment. I sat with him and he rested his head on my shoulder. "Judas, I am so tired." It was said so softly I hardly heard him. But I did know that in that moment he slept.

We stayed that way for the remainder of the night.

Next morning there was a flurry of activity as plans were made for the Passover meal. A room was hired, food bought, we were all rushing here and there and everywhere to make sure it went as smoothly as a Passover meal should, especially when we knew it would be his last one. No one said it, we were getting very good at not voicing our feelings but equally, none of us could hide the fact we knew well what we were doing. His last Passover, his last time with us, in all probability. The end was fast coming.

The women were seen in tears several times that day. The men were stern faced but calm.

And I had my task to do.

I went to the temple and asked to see the chief priest or someone close to him, saying it was extremely urgent. A busy bustling man came to see me, demanding to know why I had interrupted his Passover preparations, even though I knew well he would have many to do that for him.

Although the words all but choked me, I managed to say them. "If you wish, I will lead you to Jesus of Nazareth so you can arrest him."

The man's eyes grew large and he was lost for words for a few moments. Then he said, "I suppose you want paying."

"But of course."

"Wait here."

He was gone for some time, so long that I thought I had been forgotten, although that was highly unlikely, given the nature of my errand. Finally he came back with a small black bag. "Will thirty pieces of silver be enough for you?"

"More than enough." A single piece would have secured the bargain but it would have looked cheap. This was a substantial amount and told me how much they wanted to get their hands on Jesus.

I felt sick. Sick to my stomach, my bowels, the very depth and heart of me was sick. I tried not to show it, I stood passively by and waited until he counted out the silver, making sure there were only thirty pieces there, before handing it to me. It burned my hand, although it was nothing more than a leather pouch.

"How will we know which one is Jesus of Nazareth? The temple guards will need to be sure they arrest the right man."

"I will lead them there. The one I kiss will be the one they – and you - want."

"Then it is as good as done." He looked at me with deep suspicion. "Why are you doing this?"

"Because I have to." It was an honest answer, one he could take any way he wished. He seemed satisfied with that, because he nodded and walked away, saying: "At even, then, I will expect you back here."

"I will be here."

He could not wait to get away from me, as if I carried disease or would contaminate him in some other way. I could not wait to get away from him. I needed to lose the contents of my stomach. This I did in a quiet alley away from the temple courtyard. It didn't make me feel any better.

I walked all afternoon, pacing the streets of Jerusalem, lost in my feelings, not my thoughts. I had no thoughts left; I had nothing inside but an aching grief and sickness that refused to go. I bought pure water and that did not help. It just gave me something to retch with. I saw the sky darkening and wondered even at that point if I could go through with this. I wanted to leave Jerusalem, go far away, take my aching heart and stomach and lose myself in the desert, do penance for what I had done. But what had I done but follow his wish and the command of God?

Finally I gave in and went to the room where we were having the Passover meal. Jesus knew by my face I had gone through with it, he came over to me and quietly said, 'thank you, my trusted friend.'

"It's killing me."

"I know." His eyes were dark with sorrow and even fear. "It's killing me, too."

"What next?"

"When I tell you to go, keep your appointment and bring them to me. You know where we will be."

I had no doubt he knew precisely what had gone on, I had no need to spell out what had been said, what arrangements had been made, nothing. All was known. His abilities were astounding. It made it even worse that it had to end.

Everyone was there, waiting to begin the meal. They looked at me with puzzled faces, but no one asked any questions. We were unnaturally solemn as we sat around the large table; no one seemed to want to speak.

Jesus looked at each person in turn. "This is a strange night," he said quietly. "I have to tell you that one of you has betrayed me and it was arranged. I ask for no condemnation, it had to be done. The prophesy had to be fulfilled. I have told you often that the Son of

230

God will be handed over to the authorities, will suffer and will die. This is when it ends. But I wish you to do this for me in the future." He took up bread and broke it with his fine slender fingers and handed a small piece to everyone. "This is my body which is broken and delivered up to God for you. Remember this and do this in remembrance of me." Then he took up the wine and poured some in every cup. "This you can think of as my blood which I shed freely for you and for all who believe. Remember this and do this in remembrance of me."

I took the bread and all but choked on it. I took the wine and drank it, feeling it go sour in my churning stomach. Then Jesus looked at me.

"Go and do what you have to do, Judas."

Everyone stared as I got up, everyone that is apart from Joanna who knew what had happened. She looked at me with such hatred that I could have simply stopped breathing right there. I walked away without looking at anyone, too hurt to speak, to do anything but obey.

I went back to the temple and met the temple guards and the priests who would go with them. We waited for a time, in silence, and then walked, in silence, out of the city to the place I knew he would be. He had not told me where they would be meeting that night, I just knew, with the same certainty I knew that this was his and my destiny, that no matter how sick or grief stricken I was, this had to be done. I chanted to myself as we walked "God's will, God's will." It didn't help.

I saw them all gathered around Jesus, as if protecting him. I saw him and there was the faintest of smiles. I went over to him and kissed him. Then I turned and ran.

Chapter 28
Endless Night

The night was dark, moonless, only the stars saw where I went and how I went, in haste, in uncertainty, in blind agony and appalling pain. What can you do, where can you go when you have lost the friend you love and the woman you love through something you had to do, something you had no choice but to do? You run. You run and hope that the running will outdistance the pain, that the body will hurt so much the mind will stop.

It didn't work.

I ran for what felt like hours but probably wasn't. I was fit but not that fit. I was in a strange part of Jerusalem, a quarter I had not visited before. The houses were small, crammed together, their roofs all but touching as if talking to one another. The starlight showed me very little but I could see that, at least. I walked up and down streets, wondering why I couldn't leave the pain behind. I saw only two faces, Jesus and Joanna and they became intermingled, so the hatred I saw on her face became reflected on his. I was afraid I was going mad. Tears were flowing freely, soaking my robe, which absorbed my sorrow but did not help stop it.

I went round a corner and collided with someone coming the other way. He grabbed my arm and held it.

"Friend, are you all right? I am so sorry, I did not see you."

"No, the fault is mine," I told him. "I am blinded by my own pain at the moment and had no thought for where I was going."

"I see that." We were standing by a lighted window and he could no doubt see the tears and sadness carved into my face. I felt as if I would never smile again. "Come."

"I stopped you going somewhere."

"Yes and no. You can come with me. I was seeking a quiet place to contemplate. It seems it might be good for you, too. Come."

We walked together down a narrow dark alleyway which opened out on a small area of trees and plants, with benches scattered here and there. In the centre was a small fountain, which was full of water but was not at that moment spouting any.

"I didn't know this was here." I was trying to be polite, trying to be friendly without giving myself any relief. I didn't feel I deserved it.

"Few people do. It is a place for those of us who know it and use it properly. Come."

Again the word, just as Jesus would have said it. I followed obediently and sat down on one of the benches. There was a sense of calm about the man I had collided with and a quietness in the area in which we sat.

"Now," he said quietly. "Talk to me of what grieves you."

"You will hate me."

"No. I am not here to judge."

I looked more closely at him, wondering in that moment if he was totally human or whether he was a heavenly being come to comfort me.

"You know of Jesus of Nazareth."

"Who doesn't? The preacher who has taken Jerusalem by storm, a man who can put the authorities in their place with words taken from the Scriptures themselves. He confounds the greatest scholars, he has words for the poor. He heals and he teaches. That is the one, I take it?"

"Yes."

"Then I know of Jesus of Nazareth, even if it has not been my privilege to meet him and hear him speak. Now, friend, what is your problem with this man?"

"I am his closest friend."

"And you are here."

233

"Yes. I had a task to do for him. I had to betray him so the prophesy of his birth and his death would be fulfilled."

"He asked you to do this." It was not a question.

"He asked me to do this, out of the love I have for him."

"And you did it."

"I did, this night I took the temple guards to him and showed them which one was he."

"You, my friend, are honoured above all men. You did what few men could do. You did as a friend asked you to and you did it out of love."

"Yes."

"Then why the agony?"

"He is my friend. I love him. I cannot bear to be the one who condemned him to death."

A gentle hand rested on my arm and I was filled with some kind of light. It was not physical, it could not be seen. The darkness was as dark as ever, but I felt as if I glowed.

"You – you, Judas Iskariot, did not condemn Jesus of Nazareth to death. Let us be clear on that."

Then I knew this was no earthly being. The place where we sat probably did not exist in the real Jerusalem. I had no wish to challenge any of this, I was grateful only for his company and his compassion.

"But…"

"Do not ask right now. Consider this instead. Jesus asked you to betray him, as in he asked you to tell the temple guards, the high priest and all the others, where he was and who he was. He asked no more of you than that. Yes, you knew that when that happened he would be arrested, he would be convicted and he would be executed. But you, you as a person, did not condemn him to death. You handed him over to the authorities. No more, no less. What happens from now on is blood on their hands, not yours. They could, if they saw fit, release him. They could, if they saw fit, challenge him to a proper debate and see how their teachings fell apart. The fact they will not do these things is their destiny, not yours. All you did was do what he – and God – asked you to do."

"I cannot – is this – why do – who-"

The smile was vivid and loving. "Judas, you did just what you had to do. You will be condemned for it, for there are many now and many in the future who will not understand any of this. Jesus told you of this. You accepted it. You accepted the task of being the one to betray him, in your eyes anyway. He knew you would not fail him. He knew you would help him, out of the depths, the sheer magnitude, of the love you carry for him. God knows this, too. Now, I bid you, return to the group but stay away from them. They will kill you if they find you. If you must, follow the crowd when he is offered to the people, for he will be. If you must, follow him to the hill where he will die, for he surely will. The prophesy, as he said, must be fulfilled. He must die, for how else can he demonstrate to the non-believers that there is life eternal?"

"What will become of me?" I finally asked.

The smile grew bigger. "I wondered how long it would be before you asked that. You put him before you all the time in this conversation we are having. For this I praise and honour you. What will become of you is in your hands, Judas Iskariot. You can choose either to live, or to die. I would for the moment suggest you wait until you know Jesus is dead before making up your mind."

"There is Joanna…"

"There is indeed Joanna. She sees much but she knows not enough to make an informed decision on how she feels. For the moment, all she knows is that for the second time, the man she loves is being taken from her.

You have no way of making her see your side, Judas. I am sorry to say that love will never be yours."

"This I knew, but…"

"Yes, you knew it well and accepted it a long time ago. But you retained a hope. No, there is no hope there. Accept that now."

"Who are you?"

"Who do you say I am?"

"You are an angel and this, where we sit, is something you created for us to be alone. It was no accident we collided on the corner of the street."

"You are almost right. I am Gabriel, archangel, servant and messenger of God. I went to Mary when she was pregnant with Jesus, I told her of his destiny and she carried the burden with pride all her life – and his. She is on her way to Jerusalem now to see him, to be with him when he dies. She has been told by an angel what is to happen and she is making all haste even through the night. And you are right, I created this area for us to sit and talk. It does not exist in what you see as the real world, but to me it is as real as you are."

I sank down on my knees before him and held my hands out in prayer.

"Thank you, Gabriel, thank you, God, for your great, great honour."

He took my hands and his felt as if they were human, dry, warm and soft. "Come, get up, my friend. You are not fit to kneel before anyone. We honour you for you did what he asked. No man could ask more of a friend than he carry out the one act which his whole being fought against. Judas, you are a true friend."

In that moment he was gone, as was the place in which we sat. I was standing in a cold, narrow alley in a quarter of Jerusalem miles away from where the temple guards had no doubt carried out their arrest, miles away from where Jesus was being held prisoner. I had to find my way back. I had to see for myself.

I began to walk, doing no more than following my instincts. I was truly lost and yet my feet seemed to know the way back better than my mind. I saw again the calm, quiet face of the archangel, saw the gentleness in his eyes, heard the sound of his melodic voice in my ears, knew that he was right and that some, not all, of the intense pain had been lifted.

I knew I could tell no one of the night I had passed, for none would believe me. In truth, I had no one to tell for the group would, as he said, try and kill me if I went near them. I had to see but stay concealed. My time was not yet. I also knew my time was limited, for I doubted I could live in this world without Jesus and without Joanna. He would be dead and she would spurn me with all the hatred I saw writ clear on her face. But for the moment I was calm. My eyes were dry, my stomach quietened, my heart restored to its normal solid beat.

I know not how long I walked. I know by the time dawn broke over Jerusalem in all its radiant glory I was footsore, aching in every bone and drooping with exhaustion. And I was back where I should be, outside the temple courtyard. I had no money, I had left the communal purse behind when I left the Passover meal, I could not buy a place to stay and I could not buy food for myself, either. I still had the silver but that burned me and I could not touch it, nor would I spend it on my own comforts. I planned to return it to the temple, let them do with it what they would. It had served its purpose, it created a bargain and I had carried out my part of it.

"Fear not," a voice whispered in my ear. "All is taken care of." I turned quickly but there was no one there.

"Come." A woman stood beckoning to me. I followed her, obedient to that word, which had been said in the same tone as Jesus and then, I discovered, Gabriel. I walked quickly behind her, matching my stride to hers.

She took me to a small house where she ushered me inside. "I know you need sleep and food. Here." A room shuttered and shady awaited me, a soft bed and a tray with fruits and bread on it.

"I have no money…" I began.

"Hush. It is done. All is taken care of." Those words again. I stopped asking and gratefully sank down on the bed, asleep even before my head came to rest.

I woke, ate the fruit and bread, drank the fine clear water left for me and then went out into the house. The woman smiled at me. "You look better now. Make haste, for your friend is being displayed to the people now. You will see him if you hurry."

"I want to thank you…"

"God saw to that. I had a message, I obeyed it. Go now, and know that God is taking care of you, Judas Iskariot."

There seemed no end to the miracles that were besetting me. Before I could even begin to think, I was outside and on my way, following the crowd. Some were chanting 'Jesus of Nazareth!' Some were waving their fists and shouting words I could not understand.

In a moment of clarity I realised that the men who were shouting the strange words were agitators. They had been placed in the crowd, they were ensuring Jesus would not be released. It was a plot and one that I could do nothing about. It was a plot and I had been an essential part of it. I wondered, briefly, what they would have done had I refused to go along with Jesus' request. How then would they have captured him? Followed him, arrested him in front of a crowd of believers? They might have been massacred if they had. I began to see that my actions were not only designed to ensure the prophesy was fulfilled but to save unnecessary killings too, for the men were only servants of the regime, not men who thought for themselves.

And in a moment, we were there.

Chapter 29
Death

Our newest governor, Pontius Pilate, stood with Jesus, manacled and bound, alongside him. The imperious Roman was looking distastefully at the gathered crowd, the chanting, shouting, pushing, bustling crowd of people of several nationalities as well as native Judaeans and residents of Jerusalem. God alone knew what he really thought of us. His look was a clear indication, though, that he was not enamoured of the sight before him. Jesus lifted his head and looked across the crowd to me. He did not smile but I received the message he sent

Thank you. All is as it should be.

I did not try to return a message. In that moment the grief struck me again, the bitter heartbreak which Gabriel had lifted from me returned full blown. I had hoped it was gone but seeing Jesus in chains, in captivity, being displayed like some spoil of war by the side of a hated Governor, was enough to bring it all back into my heart.

"This man is innocent!" Pilate was shouting. No one wanted to listen.

"Kill him" The shouting grew louder and louder, drowning out the voices who wanted to dissent, those who were desperately pleading for his life. There were sufficient agitators in the midst of the people to ensure that the will of the authorities be done. I wondered if any of the group were there and if they were, what they were thinking and feeling. If they were as devastated as I was, then their pain was immense. And I could not approach any of them and offer sympathy. I had to hide. I had to remain on the edge of the crowd, ready to leave in a moment if danger loomed.

"This man is innocent!" Pilate shouted again. The blood lust grew stronger, almost physical. The crowd was baying for a death and they would have it.

Pilate turned away, reaching for a bowl of water. He dipped his hands in it and shook them dry. "I wash my hands of it," he bellowed. "Who do you want to be released in this man's place?"

"Barabbas!" the cry went up, echoing round the square, rebounding from roofs, sending the birds screeching into the air, such was the power and the sheer viciousness of the name and the intensity with which it was shouted.

Jesus looked at me again. Our eyes met across the distance which seemed to grow even as I stood there. Same message came into my mind:

Thank you. All is as it should be.

'No!' I screamed silently. 'No! Live! Live for me and for the others! Live for all the people you healed and touched with your preaching! Live, live, live!'

I hadn't realised he could receive my thoughts until I saw him shaking his head.

Thank you. All is as it should be.

No. But there was no conviction in the thought now. Three times I had received the same words, three times he had spoken to me and I had to accept it. I turned and walked away.

Did God direct my footsteps? I was back outside the house where the woman had offered me hospitality, had known my name without my saying anything, had received a message from God about me. I was outside and I had no way of knowing if I knocked she would be there, would remember me, would let me stay a little longer. I stood, uncertain and almost afraid.

The door opened without my touching it.

"So, you are back, Judas. I knew you would be. Come in. Here you will be safe, for I have no connection with your group and they know nothing of this place."

I stepped inside and she closed the door.

"Have you seen him?"

"Yes." She directed me to a stool and I sat down.

"How did he seem?"

"Determined."

She nodded. "He would. This is his destiny and neither you nor I can do anything about it." A tear escaped and ran down her face and I knew then she had seen him, been healed by him or heard him and was a believer as well as someone who could receive messages from God.

"He told me, thank you, all is as it should be." I bowed my head, trying not to show the weight of the pain I carried.

"He is right. He knew this would happen and he knows it is ordained. Nothing could stop it."

She sat down opposite me. "Judas, I know Mary and Martha. Lazarus is a friend I care about. I know Jesus raised him from the dead. Had I not seen him myself, in his shroud, in his tomb and do I not see him now, with these eyes, a whole man walking about, speaking and eating and living a normal life? Who cannot believe when these things are seen by your own eyes?"

"And you hear the words of God." It was not a question.

"I do. He told me you were coming, he told me I should shelter you and feed you, that you had done great service for his son. And so you have."

"I feel as if I have done nothing but hand him over."

"Come now, Judas, I know well God has given you more than that to dwell on in your heart."

"Yes. I have spoken with an angel and am still finding it hard to believe that I did so."

"Your lack of belief allowed the grief to come back in." She smiled and the somewhat harsh face she wore was transformed into something beautiful. "Not so much a lack of belief, more a natural reaction to the unnatural. Your love for him is great, Judas, this I know from your attitude."

"It is."

"But you must go and see him die. He will expect that."

"I could not stay away."

"No." She looked at me critically. "No, you could not, no matter how much it hurts. A true friend, you really are a true friend."

"It is a strange friend who delivers his friend into the hands of his enemies."

"It is a true friend who does as that friend – and God – bid him to do, no matter the cost to himself."

"If enough people say that to me, I might begin to believe it."

"You have already been told, Judas." She got up then and fetched wine for me. I drank it, hoping to dull the pain. It worked, for a while.

"Stay here for now. I have no other person in the house. I am a widow with means to live alone, no one bothers me. I can meditate and pray and speak with God in the privacy of this house and none need know that I do not follow the Scriptures to the letter."

"I know not even your name."

"You can call me Miriam."

"We had a Miriam who walked with us for a while, she was like a mother to everyone."

"It's a good enough name. It's safer not to know everything, Judas."

"Miriam. It may not be your name but it is right for you."

She acknowledged this with a slight tilt of her head.

"You will need to be strong to watch a crucifixion, Judas Iskariot. Would you like me to walk with you?"

243

"Are you sure you are human?" I asked in return. "You know my heart, it would seem."

"No, just using the instincts of a woman. You are deeply troubled, yet sure of your pathway. You are convinced you did the right thing for Jesus and for God but are still afraid of seeing the consequences. It is nothing clever, to work this out from your words and your manner."

"Then I accept, with grateful thanks."

"When the time comes, we will walk there together." It was said as a promise and it gave me strength. If it had not been improper I would have embraced her.

The road to Golgotha is long and steep. To walk it by yourself is hard enough. To walk it carrying part of the huge timber cross on which you will die –

The Romans knew how to draw out an execution. They knew how to humiliate, to subjugate, to crush. Miriam and I joined the crowd lining the road, standing back just enough that we did not put pressure on the people in front of us, but not so far back we could not see anything. The sun beat down, relentlessly burning us all without exception. There was a smell of dust, of bodies, of linen that was crumpled and heavily used. Food smells mixed in with the others to make a miasma that was hard to tolerate. The voices, the sound of birds, the clank of armour, many sounds, many different sounds. Some voices were harsh, others full of tears. Jesus' name was mentioned in the tears, the names of the other men who were to die were not said. They could have been invisible for all that anyone seemed to care.

My heart was pounding so hard I wondered if anyone could hear it. My throat was sore from the sheer ferocity of its beat. My heart also ached. I was standing in a crowd, waiting for the man I loved most to appear and walk to his death. I could not believe I was doing it, that I was there, that I was prepared to watch. I also knew I could not be anywhere else. I had to see for myself. I had to be there.

I had no idea where the others were; I kept looking for them so I could avoid them. I could not bear to see the hatred Joanna held for me. The woman I loved so hopelessly hated me. That in itself was a burden difficult enough to carry, without the death of my beloved friend, too. And a death that was as cruel, as barbaric as he had described the death by stoning.

The roar of the crowd told me the first person had appeared coming along the road. He was a big man, his face drawn with suffering already; he walked upright, carrying his timber as if it were a roll of paper. As he passed I could see the stripes down his back; he had been whipped mercilessly. And yet he stood proud and tall. The crowd fell silent in the face of his proud journey. He looked neither left nor right, just followed the road upward to Golgotha.

Jesus came next. He was bowed under the weight of the wood, his face drawn and showing all his agony. His robe was ripped and the stripes he wore were clear, marked in blood which trickled down his back. He wore a crown of twisted wood – with a shock I realised it was thorns. They had mocked him! I turned to stone in that moment. I could not breathe, could not feel, could not function at all. That fast beating hurting heart had stopped, I was sure it had. He turned his head slightly and I saw blood running down his face from the thorns which had dug into the skin. He did not see me, he was just turning his head. His eyes were blank; he was not seeing anything.

He staggered and dropped the wood. A Roman guard shouted and went to hit him, but a huge man stepped out of the crowd directly in front of us, bravely pushing the guard to one side.

"Leave him!" The man did not shout; he spoke quietly but with such authority the guard stepped back in fear. "I will carry the crosspiece. 'Tis a cruel enough execution without this, I tell you."

The man turned to Jesus and smiled sadly. "Friend, I know not what you have done but I feel you do not deserve this cruel death. Let me carry this for you."

Jesus did not speak, just smiled and in that smile was all that the stranger needed to know. He breathed, "this man is innocent."

He reached down and picked up the heavy timber. "In the name of the Lord God, how can anyone so treated be expected to carry this?" he roared. No one spoke. The entire crowd was silent in the face of his bravery and the stoic demeanour of Jesus.

The third man struggled to catch up with them. The spirit of what the stranger was doing for Jesus had affected the crowd, several men moved forward to help. The guards were stupefied and did nothing to prevent them.

And so the sad, bitterly sad procession made its way through the blazing sun to the hill of Golgotha.

Miriam looked at me. "Come." That word again, said in a tone that denied any discussion or dissent. I went. I wished I hadn't.

I wondered why people surged forward to see every last gory painful heart-breaking detail. Why did they want so much to see people they did not know suffering in such close proximity? Why then was I doing the same thing … except I knew one of the three, knew him as well as I would ever know anyone and loved him more than I had ever loved anyone in my life.

We pushed and elbowed and shoved and eased our way through, not so close that any of the group would see me, I made sure of that, but enough that I could see what was going on.

All three crosses were being assembled. The air was filled with the sound of hammering as men with huge muscled arms put the cross-pieces on the uprights. Then they were laid down on the side of the hill. The convicted men – this was the only way I could deal with it at that moment – were dragged over and laid on the cross. Jesus was put on the middle one. He still had his crown of thorns but little else, his robe had been taken away and he was left only with a cloth for dignity. The others were the same. I saw that he still had the faraway look, as if he had already left this life and all that was here was a body about to be killed and finish the task.

They started with the man on the left. Someone held down his arm and a man with a hammer slammed a nail through his wrist. His scream echoed clear across the crowd, silencing them for a moment. Only the birds were calling, they who had no conception or care for what was going on. The sound of the hammer began again as the other arm was stretched out, the other wrist was pinioned, another scream rent the air. The people watching began to murmur, to fill the silence with talk, what talk? What could they say? Isn't that good, isn't that bad, is that really necessary, what in the name of Heaven could they speak of? I felt anger burning me, taking the stone which had filled me earlier and exchanging it for heat, intense and frightening. If I did not control it, I would do something stupid, run at them, get myself killed, but if it stopped them…

I stopped my thoughts there, clenched my fists so that my nails cut into my palms - I found the blood pouring down my hands later when I looked – and sent up fervent prayers, the most fervent and heartfelt I had ever prayed in all my days thus far. And I sent love, pure unadulterated love, to the man waiting patiently on the second cross.

With total disregard for the suffering they were causing, they moved down, crossed his feet and hammered two nails through them, too. Another piercing scream silenced the crowd for a few moments. Then three, maybe four men got together to lift the cross up.

247

He screamed again as the weight of his body dragged at the nails. Tears poured down his face, his mouth opened in a rictus of pure agony which was made worse when they dropped, literally, the post into the hole awaiting it. Anyone could see his whole body shake and for a moment he was silenced, the agony too much even for him. Then the shrieking began again.

"Silence!" A Roman guard slashed at the man with his sword, cutting deep gashes into his legs. "You don't want to die, then don't commit the crimes!" The man's shrieks died back to muttering but it was obvious it was done with a supreme effort. He had the additional pain of the cuts in his legs to suffer as well as the nails.

I wanted to shut my eyes as they went over to Jesus but they seemed incapable of closing. The lids stayed firmly open. I was frozen again, stone, impossible to change, to move, to speak. Miriam gripped my arm tightly, far stronger than a woman should be able to hold something. That pain helped.

"Be strong!" It was an injunction. I responded by taking a deep breath and staring, as if indeed I could have done anything else.

They took one arm and held it flat. He did not move or look or react. The nail was driven in. He made no sound. I did not even see him clench his teeth to prevent the outcry. His face did not move.

But I did see, and it all but broke me to see it, his mother at the foot of the cross, sobbing in John's arms. Joanna was by her side, wringing her hands and looking with utter despair at the man on the cross. The others were there, blank faced, stunned, shocked, tearful, every sad emotion it was possible to feel. I wondered what my face showed. They nailed through his hand as well as his wrist. Why, I wondered, unless it was out of spite because he did not scream, yell, react in any way. Did they not realise he had already left, his spirit was already gone? Fools, stupid ignorant fools! You know not who you kill! Your day will come!

I did not say this aloud, I did not dare. They nailed the other wrist, the other hand. They nailed his feet. He did not scream, shout, protest, everything I expected him to do. It seemed to annoy them. One kicked him in the side but he did not even look at the man.

One of the guards came over with something in his hand. "Put this at his head," he told the man with the hammer. It was a notice of some kind. That was nailed on and then they lifted up the cross and dropped it in the hole.

It was about midday.

The third man was crucified a short time later. He screamed and shrieked and shouted and blasphemed until silenced by a guard in the same way the other man had been, slashed in the legs, causing additional pain.

It was about midday and the sun was blinding us all. Intense heat poured down on the crowd. Some began to leave, not wanting or caring to stay until the end. Others moved forward and I took the opportunity to go with them, still staying back, still not wanting to be seen. I did not know what the others would do if they saw me.

The stone melted with the anger and then went back to stone again. I had clamped down all emotions, put them in a vault and locked them.

I stood and watched for the entire time the man I loved took to die. I saw the effort it was to breathe, the chest caved in by the position of the arms, the heart beating rapidly and then slowing, the eyes flickering and then closing, the mouth opening and then closing. If he saw anything, I did not detect it. If he sent out any thoughts, I did not receive them and he must have known I would be there, that I would not let him die without my being there. He would have known the others would be there, he knew his mother was coming, he had no doubt said his farewells to her in his own way. I had no chance of a farewell, I had no chance to say 'in God's name, why did you ask me to do this?' when I knew well why he had asked me. My thoughts were foolish, stupid in the extreme, rushing hither and thither like a flood trapped in a cavern from which it could not escape.

And the entire time the woman, Miriam, held my arm, pressing herself against me so we stood like two people joined side by side, letting me feel her warmth, her strength and her compassion. I wished in a rare moment I knew her real name, that I could thank her and try and repay her but I knew that was not what she would have wanted. I knew that she had been sent by God to help me through this ordeal. I was dry of mouth and eyes. I wanted to cry, to sob, to release that which was so firmly bolted down inside me, that which was hurting beyond belief. If I had ever thought I had hurt before, it was nothing compared with the way I felt that afternoon, that endless afternoon that went on for eternity. The other two men struggled, fought to breathe, shouted at the crowd, none of whom seemed to be there to support them. But that was only at the start. Very soon their voices failed, there was no way they could speak when their chests were compressed by the very method they were fastened to the cross. I was trying to decide whether stoning was more barbaric than this unbelievable way of executing people and could not make up my mind. Then I realised how foolish that thought was too. But then, when you are standing staring at a body, a friend's body, hanging on a cross from nails, blood dripping from the crown of thorns they had compressed onto his head - or was that now dried in its rivulets down his face? - blood dripping from the nails they had hammered into his flesh, blood… stop it, I told myself. Stop it before you go completely insane. Miriam took that precise moment to press a little harder against me. I took strength from her and used it to stand straight and bid my heart to be still while he died. Slowly and carefully and seemingly lasting forever, he died.

Did the sky go black at that moment? Was there a thunder clap which rocked the buildings? If there was, it was not my imagination and my soul which heard and felt it. It seemed to me at the moment he took his last breath, which I watched so carefully and wished to treasure, everything went black. It was possibly my own senses which had given up on me right then, for Miriam was in front of me at that moment, holding both my arms, shaking me gently, guiding me away.

I turned back, in time to see a Roman pierce his side with a spear and blood gush out. He turned to his associates and made a downward sign. It was done.

Chapter 30
Resurrection

I stumbled away, hurrying almost, to escape the sight of the cross being taken down and the body removed. I did not want to know whether the nails were taken out or whether he was taken from them by force. I did not want to know where he was being buried, whether a tomb had been found, whether there was a grave. I did not want to know any of this, for I was in shock.

Stupid. How could I be shocked when I had known what was to happen, had passed the crosses myself in the past without giving them a thought, apart from sending a message to Heaven for the soul of the departed, had stood and watched him nailed to the cross, saw he was not even there any more, for not a sound left his mouth the whole time, where the others screamed and yelled and acted as a normal person would. Jesus never had been normal, even in death he was not normal. In death he had cheated them of their game, by his spirit departing before his body stopped holding on to life.

Joanna would be devastated. Joanna would not know what to do with her grief, so much had been given to Jesus, such love, such compassion, such loyalty, just as she had given John the Baptist and now he too had been taken from her. She was surely the one to be in shock.

And yet I knew I was shocked for I could not breathe properly, I was going hot and cold, I was shaking, all but incapable of taking one step after the other. If Miriam had not been there, I would have fallen and laid in the dust whilst others walked over me.

"Come." That word again, the one I was compelled to obey. We went back to her small house where she barred the door and bade me sit and brought me wine.

Then she sat by me and talked.

She spoke of her connection with God, the angels who visited her, the messages she received. She talked of healing, just as we had been taught to heal but she had no one to show her, it came naturally, guided, she said. She spoke of this person cured of the palsy, of another able to walk, what she called miracles and how the men from the temple would come and plague her with their laws and scriptures, demanding she cease these things for they were against God's law and how she would argue with them that if it were against God's law, how could it be done?

She talked on and on and I heard only a part of it but I knew the soothing sound of her words were acting like a balm on the torment I was going through. The endless circle of words in my head were breaking down, one at a time.

Jesus is dead. Jesus is alive. Jesus is dead. Jesus is alive.

They became 'Jesus is alive' after a while. I stopped shaking, stopped going hot and cold, took the wine she gave me and drank it without the cup rattling against my teeth.

It was then she looked at me and asked what I was going to do.

In truth, I said, "I do not know right now. I am awaiting his return. He told me not to go far, that he would find me. When he does, I will know what to do."

"Then you must go somewhere he will find you." She got up and went to a small room at the back of her house. She returned with a small amphora, half a loaf, a cheese and some dried meat. "This is all I have in the house at the moment. It is not much but it will suffice for a time. Judas, may I suggest you find somewhere you can stay, somewhere close by where Jesus of Nazareth will find you. I have now to let you go for this is what you have to do."

I stood up and took the food from her. "Miriam…"

253

"Don't even try." She looked at me with such compassion that I felt a rush of tears, the first I had felt since Jesus had been taken.

"But…"

"Don't even try. It was my privilege and honour to be there, to see the way he died, with such dignity and such acceptance. He is an example to us all. He foiled their plans. They wanted a scene, I know they did and he did not give it to them. His spirit departed before he died, but you know that."

"Yes."

"It has been my privilege and honour to be able to help you through that, Judas. I need no thanks for that. I have memories I can live with to help me through the rest of my life, however long that might be."

She unbarred the door and I left. It had become dark, the stars shone down on – what? A world without Jesus in it. Not in the flesh anyway, I hastily amended. The guards were everywhere, perhaps anticipating trouble after Jesus' execution, but I evaded them with relative ease. It was as if I had become invisible, no one took any notice of me as I slipped past them as they questioned people, broke up groups who were lingering on street corners or outside inns and actually walked out of the city gate without being halted by anyone.

But then I felt the weight of the silver. It was dragging at me, a heavy load I could not carry. I stopped to consider what to do with it. Drop it in the alms box for the poor, give it to the first homeless person I saw, return it…

I went back through the gate and made my way to the temple. There were people bustling about, even at that late hour, looking important and serious and pompous all at the same time.

Impossible though it seems, I saw the man I had spoken to earlier, the one who had handed me the silver.

I went up to him and put the pouch back in his hand. He looked at me and at it with surprise.

"I did not do it for money." He stared even harder. "I took your money to ensure you kept the bargain we made. You helped fulfil the prophesy. You just helped kill the Messiah and now the world will never be the same again."

Where the words came from I did not know. What I did know was they struck home. His face went white and he was speechless.

I walked away, leaving him standing clutching the silver. It was all I needed to do. I felt lighter, more confident that Jesus would find me and I would know what to do.

I spent three days outside the city walls, in a small depression in the ground which partly shielded me from the sun and protected me at night. There, without a fire or any other comfort, I sat and waited, in the sure knowledge he would come. I ate Miriam's food, drank Miriam's watered down wine and thought how wonderful she had been, how knowing, how wise. Every move she made had been the right one.

I sorrowed for the members of the group, dispersed, no doubt, hiding from the authorities, perhaps, lost in their grief and disbelief that it had happened and hating me for being the instigator of it all. There was a desperate longing to find them, to explain but I knew I would not be given the chance. It was better I stayed away.

He came late on the fourth day, walking over the grass without it bending under his sandals, smiling and holding out a pierced hand. I took it and he sat down beside me. He felt substantial, real, human again. He had donned his pure white robe, tied it with his usual plaited girdle and was just as he had been the night he was taken.

"I said I would find you."

"Yes. I have been waiting for you."

There was a small laugh. "I have been rather – busy. There were a few tasks to attend to, a group of sorrowing people to console, a heartbroken mother to visit, some women who met me in the garden who need reassurance. Oh, you did not know where I was buried, did you? Joseph of Arimathea, a rich businessman and secret follower, donated his tomb to me. I lay there for three days or rather, my body lay there for three days whilst I went back to the Father and rebuilt my energies. Then I came back and was just about to leave the garden where the tomb is when the women found me. Mary of Magdala, Joanna and Susanna. They were a bit surprised, even though I had told them, how many times had I told them? I would come back. So I have been rushing here and there and am grateful I am spirit, it made the rushing about much easier."

I smiled. "Perhaps now she has seen you, Joanna will not hate me so much."

"Ah, poor Judas, of course she does! Is she not woman through and through? Does she not need a scapegoat for my death?"

I laughed for the first time since his horrific execution. "You're right, as always."

"Tell me, what did you do with the silver?"

"Handed it back. I told him he had helped kill the Messiah and the world would not be the same again."

"Where did the words come from? They were not yours, I know."

"I don't know. I was going to shout something about 'you killed an innocent man' but instead those words came out. They shocked him and I think struck home, for he went white and was silent."

"Such arrows of truth do much good. He will think on that in the darkness of his night and perhaps believe. You did well, Judas. But then you did well for me

256

throughout my time, throughout all I asked you to do, all that you suffered for me. Your love for me is immense. Now, my question is, what do you want to do?"

"Are you giving me the choice of living or dying?"

"I am."

"I have thought long as I have sat here waiting. I think you knew that too, you gave me time to consider what I really wanted, what future I really had. I want to go with you. I have no life here without you."

He nodded and his hair moved in the evening breeze. If I had not seen him die with my own mortal eyes, I would not have believed he was spirit.

"If you wish to end your life now, I will understand. I will welcome you into the Kingdom of Heaven as a true man of God, a true friend, a man of great love and understanding. Come, Judas, join me."

That word again. The eyes blazed just as they had when I first saw him in my vision.

There was no need for second thoughts. No need for sadness. No need for regrets ever again.

A convenient tree branch, my own plaited girdle and…

THE END

Thanks go to:

Judas Iskariot, for entrusting me with his story and in consequence of that, his future happiness and progression as a spirit:

Ann-Jacqueline Davies, talented medium and psychic artist, for the beautiful portrait of Judas, the in-depth reading which came with it and for being a trusted and loving friend.

Paul Dobree-Carey for his research, support and guidance throughout the writing of this book. His encouragement meant a lot.

Mary Holliday, devoted friend;

Karen Jones, who travelled the 'journey' with me. Her prayers for strength for me at the critical moments were heard and I got through.

Terry Wakelin because he is Terry Wakelin, my rock and my anchor as always;

My Inner Circle for support, love, guidance, laughter and for always being there.

Recognition must go to Columbia International University for the superb production of "Walking In Their Sandals", a multimedia journey through the land of the Bible. It was a tremendous help in bringing the country alive to one who has never been there – in this life.

A percentage of the royalties from this book will be sent to the Earl Mountbatten Hospice here on the Isle of Wight at Judas' request.

Author's note

Judas came as a complete surprise, arriving as he did amongst the kings, queens, aristocrats and leaders who populate our history and who are queuing for the chance to give the world their side of the story. It took me a while to accept that someone from what I would think of as 'religious history' had come to me but then I thought, why not? Those for whom I work are mostly the misunderstood and/or maligned, is there a person in history so maligned as Judas Iskariot? He was - and is - anxious to explain his version of events, to lift the stigma that has haunted him since that incarnation.

Judas' book was written in record time. I found myself writing a chapter a night, when I could. One night we wrote a chapter and then half of the next, such was the intensity of his emotions and the power of the channelling. It came through with virtually no editing needed; I just received the flow of the story. As if to make my life really challenging, Judas would say yes, the chapter is done, I would Save and then store on an external drive for backup, at which point he would tell me what was coming next...

We did laugh, often, it was not all gloom, doom and intensity but the book itself is intense and passionate. There will be many, established church people and otherwise, who will disagree with virtually every part of it. That doesn't matter. What matters is that Judas has had the chance to put his side of the story in front of the world for the first time in approximately two thousand years. Whether the world accepts it or not, the story is told. It is to be hoped some people will understand and accept his words, for only now does the bible story truly make sense. Random sayings of Jesus, faithfully recorded, now fit into the great scheme, what I think of as the Master Plan of the spirit realms.

It was a tremendous experience and an honour to write.

You may well decide not to believe that this is a channelled book direct from spirit, that I am a good author and wrote an interesting work of fiction, in which case I hope you enjoyed your read. If you choose to believe that I channelled the work, then you will have had an insight into a period of history usually only seen through the distorted eyes of historians. There are more such insights to come from a great variety of people who have approached me with the same request, to tell their story and put the truth in front of the world.

Thank you for buying this book and for reading it to the end. If nothing else, you should have a different opinion on the giant of a man known as Judas Iskariot, which is what we set out to achieve.

Dorothy Davies
Isle of Wight, the year of Our Lord 2011

NOTES:

I am asked to pass on the following observations which either had no place in the book, as they were not understood at the time, or would have interrupted the flow of the story.

Iskariot is the correct spelling of Judas' last name; it means Judas of Kerioth, which is spelled with a K.

Jesus' 'transfiguration' was the result of his communicating with his guides, Moses and Elijah. We all have guides, not everyone knows who they are or works with them. Sensitives and mediums do. Jesus was one of the finest mediums who ever walked the earth. In today's understanding, transfiguration is when a spirit overshadows the medium and can be seen by others and recognised. It seems, from the descriptions given, that Jesus was enveloped in the white light of spirit and Moses and Elijah were seen standing beside him and speaking with him. This is not true transfiguration but probably the only way it could be described at the time.

Judas is not aware of any person named Mark, or otherwise, who was an eye-witness to every single event of Jesus' life. He is inclined to think the person was a sort of reporter who went round and collected statements from witnesses before writing them up as his own record of the time.